Courtney's Wench

by
Jeanne Montague

Dales Large Print Books
Long Preston, North Yorkshire,
England.

British Library Cataloguing in Publication Data.

Montague, Jeanne
 Courtney's wench.

A catalogue record for this book is
available from the British Library

ISBN 1-85389-485-0 pbk

First published in Great Britain by Robert Hale Ltd., 1973

Copyright © 1971 by Joan Hunter

Published in Large Print 1994 by arrangement with the
copyright holder.

Dales Large Print is an imprint of
Library Magna Books Ltd.
Printed and bound in Great Britain by
T.J. Press (Padstow) Ltd., Cornwall, PL28 8RW.

COURTNEY'S WENCH

To my mother, and my daughter, Vanessa, for their help and encouragement, always

BIBLIOGRAPHY

Rebuilding of London after the Great Fire
Of London and Londoners. Weymouth
Home Life under the Stuarts. Godfrey
House Keeping in the Eighteenth Century.
   Bayne-Powell
A Short History of the West Indies. Parry
   and Sherlock
Plays of Vanbrugh
The Diary of Samuel Pepys
A History on the Most Notorious Pirates.
   Captain Charles Johnson
Pirates of the Eastern Seas. Wycherly
Buccaneers of the Pacific
Life in Shakespeare's England. J. Dover
   Eilson
Wesley's England. Whiteley.
The Road to Tyburn. Christopher Hibbert
Historic Costume. Kelly and Schwabe
The European Nations in the West Indies.
   A.P Newton
The Chronicles of Newgate. Arthur Griffiths

PRELUDE

The candles in the wall-sconce dipped at the sudden rush of air into the panelled hall. Roxanna Marshal, wearing a vizard-mask, a black velvet cloak wrapping her completely, stealthily closed the heavy front door and leaned against it for a moment, listening intently. Outside, cries of the link-boys, the rattle of a coach on the cobbles, mingled with the swirl of rain on this stormy September night. From the parlour across to her left she could hear the murmur of voices. This was unusual; the family were nearly always in bed by nine and it was well past that.

Gathering her voluminous silk skirts about her so that they should not rustle, she lightly sped across the hall hoping that, by reaching her bedroom undetected, she might postpone the inevitable unpleasant interview with her father.

She had almost reached the dark stairs when, in her haste, she dropped her fan. At once the parlour door flew open and

11

Gerald Marshal's bulky figure was outlined on the threshold.

'Roxanna!' His voice was hard and impatient. 'I wish to have a word with you!'

Slowly, a sullen expression settling on her face, she turned and followed him. In the parlour she saw her sister Paulina, seated in a straight-backed chair by the fire which blazed in the huge, heavily-carved stone fireplace.

She wore such an expression of smug self-satisfaction that Roxanna's palm itched to slap her. She had been to the theatre that afternoon, and while leaving in the rowdy company of several over-painted, giggling young women and a group of be-ribboned, explosive dandies, had looked up archly to laugh at some bawdy jest made by her own escort. But across his raffishly handsome face and velvet-covered shoulder she had suddenly seen Paulina smirking down at her from a hackney. Too late, she had clapped on her black vizard.

Alert, but wearing an air of unconcern, Roxanna sauntered over to spread her hands to the flames, and her watchful, tilting green eyes scanned the family assembled there so solemnly. Her brothers' expressions were reproving. Their wives gave her a brief glance, lips pursed, before bending their heads back over their embroidery. Roxanna's full red mouth drew down slightly at the corners. She began to peel off her long golden gloves with leisurely insolence.

It had been her habit, during the past three months since she began to go on these clandestine outings, to change her clothes at her friend Lydia's apartment, always donning her dull, unfashionable garments before returning to Holborn and her father's solid Elizabethan mansion. But tonight, with the knowledge that Paulina would undoubtedly betray her, she had been seized with a reckless defiance, and she tossed back the fur-lined hood of her cloak, displaying the green gown beneath.

She caught Paulina's envious glance at her bronze ringlets on which, only that day, Lydia's coiffeur had worked so that they gleamed like coppery satin. Roxanna gave her a little superior smile and deliberately lifted an eye-brow at her brother-in-law, Nicholas, who answered her with a quick wink. She knew that he wanted her; several times he had waylaid her in the dark hall-way with kisses panting and ardent, hands fumbling for the fastening of her bodice. Paulina had not taxed her with this, but her glowering glances told that she knew all about it.

Gerald Marshal's heavy voice cut like a lash as he began to upbraid her. 'What is this tale Paulina brings me of your going to the play, and meeting with that whore, Lydia Ward? Have you not been strictly forbidden ever to speak with the wench again?'

' 'Tis plain, sir, that Paulina has given you details enough.' Roxanna's voice was low and rich, slightly scornful, and she used the indolent drawl affected by the fops with whom she had been associating. 'What more can I add?'

'Do not be pert, hussy!' Marshal's darkly-jowled face flushed.

Although his bulk dominated her slender five feet four inches she showed no sign of cringing from him and, for an instant, he had a clear, uncomfortable picture of her mother. He had been considered very fortunate that, in a match arranged by his father, his bride should be so fair. But she always held herself remote from him, although she bore him a child for seven of the eight years that they were married. The only time he ever saw her betray emotion was after Paulina was born, when she had pleaded with him to let her sleep alone. He had dismissed her entreaties as silly, womanish fancies. Ten months later Roxanna was born and his wife died.

A spasm of grief and rage against himself and this daughter born of an unwilling mother, set him shouting so that the glasses chinked on the table and the women jumped nervously. His temper was notoriously short and the whole house quailed at his outbursts of fury.

'I'll not tolerate it, Roxanna!' he thundered, jabbing a stubby finger at her. 'Nor will I have you painting your face and making a show of yourself at that cursed playhouse. Lydia brought disgrace to her father, running off with that young spark last year, and living like a whore since. She is naught but a common drab, and that is how you will end!'

'She is my true, dear friend!' Roxanna rounded on him, blazing and indignant, her curls bouncing, the pearls threaded among them gleaming in the candlelight. 'She is not a whore, but an actress! I saw her perform today! I went escorted by a nobleman,' she added testily.

'So you may have been,' Marshal answered sardonically, rocking on his heels, hands clasped behind his back under the skirt of his dark, broadcloth coat. 'But one of those young bucks will be your ruin, my lass. I'll engage that none of 'em mean to wed you. They'll give you naught but a clap or a bastard, or both!'

'Pa!' This horrified exclamation came from his eldest daughter, Margaret, and Roxanna grinned at the shocked tone, but she knew very well that what her father said was perfectly true. Marriage was considered a most dull fate by the young bloods who courted her. They undertook it only when driven to by the necessity of obtaining a large dowry. With this, they settled their debts, packed their unfortunate brides off to the country and took a wench into keeping. It was definitely unfashionable to do otherwise. Roxanna had accidentally met Lydia at the Royal Exchange, where she had gone on a rare shopping spree, and had been dazzled by the air of sophistication, the modish clothes and speech, the worldly morals and laxity, the preoccupation with a round of pleasure. The young men spent their days in gaming, ogling the actresses at Drury Lane, watching wrestling, bear or bull baiting and cock fighting. After a time, the novelty of many of these amusements began to pall for Roxanna. Lydia wanted to find her a wealthy man who would be willing to set her up in an apartment and keep her as his mistress, which was what she herself had done, but Roxanna hesitated. So many of Lydia's friends were diseased, openly discussing their symptoms, the latest remedies and nostrums, that this alone was a strong deterrent.

Marshal, looking down in baffled anger at his youngest child, admitted unwillingly to himself that she was pretty enough to set the whole town by the ears. There was more than a touch of the wanton about her, the way she had of glancing up from the corners of her compelling eyes, the tilt of her brows, the provocative movements of her hips as she walked. Her mouth was red and sensual, and her body disconcertingly well developed for her sixteen years, with breasts high and pointed, waist very narrow, and legs, though concealed beneath full skirts, which could only be long and slender. She moved with a fascinating half-conscious allure, which even he acknowledged as seductive.

His bushy grey eye-brows drew together in a deeper frown.

His worried concern found a fresh outlet and he scowled at the gentle Margaret, in whose small, capable hands lay the management of this large household. It was a formidable task with so many relatives, servants, apprentices, as well as ten young children to be cared for. 'Nan Dobs should have had her wits about her,' Marshal continued to grumble. 'She well knows the tricks madam here is capable of playing!'

'Nan has been helping me with the babies!' Margaret's face was pale, anxious but determined. 'They have been mighty sick. We all but lost Paulina's little Will.'

Roxanna gave a disdainful flick of her curls, remarking spitefully; ' 'Tis a thousand pities that Paulina was not so engrossed with him also. Perhaps she would then have kept her nose out of my concerns!'

'It is her duty to see what you are about!' Marshal swung back to her with a roar. 'Damn me, I'll not see one of my girls play the harlot!'

'I have no mind to do that!' Roxanna's voice rose stridently. 'I like fine clothes, yes, and to enjoy a few pleasures... Is that so very wicked? Do I have to remain tied to the house? I'll warrant if I were a lad I could do far worse things than the sins you tax me with, and you would turn a blind eye to 'em!'

She stabbed a knowing stare at the only unmarried brother present. Lydia had told her that he was a regular visitor to Mrs Fugg's brothel in Shoe Lane. They had giggled about it together.

'Enough of this!' Marshal cut in conclusively. ' 'Tis time you were wed. Edmund Raynal came here again this afternoon to ask for you. I shall accept his offer!'

Fear collapsed Roxanna's new-found confidence. She had only once met Raynal, a planter from Jamaica in England on business, and her dislike of him had been instantaneous and instinctive.

'You will marry me to him just to be rid of me,' she said bitterly. 'It doesn't matter to you that I shall go miles away to some savage island, with a man who is a stranger.'

'I am not prepared to discuss it further,' Marshal's tone brooked no argument. 'He dines here tomorrow, and I shall tell him that you are honoured to accept him.'

'You cannot force me to marry him!'

She whacked her fan down on the polished surface of the table with such force that the ivory sticks snapped.

'If you go against me, you leave this house tonight...for good! Out into the streets where you belong, you sorry slut!' The contempt in her father's voice sent the tears smarting to her eyes, but she glared up into his face which had gone beet-red, the veins standing out on his forehead.

Roxanna spun round, her long train swishing, and fiercely raked the faces ranged solidly against her. And she hated them, loathed their air of prosperous, smug respectability, their orderly, industrious lives. She doubted if any of them had ever made a foolish, impulsive action. Not for them, it seemed, the frustrated yearnings, the unnamed desires which racked her and sometimes sent her down to the wharves to stare, be-dazzled, at the high-pooped, romantic ships, aromatic with the scent of spices, telling of voyages far away, and adventures that were like a different world to the safe routine of the merchant Marshals.

Roxanna gave them one final, searing glance, and then stormed to the door. In passing Paulina, she ground her heel down on her toe. 'I'll take a course with you on this. Bitch!' she hissed through clenched teeth, before the door crashed shut behind her.

Outside, a manservant, who had been eaves-dropping, leaped back guiltily. She gave him a withering look and brushed past him, high heels rapping the bare wood, skirts held high as she ran up the stairs, borne on by the impetus of her rage. On the first landing she paused to get her breath, before going along the candle-lit passage to her own room. She wrenched open the door, flounced in and kicked it savagely shut.

'Now then, hoyden, enough of this noise. D'you want to waken the whole house!' It was Nan Dobs, standing waiting for her, with lined face severely set, arms folded over her withered breasts.

Roxanna flung her an aggrieved glare; the last thing she wanted was to be scolded further. Sulkily, she moved across to the dressing-table, tossing her cloak onto the bed.

'And where, pray, did you get that gown? Gracious Heaven, look at the bodice! Your bosom is all but naked!'

Roxanna glowered at her in the mirror,

reaching up to slide the jewels from her ears. These gowns, made by Lydia's tailor, had been her especial delight. In them she felt different; no longer the unfashionable, countrified little merchant's daughter, bred from a strict family almost Puritanic in dress and outlook. Lydia, delighted to meet her friend again after more than a year, was only too happy to supply the money to buy gowns, petticoats, lace-trimmed shifts, velvet gloves, silk stockings and stilt-heeled satin pumps; anything and everything which the luxury-loving Roxanna wanted.

Nan Dobs came up behind Roxanna to unlace the strings of the busk, that tight, short corset worn beneath the bodice to nip in the waist and force up the breasts. Roxanna heaved a sight of relief.

'Where is Lucy?' she asked, slipping her arms out of the full, slashed sleeves.

'Lucy has gone to bed with a buffet on the ears that she will long remember!' Nan replied crisply.

Lucy Knapp was Roxanna's personal maid. She was a year her senior and had fast become a friend and confidant, her high-spirits and zest for life finding a match in her mistress. A fresh-faced, snub-nosed country girl, with merry blue eyes and short, springy brown curls, she had entered with relish into all Roxanna's intrigues.

Roxanna did not bother to reply, but looked at her image in the glass. She stared critically, head to one side. Her face was like that of some elf-child, small, heart-shaped, with strange green eyes oddly slanting at the corners under thick black lashes. At a time when so many women were cruelly marred by small-pox, her skin was faultless. She crossed one shapely leg over the other, swinging her shoe on the tip of her toe, only half-listening to the nurse's drone.

' 'Tis because you were born on a Friday. I have never known one with it for their natal day who was aught but a trouble. Is that paint on your cheeks, and a black patch! Merciful Heaven, what next! Is your maidenhead still intact?'

Roxanna twisted away from her, petulantly. 'Have done do, Nan! Why do you din a body's ear so?' Angrily, she stood up and the yellow taffeta underskirt and stiff white petticoats whispered to the ground. 'Rest easy. I'm still a virgin! D'you think I have no sense at all? I can look out for

23

myself, I'll warrant you!'

Wearing her knee-length shift, she padded across the burnished oak boards on bare feet, to the large panelled bed with its carved posts and tester, tapestry curtains hanging on each side. Nan put the candlestick on the bedside table, held back the bedclothes and Roxanna jumped in, shivering a little and drawing the feather quilt up under her chin.

'I've done my best to bring up your saintly mother's little forlorn partridges.' Nan was now launched onto one of her favourite subjects. 'I've tried to make an honest wench of you, teaching you all I know of housewifery, as well as seeing that you studied your horn book, and trained you in the skills of neat stitchery. Tho', Lord knows, you were never over eager to learn!'

'Why all this pother, Nan? I've done nothing.'

'You've disobeyed your father by meeting Lydia, in the first place.'

'But she has always been my friend.'

'She disgraced her family!' Nan's face was relentless. 'And she should be whipped through the streets at the cart's tail for a whore! She'll end in Bridewell, and so

will you if you follow her example!' Her
voice softened. 'Come now, poppet...you
will be a good daughter and marry Mr
Raynal.'

Roxanna's lips began to quiver. 'But
he is so old, Nan,' she sniffed, 'I shall
go away, miles away to the Indies. You
wouldn't wish that on me, would you?'

'He's very rich.'

'I'll not be bought!' Roxanna's chin
lifted stubbornly, but she stopped crying,
resting her arms on her raised knees, her
eyes thoughtful.

'A man with wealth is not to be
despised,' advised Nan, adding artfully:
'You'll have blackamoor slaves aplenty.'

'Shall I have a fine bridal?' Roxanna
demanded, inclined to bargain if she was
to be driven into this match.

The nurse raised her eyes and hands to
the shadowed ceiling. 'Lord! You can leave
me alone to see to that!'

'Finer than Paulina's?' There was a tart
edge to Roxanna's question.

' 'Uds Lud, no one will remember that
Paulina was ever wed at all.' Nan promised.
'You shall have a fine wedding-gown, boxes
of linen and plate to take with you to the
Indies, all the new clothes you desire.

And,' she added archly, 'I've a set of infant's garments in readiness. I'll swear that within the year you'll be in need of 'em!'

Roxanna eyed her narrowly as she got stiffly to her feet, the keys at her girdle jangling faintly. 'And can I take Lucy?'

'If her parents be willing.' Nan stooped to kiss her, and then hobbled to the door.

'I'll sleep on't,' Roxanna muttered guardedly, but she had already made up her mind to comply.

'That's my moppet,' with her hand on the latch the old woman paused. 'When you have little ones of your own, you will be too busy to notice whether your husband is handsome or no. And refrain from bantering Mrs Paulina, you two have ever given one another the spleen!'

This was true enough, Roxanna had hated her even in the nursery when the brass-bound horn book, from which they were supposed to learn their letters and prayers, had made an excellent weapon. Lydia had always taken Roxanna's part in the vicious, spiteful battles which had often raged. Their tempers had been in no way improved by Nan's pinches and slaps if mistakes were made in their embroidery, or her shrill scoldings if their behaviour was unladylike.

Roxanna reached out to snuff the candle and then instantly tucked her head down under the sheets, convinced that the darkness was peopled by hobgoblins.

Jamaica! Suddenly the full realization of its great distance from England swept down on her. She forgot that she had been bored with the secure life in this house where the Marshals had been firmly established for several generations. All that she remembered was that her room was so safe and familiar, with its dark panelling, the mullioned windows which looked out over the large pleasant garden, and beyond it the fields of Holborn. A picture of Edmund Raynal's cold, cadaverous face floated behind her closed eyelids, and abruptly she turned her face into her pillow and began to cry like a lonely, despairing child.

The wedding took place three weeks later on the first day of October, 1679. As Nan had promised, no expense was spared, and the women of the household were reduced to a state of hysterical turmoil by the speed with which all the arrangements had to be made. Roxanna was kept virtually a prisoner.

Arley House was crowded with guests on the wedding day, many of them complete strangers to the bride. They put away their unimposing garb and, wearing unusually gay apparel, arrived early carrying sprigs of rosemary and flourishing true-lovers knots. Nan Dobs had driven the servants hard and the whole house had been thoroughly cleaned from attics to cellars. The pewter and silver were burnished, the waxed oak glowed warmly, hung with gilded bays and rosemary.

The ceremony and the feast which followed passed in a nightmare haze for Roxanna. She moved like an animated doll, pale, in a white satin formal gown, the bodice long and pointed, the sleeves short, full and slashed to show the lace-trimmed chemise beneath. The underskirt had a wide silver centre panel embroidered in silver thread and seed pearls. A fragile orris collar buttoned to her throat, fastened by a pearl choker, and Roxanna, seeing her reflection in the mirror could not believe that it was herself. She felt numb, frozen with dread.

Raynal did not once speak directly to her during the whole long afternoon and, when the rooms were made rosy with scores of candles sparkling in the chandeliers, her fingers curled with revulsion as they rested on the hand extended to her to lead her on to the floor in a coranto. His vein-knotted flesh had the chill of a reptile, but he trod the measure faultlessly, upright and courtly. After this, the dancing became wilder, as the excited, drunken throng skipped to the livelier music of a jig. And, at last, the moment which she had been dreading was upon her; the time when she would be left alone with her husband.

Roxanna sat stiffly on her side of the vast four-poster bed which dominated the wedding-chamber, shivering violently, although a fire blazed between the andirons on the wide hearth. Miserably she shifted the sheet up to cover her more closely, certain that any fate would have been preferable to marriage with this man.

For a moment, neither spoke or moved and they listened to the shouts and laughter as the guests ran back to continue the merry-making. Suddenly, Raynal turned to her. Involuntarily, she started and shrank

29

back. A gleam of amusement flickered in his dark eyes.

'Madam, now that we are alone there are several facts which you should know.' His clipped voice was precise, long yellow teeth glinting briefly. 'Firstly, I shall make no connubial demands on your body,' his lips had an ironic twist. 'I doubt that this will distress you over much.'

Roxanna was so astonished that her mouth dropped open. A great up-rush of relief flooded her and with it, curiosity.

'In truth, madam,' he went on, 'I find the female obnoxious, and prefer to take my pleasures in another fashion. I married you because I have recently had occasion to take a Dutchman into partnership on my plantation. He is of a conventional nature, and objected to the gossip which was being tattled in Port Royal concerning myself and a certain young man. A wife will still those virulent tongues. Also, your dowry was not ungenerous. Play your part as a wife should, leave me to follow my own devices, and you shall have nothing to complain about in the treatment you receive.'

Roxanna was rendered momentarily speechless. When she did speak her voice

30

shook with loathing.

'Very well, sir, that arrangement will please me mightily. I take it that I, too, shall be at liberty to follow my fancy?'

He glanced up with an expression of impatient dislike. 'You misunderstand me, madam. It would spoil my design if you get yourself talked about. We are purporting to be a respectable wedded couple. If you go playing the bitch around Port Royal I shall be in a sorrier fix than before!'

Viciously, she rounded on him, her eyes flashing. 'You can't prevent me from taking a lover!'

He watched her contemptuously. 'I have told you what is to be done. Do not forget that you are coming to the West Indies. We are not very civilized there.' He gave a remote, chill smile. 'A wife is her husband's property. I can do with you what I will, and I am not a man to be disobeyed, madam. On my plantation we burn alive slaves who dare to mutiny!'

On the following week her father's ship, *The Mary of Guilford,* was ready to embark and, on the tide of early morning, misty with rain, they sailed down the Thames on the start of their journey to the West Indies.

CHAPTER 1

The ship moved lazily, its bows carving the green-blue Caribbean water.

In the stern cabin, Roxanna was beginning to wake. As the awareness of her surroundings pressed in on her dreams, she turned over, thumped her pillow and tried to settle down to sleep again, then, realizing that this was impossible, she lay gloomily thinking. Her husband, the unconscious object of her sullen conjectures, was snoring at her side.

She propped herself up on one elbow, the sleeve of her nightgown falling back over her rounded arm, an ugly expression on her face as she considered Raynal, coldly and critically.

Before they had left England, Roxanna had realized that his valet was his paramour. He travelled with them, and she grew to loathe this plump, femininely simpering young dandy. Her flesh crawled every time he came near her. Raynal called him Phoebus, but she did not know if this

32

was really his name.

At first, Roxanna was very sea-sick. When she was recovered she took a lively interest in the ship and the vast ocean which surrounded them. This soon paled into deadly monotony, the days hanging wearily on her hands. To pass the leadened hours she taught Lucy to read and write.

Raynal took a delight in frustrating anything in which she showed pleasure. She had brought her spinet with her and enjoyed it, but Raynal ordered her to cease, complaining that the noise made his head ache.

With a sigh, she flung back the sheet and swung her legs to the floor, briefly comforted by the sight of their slender length, the delicacy of her small-boned feet and ankles. She tucked her toes into high-heeled mules, crossly remembering that no man but her vile husband was ever likely to view her.

She dragged on a white satin dressing-gown and called for Lucy who slept in the adjoining cabin. The maid came in quickly, smiling and neat in a brown calico dress, the skirt tucked up over a striped petticoat. At once, she went to the bed to smooth out the doke, the impression of Roxanna's body where she had lain, so that no evil spirit might lie in it and gain ascendancy over her forever. She then fetched in a pewter ewer and bowl. Roxanna washed and scrubbed her teeth with salt.

She sat moodily on a stool before the mirror and Lucy brushed out the snarls from her long locks, twisting a great braid which she pinned with turquoise and gold bodkins, high on the crown of her head. Roxanna pulled off her sweat-soaked nightgown and Lucy dropped a clean shift over her head. Suddenly the cabin rocked with cannon-fire which set them clutching each other, thunderstruck. The decks were in an uproar.

Protesting, Lucy was sent to find out what was happening. Roxanna began to struggle into her clothes, fingers tearing at ribbons and lacing. She was standing in her flounced petticoats when Lucy rushed back.

'Oh, Ma'am!' she cried breathlessly. ' 'Tis another ship firing on us. The sailors say they may be pirates, Ma'am!'

Lucy was trembling violently as she fumbled with the fastening of the yellow taffeta gown, giving a perfunctory shake to the spreading skirt.

'Heaven help us, Ma'am!' she wailed. 'But I've heard such dreadful tales about them!'

'Well, do not repeat them to me. I don't want to hear them!' Roxanna snapped. She'd heard enough about the marauders who haunted these waters. Her father and brothers had often gloomily discussed the difficulty of obtaining insurance for their vessels when it was known that they were to cruise in the Caribbean.

Roxanna flew to the bed and fumbled under her pillow, bringing out a paper-backed booklet. Hurriedly, she flipped through the dog-eared pages till she found the right one. It was an almanac and she had adopted Lydia's habit of religiously studying it every morning to see if the planets were favourable. She ran a finger-nail down the closely printed page, then swirled round to her maid.

'See, Lucy,' she waved the book under her nose. 'The stars are in my favour! Now wake that wretch! Gad, what a damned rogue to sleep at such a time!'

Gingerly, Lucy leaned over to shake Raynal by the shoulder. He groaned and shook off her hand. Roxanna, angry and impatient, gave him a hard, vicious punch and shouted close to his ear:

'Wake up! Do you hear? The ship is being attacked! Jupiter! Sirrah, awake!'

His eyes snapped open and he sat bolt upright, his cropped brown hair showing under the night-cap which had slipped over one ear. Roxanna thought she had never seen such a despicable sight.

She tossed over an armful of clothing and he began to dress, tucking night-shirt into breeches, dragging on waistcoat and coat, stockings and buckled shoes. He swept his peruke from the wig-block and clapped it onto his skull.

'You must do something!' Roxanna was frantically thrusting clothes and jewellery into a portmanteau when the door was suddenly wrenched open and Phoebus fell in. He had just left his bed, his eyes scared and bleary, his brassy hair still with curling papers stuck in it. He rushed over to Raynal, gabbling excitedly, his fat cheeks shaking.

Roxanna watched them, her hands on her hips. Her eyes were bright with scorn.

'Well, well,' she drawled with heavy sarcasm. 'Here's as pretty a pair of cowardly dogs as I've ever seen!'

'Shut your spiteful mouth!' ordered her husband curtly. He unsheathed his sword, ignoring the gibbering panic of Phoebus.

'Will you fight?' Roxanna eyed the length of steel with sudden hope.

'Fight?' he rejoined. 'We shall see. I am no knight errant, madam.'

A sickening crunch shook the vessel and knocked them to the floor. When Roxanna looked up, it was to find Lucy and Phoebus in hysterics and Raynal scrambling through the door. She slapped her maid's face hard, and propped her on the locker sobbing into her kerchief, then she aimed a vindictive kick at the prostrate youth and ran out into the great-cabin.

The captain and his officers were too busy to be bothered with passengers. Roxanna had great faith in the brisk Captain Brownrigg, an energetic and very practical man. He had been master of her father's ships for over twenty years and knew the family well. Completely dependable and trustworthy, his craggy face was lined by constant exposure to the elements and the unrelenting vigour of maintaining strict discipline.

A young sailor, stripped to the waist and wearing the calico breeches of his trade, appeared on the threshold.

'Cap'n, there's a great fellow a' callin' for yer from the deck of yon rover!'

Raynal and Brownrigg exchanged a brief grim glance before the captain went on deck. Roxanna rushed after him before anyone could restrain her, and stood on the quarter-deck gaping at the ship which she had not realized was so close to them. A huge, blonde bearded man was hailing Captain Brownrigg. He hung out on a rope and roared across the dwindling stretch of water;

'Ho, there, cully! Have you Edmund Raynal aboard?'

The tawny giant bared white teeth in a wide grin and his voice held good-natured warning. 'Come now, we are much stronger than you...all that we want is Raynal! My lads will not harm you. We are buccaneers, not pirates, we don't wage war on any but the cursed Spanish. Give us Raynal!'

His men took up the cry in an ominous undertone which swelled to a roar. Weapons bristled in their great fists and across sun-burned shoulders. Several of them wore long rat-tailed moustaches and heavy beards, while tawdry scarves

38

bound back their greasy locks. They stirred restlessly, impatient for a fight.

Brownrigg cupped his hands and bawled his answer. 'Get away from here, you misbegotten swine! I'll see you swinging in chains in Port Royal!'

The buccaneer Captain shifted his position on the rope. 'Very well, mate, but I give you fair warning. My men will not harm you. They have their orders to shed no blood!' His cutlass flashed in a signal.

Glittering iron hooks snaked out to bite into the merchant-ship's side. Men swarmed across the chains and at the same time Brownrigg's confused sailors fired a few wide shots. Brownrigg curtly ordered Roxanna inside, his cutlass leaving its sheath with a hiss.

It was an oddly bloodless combat. True to his word, the corsair Captain saw to it that none of Brownrigg's men were killed. They were outnumbered and the struggle was brief. The sailors were either disarmed and pinioned or knocked over the head if they proved troublesome.

The buccaneer leader was the most powerfully-built young man Roxanna had ever seen. Well over six feet tall, with the great shoulders of an ox, and he exuded vitality. He wore a torn, stained red shirt and baggy blue breeches with a yellow sash spanning his waist and scarlet leather jackboots on his feet. His hair, bushy moustache and beard were a golden-bronze, and his jovial, reckless face was tanned a deep copper.

When his eyes lighted on Roxanna he gave a long, low whistle. He looked over her face and figure, lingering on her breasts. She felt the warm flush spreading up over her neck and cheeks at his frank appraisal.

'What have we here?' His full lips widened into a grin. 'How now, sweetheart. My luck was in this morning!'

His voice had the accent of one West-country born. Roxanna stared at the jewels in his ears and on his large brown hands. Her eyes met his bold ones and her fear vanished. So this was a buccaneer! He was only a man and she was confident that she could handle him as well as any city-bred fop! She gave him a smile, arch and flirtatious and he strolled over to stand very close to her so that she caught the heavy reek of his sweat.

'I am the Captain, Johnny Comry, at

your service at any hour of the day or night,' he murmured and his gaze went down again to the deep valley between her breasts, half hidden by the gauzy shift. 'What's your name, darling?'

'The lady is my wife!' Raynal pushed between them, his voice level but his eyes shining with a virulent fury.

Johnny flickered an insolent glance at him.

'Your pardon, sir. And may I have the honour of knowing your name?'

'Edmund Raynal!' There was no hesitation in her husband's voice and Roxanna almost admired him at that moment.

A deep-throated growl rose from Comry's men who crowded the door-way, clattering their swords. He silenced them with a stream of pungent oaths before giving Raynal a menacing smile.

'What do you want with me?' Raynal's tone held all the contempt only a planter could feel for these men, mostly deported convicts, escaped slaves, the dregs of many nations, who made the Caribbean waters very unsafe and, therefore, bad for trade.

'I have no quarrel with you,' Comry assured him. 'But my matelot has the greatest desire on earth to clap peepers

41

on you!' He swung to the door, moving, for all his bulk, with agility, and they heard him thunder across into the waist, 'Dirk! Here's your man.'

A voice answered him, there was a quick step on the stairs and another man ducked his head under the lintel. Roxanna could do nothing but gape at him, completely stunned. He was so overpoweringly handsome that even Johnny faded into insignificance. She could not drag her eyes from him, and continued to stare, mouth slightly open.

He was very tall, his head at least four inches higher than his Captain, and with great width to his shoulders, a narrow waist and long muscular legs. His black hair fell in heavy waves to the shoulders of his soiled white shirt, where it rolled under into thick curls. He had a short, straight nose and his mouth was finely-moulded, the upper lip curved and sensitive, the lower full and sensual, his chin square and determined.

Grey eyes stared out keenly from under black eyebrows. They were turbulent and wild, oddly pale against his bronzed face. There was a hauteur in his bearing which suggested aristocratic birth, and a hint of arrogant pride and ruthlessness which sent a chill of pleasurable fear down Roxanna's spine. The newcomer wore black velvet breeches which fitted his sleek hips closely and his waist was girded with a wide, brass-studded belt. Thigh-length black leather boots encased the handsome legs.

There was silence in the cabin for an instant while he and Raynal exchanged a glance of recognition and dislike. Roxanna saw her husband's face turn a muddy-grey as a deep, resonant voice cracked out:

'Raynal! Do you remember me?'

'Yes, I know you, Dirk Courtney.' Raynal's voice was quiet. And all that was revengeful in Roxanna took delight in knowing that he was afraid. Dirk strode over.

'The last time we met I was hanging by my wrists from a whipping-post. I had just been flogged. You found it amusing to hear me scream as they rubbed lime-juice and chile-pepper into my raw skin! I shall carry the scars until I die! While you had me tortured, I swore to kill you. My men are eager to lay hands on you. More than one has suffered from your brutality and they have many pretty methods for making a man pray for death. But I'll give you a chance to die cleanly with your sword in your hand.'

Raynal recovered his composure and with it his scorn. 'You are still my property!' he snarled. 'I'll not cross swords with a base-born slave!'

Dirk's face was taut, a muscle jerking at the side of his mouth. His hand shot out and slashed across Raynal's cheek, making his head snap back.

'Now will you fight!' he ground, through clenched teeth. 'Up with your sword and fight me! You bloody slaver!'

Raynal put up a hand to his face, where a vivid red mark burned. Without a word, he followed the young buccaneer out onto the deck and down into the waist where an ever-increasing crowd of men gathered to watch the fight. They formed a noisy, ragged circle. Roxanna stood on the quarter-deck, her attention riveted on Dirk Courtney.

At a signal, the swords crossed and then they circled, their weapons extended to arms' length. Raynal was an expert swordsman, trained by an Italian fencing-master. He was quick and light, desperately fighting for his life, and he delivered

44

a ferocious lunge which pinked Dirk in the arm. The onlookers bellowed their excitement.

Raynal's method was one of attack. He used his energy aiming whistling cuts at his opponent, which were always neatly turned aside. Again and again, Raynal tried to beat down that baffling, glittering barrier that was Dirk's sword and his breathing was harsh and rasping, while froth smeared his lips, the sweat running in rivers down his lean, hatchet-face.

The throng of spectators, kneeling, standing or perched up on the gilded sides, were silent and expectant. A sudden gasp went up as the swords of the two opponents engaged and locked. Suddenly, Dirk's shoulders bunched and he gave a tremendous heave, forcing his steel free. Raynal stumbled back, off his guard, Dirk lunged, driving the blade into his chest until the tip appeared between Raynal's shoulders. Dirk straightened with a lithe, graceful movement, withdrawing the sword, crimsoned and slippery.

A cheer shattered the tense silence. Raynal stood as if stunned for a second, his rapier clanking on the deck, then, amidst the excited yells, he slumped to his knees, bloody foam bubbling from between his lips.

Without moving, Roxanna kept her eyes fixed on Dirk. His wide chest heaved with the recent exertion, the sweat making great dark patches on his shirt and running from his hair. The blood on his arm had spread into a wide scarlet circle.

'Are you satisfied, lad?' Johnny clapped him affectionately on the shoulder, while his jubilant comrades shouted their congratulations and praise.

Dirk shook his head, seeming doubtful and a little perplexed. 'Revenge doesn't hold the satisfaction I had expected,' he said slowly.

'What about his widow?' Johnny's eyes crinkled at the corners as he saw the way in which she was staring up at Dirk.

Dirk shifted his attention to her for the first time, and she had the sensation that all her bones and muscles were dissolving and turning to jelly. As their eyes locked, it seemed as if the ship and all about them disintegrated. She had the most extraordinary conviction that since the very beginning of time she had known this man. Certainty swept through her that, in ages yet to come, she would always be incomplete until she was united with him. But this sensation lasted only for the fraction of a second. She became conscious of the clamour of her blood which demanded that she be swept up against him, crushed into his arms. He had not moved, but she felt that he had come suffocatingly close. She shut her eyes, then raised the long lashes to peek at him again.

Dirk's glance travelled slowly, speculatively, down her body with a look which made her feel hot all over. He raised one dark curved eyebrow, an amused, faintly mocking twist to his mouth.

Abruptly, he turned away to issue curt commands to the buccaneers.

Roxanna was hurt and disappointed. Dirk made her feel as if he did not care to be troubled with her.

'Who *is* he?' she demanded.

Comry grinned. 'That good-looking bastard! He always steals the hearts of the wenches I have a fancy to lie with,' he teased. 'Well, he is my matelot, my lieutenant. I couldn't run this ship without him. I met him, oh, must be five years ago, when I was a boucan-hunter. We worked together, shared the fortunes and hardships. But don't fall in love with him too deeply,

47

my pretty. He's a mighty strange fellow!' Then he went on, 'But you. You don't seem over-concerned that your husband is dead.'

'My father arranged the marriage. Indeed, it was never consummated. He didn't fancy women. His pretty male popinjay is even now cowering in his cabin.'

Johnny threw back his shaggy mane and roared with laughter. 'Poor wench! No wonder you find the lusty Dirk to your liking. I'll warrant he'll make up for your husband's lack.' He gave her waist a squeeze and his face was kind and full of good-humour. 'Nay, don't blush so furiously, sweetheart. Come over to our ship and I'll get him to give you what you want. Tho' I doubt he'll need very much persuading.'

CHAPTER 2

Lucy was in the great cabin chattering animatedly with a sturdy, bandy-legged Irishman who was staring at her with awed wonder on his likeable, battle-scarred countenance. There were six buccaneers on guard over Brownrigg and his officers, who stood in glum, sullen silence, while their conquerors swaggered and rattled their weapons, bragging loudly for the benefit of Lucy. She was obviously favourably impressed, while Danny Harrigan just grinned at her vacuously, as considerate as if she were made of china.

Johnny explained to Brownrigg that they would do them no injury. The Captain, his face as hard as a coral reef, still scathingly referred to them as 'pirates', but Johnny maintained his cordial manner, saying that he would put a prize crew aboard, and would entertain Brownrigg and his officers on his own ship. He promised that as soon as they reached the shelter of Tortuga they would be free to continue their journey, offering to pass the word among 'The Brethren of the Coast', that they were to be molested no more.

The buccaneer vessel was a captured Spanish galleon which had been renamed the *Hopewell*. It was an impressively magnificent ship, rich with gilt and carving. The buccaneers had made alterations on capturing it, so that it was now speedy, much lighter, and generously fitted with cannon. Under the methodical command of Dirk, supported by Johnny, the decks were as orderly as any man-of-war.

The Captain stood back to let his enforced guests precede him into the state-cabin. Brownrigg entered with stiff caution, but Lucy and Roxanna were entranced by the opulence of the furnishings. The cabin was long and low-ceilinged, with painted panels, gilded scroll-work and velvet curtains at the curved horn-paned windows which ran almost the width of the stern.

Johnny waved Captain Brownrigg and his crestfallen companions into seats, and begged Roxanna to tell him her name, before introducing her to his mates with a great show of gallantry.

When the food was brought, the buccaneers ate heartily, their prisoners with more reserve, but presently the merchantman's Captain relaxed a little under Johnny's jovial cordiality, and the constant replenishment of his glass.

'Now, sir,' Johnny waved a piece of beef speared on the point of his dagger. 'Tell me how you like our meat!'

'Very good,' Brownrigg conceded cautiously. 'Much better than we can obtain.'

'That is because of the way in which we preserve it.' Johnny hacked off another chunk. 'Far superior to the salted pork which you have lived on for months, I'll warrant! In the beginning, we buccaneers were simply hunters and settlers, wanting to farm and trade and make a living by going after cattle.'

Johnny sat far down on his spine, his booted feet up among the silver dishes, gulping back his third straight brandy.

'Then tell me, Captain Comry,' Brownrigg enquired, 'why do the Spaniards hate the buccaneers so, if they are only harmless traders?'

Johnny pulled a thoughtful face. 'The Spanish are greedy, they want no other nations here, and maybe our lads did sometimes take a few of the cattle from the Spanish settlers. When our countries are at war they are glad enough to use us as a kind of militia. When peace reigns we are supposed to be hanged if we are caught! Usually the governors of the islands will back us if they are given a large enough share of the loot!'

Roxanna toyed with the food on her plate. Slowly she raised her wineglass and over it looked into Dirk Courtney's cool grey eyes. He was seated directly opposite her, and stared back unwinkingly. His face was moodily pensive, perturbing gaze sombre under the black brows. The neck of his shirt was open showing a tanned chest, and there was a long red scratch running down his forearm where Raynal had pinked him.

She gave up the pretence of eating and warmth surged in her body on a steadily rising tide of excitement. A new expression crept into his face, intense and alert, while his eyes narrowed slightly as they slid to her naked shoulders and half-concealed breasts. She drew in a sharp breath while her heart raced.

One of his long, oddly-aristocratic hands, was resting on the table and in the other he twirled the slender stem of his goblet. The light gleamed on the heavy gold ring he wore on his little finger. Set with a carved garnet it sent out a sullen, reddish fire. Roxanna wondered how it would feel to have those strong brown hands closing over her, fondling her body. There was half-derisive amusement in the curve of his mouth and she flushed scarlet, convinced that he guessed her thoughts.

'Where are you taking us, Captain Comry?'

Brownrigg's question drew her attention back to the conversation which was flowing around them. Johnny heaved himself up in his carved chair, swinging his legs to the floor, gripping a tankard in his great fist.

'Tortuga!' he answered.

'That's a French island,' remarked Brownrigg's first-mate.

A wide grin lifted Johnny's bushy moustache. 'Aye, the governor was pleased to give us a bundle of commissions against the Spanish Crown! Very pretty they are, too, aren't they Dirk?' He raised an eyebrow at his lieutenant who responded with a sardonic grimace. 'All duly beribboned and certified with most impressive red seals! And they cost us a rare amount, by God!'

'The governor must be a blaggard!' Brownrigg snorted, shocked.

Johnny grunted. 'He's a wise man with an eye to business! Port Royal is closed to us now that Harry Morgan has been knighted and made the Lieutenant-governor! Although he was the greatest buccaneer of us all, he's now turned bloody

53

respectable, and is nubbing his old cullies. Devil rot his guts!'

'Amen to that!' vehemently agreed his quarter-master, Jim Rackham, fingering a bristly chin. Roxanna had been revolted to notice that the tops of both his ears had been cut off.

'So we find a convenient refuge in Cayona,' Johnny flung wide his massive arms and stretched till his joints cracked. 'The governor encourages the Brethren of the Coast to come to his snug little harbour and spend their money.'

Roxanna heard Lucy whisper and looked across to see that the Irish mate was grinning and ogling her maid. Roxanna leaned closer to her and murmured:

'Gad, but he appears to be mightily smitten with you, Lucy.'

A tobacco jar was passed around the table and soon the sweet-smelling smoke was rising from half-a-dozen pipes while the tankards were filled again. They were, suddenly, abruptly disturbed by an infuriated uproar from the quarter-deck.

The Captain flung wide the door and a ragged group tumbled in, dragging with them a struggling youth who was bawling insults and aiming vicious kicks at his captors.

'What in hell's name ails you, stinking bastards!' shouted Johnny.

'There's a doxy aboard, Cap'n. This 'ere is a plaguey mort what was servin' on the marchantman. All done up in men's lurries! Says she was cabin-boy.'

The captive rose slowly from the floor, assuming a half-crouching wholly defiant attitude. She was gaunt, raw-boned, tall and flat-chested. Her clothes were patched and filthy, her hair concealed beneath a knitted cap. Her thin, pinched face had the ferocity of a wild animal at bay.

Johnny ran an eye over her.

'I assure you, Captain, that I had no idea of her sex,' Captain Brownrigg interposed. 'She has served us well as a cabin-boy.'

Roxanna and Lucy stared with distaste at the uncouth female who now stood glaring about her.

'Well, my lass, what's all this?' Johnny cocked an eye at her.

The girl stood in front of him, face sulky eyes vivid in her grubby face.

'They bubbled my secret out of me, that's plain enough.' She had a harsh truculent voice. Roxanna recognized the strong, nasal accent of the London slums.

Johnny was sceptical. 'Come now, after all these weeks, d'you expect me to believe that you were so careless?'

She suddenly relaxed and swung an angular leg over one of the chairs, seating herself adroitly.

'If you must have it, I was on the run from being habbled. I was on the buttock and twang lay but some bloody thief-taker run rusty on me. My bully was taken and scragged at Tyburn but I lay low and shipped aboard the merchant. If they had caught me I should have been for that last ride in a rattler too!' She lifted her lean shoulders. 'As for why I let those bastards see I was a wench, well, I chose to!'

Johnny leaned forward, his eyes like glowing topaz. 'You took a risk. You know what they're like when they see a woman!'

'I can look after myself.' She tossed her head. 'I wanted to be brought to you!'

'You might fare no better with me,' Johnny gave a wicked smile, baring large even teeth.

She rested her palms on each arm of his chair and bent towards him.

56

'Maybe that is what I wanted,' she told him softly.

For a moment their eyes held, while Johnny pensively tugged at his golden moustaches.

'What is your name?' he questioned at last.

'You can know me as Kate Johnson!' she said crisply. Then her voice warmed with admiration. 'I want to be your woman, Johnny Comry!'

Johnny screwed up his eyes in mock suspicion and then opened them wide, pleased and amused.

'I know what you are thinking!' she railed. 'But I don't mean to share your pad just for a night or so! You take me on and it will be for good! I'm no simpering virgin. I've been a prig all my life and seen the inside of the Whit more'n once. My bully was a bridle cull in the summer, holding up the coaches on the heaths. He was a fine, gallant lad and I loved him. But I can now love you just as strongly. You'll have my loyalty don't doubt that! I like you. You're a big, handsome animal and about as stupid, I'll lay a groat!'

Johnny bellowed with laughter at this

57

outburst and slapped her across the buttocks.

'A lass after my own heart!' he grunted. 'Newgate Jail, eh? I've been lodged there too, so we are almost old cullies already! See this,' he held up his left hand, palm uppermost. An F for felon, had been deeply branded there.

'You've been glimmed,' exclaimed Kate.

'Aye,' he answered with his ironical smile. 'Glimmed and transported. I should have been scragged, but was sentenced to transportation instead. There's no doubt that the judge had a cut of my sale-money. But 'tis the nubbing-cheat for me next time I'm caught!' He put his hands round his throat in imitation of a noose and pulled a ghastly face.

'How did you get to be a prig?' Kate wanted to know.

'I was a farmer's son. But I got restless, it wasn't exciting enough for me. So, I went up to London. The first day I got there I fell for the very same buttock and twang lay as you were on, Kate, my love.'

He reached out an arm and pulled her down on to his knee. 'I went into a tavern and this lively little jilt came up to me.

She got me lappy, I wasn't used to strong drink in those days, then she invited me to go outside with her. But hardly had I got my arms round her, there in the dark alley, afore down comes her bully's cudgel. When I woke I found myself face down in the road. They'd milled me of every penny I owned.'

'Yes, that is just how my bully and I worked.' Kate said with a slow, reminiscent smile. 'But how did you shift?'

'I starved,' he replied. 'I fell in with a battalion of foot-scamperers. It seemed an easy way to make a living and I had a good run for well over a year till I was whittled on by some damned thief-taking dog!'

Kate wound her arms about his neck, pulling at the gold hoops in his ears. 'I'm sick of being poor. Tired of emptying slop-pots for bunters like her!' She jerked her head at Roxanna, darting her a venomous look.

Dirk stood up and stretched and Johnny gave him a brief glance. 'We must get down to business, Dirk. The lads want the share-out as soon as maybe. I shall need your wits out there.'

'You shall have them, too, Johnny,' Dirk answered levelly. 'But first I must wash off this blood, put on a clean shirt.'

Johnny lowered his lid in a solemn wink. 'Aye, preen yourself for her ladyship here.' His glance encompassed Roxanna. Dirk returned his look with a smile, as if they shared some joke between them. When the door had closed behind him, Johnny said to Roxanna. 'He has had your box taken to his cabin!'

Roxanna flared up, her chin went out and her red lips drew back over her small white teeth.

'Oh, has he! He's mighty confident!' she retorted.

'Dirk desires you,' Johnny stated flatly. 'And what Dirk wants he always gets! He no doubt recognizes an amorous little baggage when he sees one!'

CHAPTER 3

The share-out was the climax of a buccaneering trip, when the gold and jewellery, silver-plate, weapons and ornaments were fairly divided. Bales of cloth and other merchandize were sold in port with any slaves captured, and the money shared after. A sum was set aside for the merchant who had provisioned the ship on credit, and a bribe for the governor of whichever island they were allowed to use as a base.

There was almost one hundred men aboard and they each came forward as their names were called. The Captain and officers received the largest portions, others were allotted a share according to their conduct or wounds. Roxanna stood forgotten in the lust for wealth. She fidgeted in the heat, the sweat starting out on her face beneath her rouge. Languidly, she waved her fan and talked to Lucy. Her lips drooped crossly. Try as she might, she could not get Dirk to look at her.

Homesickness suddenly swept over her and she felt tears smart under her eyelids, until she looked up and caught sight of Dirk with his proud bearing and powerful attraction. Then Roxanna knew that she would rather be with him than anywhere else on earth.

At last Johnny wiped his wet face with his shirt-sleeve and spoke, his voice butting across the din.

'That's the lot, my bloods! In a day or

so we shall be in Cayona where the brandy-shops and bawdy-cases will be ready for you to spend your cole!'

'Hey, Cap'n, what about the women prisoners? Aren't ye goin' ter put 'em up fer auction?' A shaggy lout slouched forward to mouth up at Johnny.

A deafening clamour rose, as the marauders supported their mate, demanding the women. Johnny's officers closed up behind him, mouths inflexible, hands on their weapons.

'Order there!' Johnny snatched up a leathern speaking-trumpet which he generally used to issue commands in battle. 'Order! You misbegotten slobs! By God, I know that you are a pack of crass dogs and not over-blessed with wit, but surely you can see that we can't treat these people from an English ship as prisoners or we shall be marked as pirates! And that we are not! Do what you like with the Spanisher wenches, but these you can't have!'

'She was wife to that devil Raynal!' yelled a hulking, sandy-haired veteran.

The first speaker mounted the companion-way waving a cutlass round about his head. 'He's dead, bullies!' he bawled. 'But this flash jade is here! We'll have sport with her and then kill her by inches!'

Johnny swung his pistol like a club and brought it down across the man's head. The rioter fell back on top of the men who crowded behind him. Roxanna backed away in blind panic.

She felt arms about her and with a quick, breathless glance up, saw Dirk's menacingly angry eyes. She buried her face against him, blocking out the yelling rabble. His chest and the powerful muscles of his thighs felt iron-hard and she clung with her arms about his waist. The heavy masculine odour of sweat on his clothes, the scent of leather from his jackboots sent a violent yearning sweeping through her, thrusting out all other thoughts.

His bitingly contemptuous voice rang out to quell the uproar.

'I settled a score with Raynal! If anyone has a claim to this woman it is I! Any man who feels that it should not be so can cross swords with me, if he has a mind!'

A fierce rush of joyous pride made Roxanna throw back her head to look up at him adoringly. The men muttered and growled, but they respected his reputation as a duellist.

Johnny swung round to mutter: 'Get

63

her out of this quickly, Dirk. I'll talk 'em round, the insubordinate swine! A couple of bullets in their hides will change their tone.'

He grinned to see the way in which she was clinging to Dirk and gave her a monstrous wink. Dan stood guard on the stateroom door, ready to fight to the death to protect Lucy. Without a word Dirk hurried Roxanna to his cabin.

It was comfortable and richly furnished, with a Turkish rug on the floor, a carved chest, gilded mirror and scarlet-upholstered chair. There were books on a shelf, pistols and a rapier in one corner. The bed was wide with embellished head and a coverlet made from matched jaguar pelts. Roxanna's leather, brass-trimmed trunk stood under the curved windows, which were flung wide in the broiling afternoon heat.

Roxanna was sick with shock from the scene on deck. There seemed to be a lump in her throat and she swallowed hard. The veneer of sophistication and coquetry, acquired under Lydia's expert tuition, had deserted her completely, leaving her tongue-tied. Dirk watched her seriously, unsmiling. Reluctantly she met his eyes, her hands wet, languor creeping over her limbs.

Every movement he made, seemingly unhurried but swift and lithe, heightened her desire, yet at the same time she was petrified. He was a stranger, no doubt as ruthless as the men he commanded. The tension was mounting unbearably between them and she suddenly swayed towards him, lids half-closed, almost intoxicated by his close proximity. He reached out and drew her hard against him. She let her head tip back, supported by his arm, her lips parting to receive his kiss.

It was some time before he raised his head and she opened her eyes as completely stunned as if there had been a violent explosion. He was looking down at her with a curious expression, a mixture of puzzled tenderness and faint anger. Roxanna felt cheated, incomplete, and her arms tightened demandingly about his neck. In a swift movement he picked her up and carried her to the bed.

Roxanna, her terror almost as great as her desire, struggled to get away from him. The control he had shown so far gave way to a passion that was tempestuous and relentless. Beneath his quiet exterior lay a nature at once completely selfish, sensual and rather cruel. But soon the knowing caressing of his hands and the strong sweetness of his kisses crushed down her fear, rousing her to an urgency which matched his own, and she relaxed. She could feel the sweat soaking through the back of his shirt and the pungent male smell of him was in her nostrils, mingling with the taste of wine on his mouth. His face above her was darkly absorbed and, thrusting her hands up into his thick black hair, which she had longed to do since the very first moment she saw him, she drew him down to her.

Unprepared for the searing pain which accompanied the ecstacy of their first embrace, she lay trembling and sobbing in his arms when it was over. His breathing grew quieter, he stroked her hair gently, all violence gone from him, and his lips were tender against her cheek.

'What's wrong, sweetheart?' he asked. 'I am sorry if I hurt you, but I had no idea you were still a virgin.'

Roxanna shook her head, her hair, which had all come tumbling down, falling across her face. She pressed her cheek into his shoulder and then her sobs stilled as a great joy seemed to burst inside her. She looked up at him radiantly. 'Oh...I love you so much!'

He made no reply and she was disappointed. Surely, during those moments of intimacy he must have fallen in love with her, too! She glanced anxiously into his face. His expression was grave, there was already a remote detachment about him. Then, mercurially, his mood changed and he smiled with extraordinary charm, bending to kiss her before getting up. Warily, she watched him while he tucked his shirt into his breeches and fastened his belt.

'Dirk.' She spoke his name a little shyly, still in awe of him. 'Where are you going?'

'I must go over and see how Johnny is faring with those wild rogues of ours.' His voice was maddeningly matter-of-fact.

Instantly, she was on her feet clutching at him. 'Don't leave me! Stay with me!' She wanted to be with him all of the time, longing to sleep with him there close beside her. Quite irrationally, she began to sob again, beating her fists against his chest. He caught her under the elbows and gave her a little shake, a scowl creasing his eyes.

'Hold there, Roxanna darling!' His warm voice, speaking her name for the first time, sent a vibration down her spine. 'Be still!' he urged. 'I shall not be long, then I will stay with you as long as you want. I'll send your maid to you.' He dropped a light kiss on the crown of her head.

Reluctantly, she let him go and Lucy came rushing in, anxiety on her round, freckled face.

'Oh, Ma'am, are you all right?'

Roxanna nodded, confused and dizzy, with the sudden impression that the walls of the cabin were pressing in on her.

Lucy fussed around her. 'Oh, the great brute! Did he hurt you, my poor lamb?'

'Yes, no! Oh, I don't know!' Roxanna was impatient under Lucy's tender ministrations, wanting only that he should return to her. Lucy patted and soothed.

'There now, rest easy, Ma'am. 'Twill be easier next time!'

Roxanna flashed her a sharp glance. 'And how do you know, pray?'

Lucy's laughter peeled across the cabin. 'Lud, Ma'am, do you imagine I'm still a maiden?'

'What do you think of him, Lucy?' she

questioned, wanting to talk of nothing else but him.

Lucy rolled up her eyes to indicate her vast admiration. 'Marry! But he's a mighty fine fellow, to be sure! And he seems to be a person of quality, too!'

'I'm in love with him to desperation!' confided Roxanna with a deep sigh. Lucy grinned at her woeful expression.

'If you love him, dear ma'am, then why the flurry?'

'Tell me, Lucy, do you think he loves me?' The insistence lingered in Roxanna's voice.

'Lord knows, Ma'am, men be mighty odd creatures!' Lucy gave a sage shake of her head.

Roxanna suddenly clapped a hand to her mouth. 'Maybe he'll get me with child! Would he marry me, if he did, think you?' Without waiting for a reply she was at once plunged in gloom again. 'Maybe he's already wed!'

She jumped up and began to pace the cabin restlessly. Lucy shook out her gown before hanging it up, clicking her tongue.

'Jupiter, my lady! But he made a sorry mess of this. I doubt that I can mend it.'

'A pox on it, he'll buy me a dozen more!' Roxanna snapped her fingers, and stopped dead in front of Lucy, her breasts heaving under the chemise which was all that she had on. 'Tell me what you think, Lucy! Say, has he a wife already?'

Lucy looked up from folding away the clothes, with love and pity on her features. 'I don't think so. He doesn't strike me as a marrying sort of man!'

Before departing from England she had received a gift from Lydia. This was a black nightgown, made of flimsy tiffany. Roxanna knew very well that Lydia intended she should wear it when she took a lover and now she ordered Lucy to get it out of her box. She stripped off her chemise and Lucy dropped the revealing garment over her head.

The mirror gave back an image which made her grin with satisfaction.

'Lucy,' she said with a determination that brooked no argument. 'If that man doesn't love me now I'm going to see that he soon damned well does!'

She repaired the paint on her face, and drawing out the crystal stopper of her perfume bottle, quickly touched it behind her ears, at her wrists and breasts. Lucy

70

straightened the rumpled bed and Roxanna jumped in.

She gave Lucy a quick, mischievous nod. 'You did not come to aid me, Lucy! I suppose that you had your ear pressed to the door throughout!'

'I did not!' protested her maid, indignantly. 'I waited for a moment but, as you didn't start screaming, I gathered that you were not taking amiss what he had in mind to do! So, I went on deck again.'

'To seek out the Irishman?' Roxanna sat up, hugging her knees.

'The very same,' Lucy's eyes were alive with merriment. 'Do you know, Ma'am, he is mightily besotted with me! Says that he wants to wed me! Proposes to retire from the sea and buy a tavern in Cayona. Should I accept him?'

They talked for a while, exchanging the most outrageously intimate confidences, until at last there were voices in the great-cabin.

Roxanna hastily shooed Lucy out when they heard Dirk's step and lay back, trying to compose her features while her heart thumped. He closed the door and smiled over at her, putting down a bottle and tankards on the table. She watched him, eyes glowing with admiration, while he unclasped his wide leather belt and kicked off his boots. He paused, pouring out the rich brown liquid and swallowing it down.

When he stood beside the bed her blood began to rush dizzily. He slowly scrutinized her face, abundant hair splayed out over the pillow and the shapely shoulders which rose from the black flounces. He reached out and drew back the covers. His eyes changed, slate-dark, as they went down over the rounded curves of her body, the slender thighs and legs visible through the transparent silk.

'How very fair you are!' he said softly.

Roxanna drew in a breath that was almost a sob as she held out her arms to him.

CHAPTER 4

Roxanna was playing the spinet. It was the afternoon of the following day, sultry and humid. Dirk lay on his back on the bed, his hands clasped behind his head,

72

watching her and listening to the music. She moved her fingers indolently over the keys, plucking out the mournful little air of 'The Earl of Salisbury's pavanne'. Its faint melancholy matched her mood. She had yet to hear Dirk say that he loved her. He had made love to her most of the night, but still those magic words had not crossed his lips.

She was completely infatuated with him, he had become everything to her, lover, guardian and idol. She thought him the most fabulous person in the whole world and was jealous of every moment he spent away from her. He in turn intrigued, delighted and infuriated her. She discovered that he could be charming and tender or moody and irritable. Leashed, but just there beneath the surface, was an inflexible will and savage temper. Of his past life he would say little, becoming silent and withdrawn if she probed. He did tell her that he had been called after his maternal grandfather who was Dutch, when she remarked on his unusual name; adding that it meant 'People's Ruler'. She thought it very apt. She gathered that Dirk's father had been an English nobleman, but he seemed averse to giving her further enlightenment.

Dirk's love-making was so experienced that she was forced to admit reluctantly to herself that he must have known many women. He was twenty-eight and she was unreasonably dismayed because he had lived for so long without her. She wanted to possess him entirely; to absorb him and be engulfed in return and gave herself whole-heartedly, without any reservation. Every fibre of her volatile being quivered in response to him, roused to an extreme of emotion which amounted almost to worship.

They had breakfasted in the main-cabin, although she was unwilling to share Dirk with anyone even for a brief period, and she had suffered a deal of teasing from Johnny. The grim castigation of the seamed face of Captain Brownrigg caused her a moment of embarrassment, reminding her of how her wanton behaviour would be received at home. But she was so deliriously happy that it did not disturb her. She was relieved to learn that Johnny had given Brownrigg permission to return to the merchantman with his officers, under the supervision of the buccaneer's first mate and a prize-crew.

Roxanna came over to Dirk, never tiring of his magnificent body, tanned a deep coppery brown.

'The music pleases you, darling?' she asked, her voice warm and low.

He stirred, reaching for the bottle on the table and tipping it to his lips. 'Aye,' he answered. 'I like it well. But it moves mawkish sentiments within me which are best forgot! You are a very accomplished little witch.'

She lay beside him, tracing his features with tender fingertips. His lean, bronzed cheeks were smooth-shaven, and the sunlight slanted across his eyes, making them translucent, their colour opalescent, speckled with silver, shadowed by lashes which were black, thick and curling. She ran a hand through his dark coarse hair, bending to press her lips where it sprang back from a peak on his forehead, her throat aching with rapturous tears.

'Dirk, I love you!' Her voice shook with intensity. 'Do you love me, too?'

The half-taunting smile deepened on his face, and he reached up to pull her down to him, brushing his lips across her bare shoulders, his hands going under the robe.

'Love!' his voice was caustic. 'Women always find it easy to prattle of love! Thinking that because they give a man their body they can possess his very soul in return!'

Roxanna lay still and unresponsive while he caressed her, despair jabbing at her peace of mind. Realization swamped her that here was a man quite independent, who did not really need her at all.

Self-pity, frustration and a hot wave of anger and indignation sent her twisting from his arms.

'What then, am I to you?' she demanded, eyes hard as agates. 'Just a passing fancy?'

He flickered an impatient glance over her and got to his feet.

'My dear, mine is a roving life. I cannot be bound. I shall have to go away again after we have been in Cayona for a week or so. Let me arrange for you to continue to Jamaica with Captain Brownrigg. Later, perhaps, you will wish to return to England.'

With a shocked expression she sprang to her feet staring at him in dumbfounded consternation while her lips framed a denial.

'No!' She gripped his bare arm, very tiny against his height, glaring up at him. 'You can't send me away! I shall die without you now!' Her face crumpled and she dissolved into a flood of sudden tears, throwing herself into his arms, the brass-studded leather of his belt digging at her flesh. 'I've never felt like this about anyone before. You must let me stay with you.'

His brows knit as he looked at her, as if angry with himself for bringing about this situation.

'You would fare better at home,' he cautioned. 'Nothing need be known of this episode. I suppose you would be kicked out if your family learned that you were my leman.'

Roxanna nodded vigorously, blowing her nose hard on the handkerchief which he had dragged from the pocket of his breeches.

'Yes, they are mighty prudish,' she sniffed.

His eyes narrowed to slits and she felt his muscles tense; 'They have not Parliamentarian sympathies, by chance?' he jerked out.

She was alarmed by the vehemence in his voice, his fingers dug into her shoulders. Quickly she shook her head.

'No, they are loyal to King Charles, but they do not approve of his way of life. I should be in a mighty straight for lying with you!'

He laughed, relaxed again, the tension gone, 'Do you regret it?'

Her face was grave and very earnest. 'I think I was not really alive until you kissed me!' she replied with passionate conviction.

A while later, Johnny's mop of hair appeared around the cabin door. He came in and the bed sagged as he sat down.

'Dirk, the helmsman is bellowing for you,' he informed him. 'Will you go and take the wheel through that bloody channel into the harbour? Jake can't manage it, he'll run her aground.'

Roxanna attempted to cover her nudity with the sheet. Dirk slapped her carelessly and stood up. He and Johnny exchanged that superior male smile which she found so exasperating.

'I'll keep madam warm against your return,' offered the Captain, with a lift of one eyebrow.

Roxanna assumed that he joked, but when he stretched out full length and slid an arm about her, his other hand closing over her breast, she struggled up and gave him a resounding smack.

'Fine friend you are!' She was bristling with indignation, and got up, drawing her robe tight about her. 'I trow, Dirk would call you out if he were to hear of it!'

Johnny howled with laughter. Furious, she hit him again and he raised his arms to shield his head in feigned terror.

'Have done, sweetheart, do! That's my ear you are buffeting! Don't be in such a passion. D'you think that Dirk would care if I laid his trollop?'

Roxanna fairly danced with rage. 'How dare you! I'm not a trollop, you vile knave. I come from a good family! I'm much better than you! You damned pirate!'

'How now, darling,' he seized her wrists. He was a massive giant who could have killed her with a single blow but he held her gently. 'I don't doubt that you are an honest trull...eh, girl,' he hastily corrected himself, as her eyes commenced to spark. 'But really, I admire you greatly!'

Somewhat mollified, Roxanna sat down again, warily keeping the width of the bed between them.

'And what of Kate?' she asked.

'Kate is well enough, and a good wench. But I like something with a little more flesh to it!' He grinned so disarmingly that she found herself smiling back, pleased to score over Kate.

Johnny teased her. 'Dirk tells me you have kept him mighty busy in here!'

Roxanna flung him an annoyed glare. Neither he nor Dirk ever seemed to take her seriously. They treated her as if she were a pretty toy, and not too bright at that!

'I love him!' she declared, spine stiff with dignity. 'So you see I could not lie with another man. Not even his matelot!'

She was quickly beginning to adopt Dirk's mannerisms and curse-words, as well as the underworld cant, which was at first almost unintelligible. She possessed the ability to adapt herself speedily to her surroundings, to absorb new experience and make it a part of her personality.

Johnny scratched absently at the matted pelt on his chest while he looked at her with compassion and an unusual gravity in his amber eyes.

'Sweetheart, you are very young. Dirk and I have roamed this wicked old world for years. Maybe, once, we felt as you do. Perhaps you are right,' he reached over and collected one of her hands in his calloused fist. 'Poor little bitch. You are going to suffer cruelly if you love him too deeply. He will not give his heart into any wench's keeping. And he can be completely cold-blooded if his wishes are crossed.'

'I want to be his wife,' she announced in a quiet voice.

Johnny gave a soundless, wry whistle. 'You have set yourself a sorry task there, my lass.'

With sensitive hands and the observant eye of an expert, Dirk piloted the *Hopewell* into the crescent-shaped harbour of Cayona. On a reach and at the slack of the tide, he negotiated the narrow, dark-blue streak between coral reefs, which marked the only passage to the land-locked port of the tight little fortified island of Tortuga. In the frothing wake several petrels circled and dived after the small flashing fish. Aboard the *Mary of Guilford*, Captain Brownrigg's navigator set a course to follow closely behind the buccaneer sloop.

At a signal from Johnny, the grinning gunners convivially fired a culverin, its heavy report echoing across the warves to reverberate among the wooded hills beyond. A flock of disturbed gulls rose, wheeling and screaming, from their perch on the festering debris littering the silt between the weed-slimy piles of the jetty. Half a dozen ships, swinging easily at their moorings, gave answer in a thundering volley. Roused from the somnolence of the torrid late afternoon, the inhabitants of Cayona turned out to welcome the newcomers.

With a rumble of chain the massive anchor plunged down into the glassy green depths of the water. The crew needed no urging from the boatswain to get the longboats launched, eagerly tossing in knapsacks and bundles of loot with raucous, cheerfully bawdy jibes. There would be no lack of opportunity to spend their money in the brothels and taverns of the most lawless, licentious port in the West Indies.

In Dirk's cabin the women prepared to go ashore in a flurry of excitement. They were to sup at the house of Henry Dubois, the merchant who had provisioned the *Hopewell*.

Roxanna fretted restlessly as Lucy worked

on her curls. A qualm of uneasiness jabbed her; she knew very well that she should be wearing widow's black, now, and for at least a year. But she shrugged away the thought defiantly, no one knew her here, so why should she be such a hypocrite as to pretend to mourn a man she had thoroughly detested?

Dirk came in just as she was sticking a black heart-shaped patch on her chin. He glanced over the gold damask gown, looped high above a black taffeta skirt.

'Quite the grand lady,' he observed, with his singularly winning smile.

She whirled round, skirts whispering.

'I must be a credit to you, darling. After all, we shall meet people whom you know.' She did not add, perhaps women who might desire him, and in whose teeth she would flaunt her confident beauty.

He produced a flat leather case from behind his back and put it into her hands. Wonderingly, she pressed the catch and lifted the lid. He was smiling, his hands thrust deep into his pockets, rocking back on his heels, watching as she opened it.

The candlelight winked on emeralds set in heavy gold, which shimmered against the dark velvet lining. Dirk's smile was tenderly amused and she went into his arms, almost unbearably happy because he had given her such a present.

His cheek was cool and smooth to her lips. She kissed him quickly and turned back to the glass. With reverent fingers she picked up the pendant ear-rings, the green stones surrounded by a filigree of gold, and hooked the wires into her lobes. Then she stood back to study the effect.

She had bloomed under Dirk's practised guidance. He had brought to full flower the innate carnality of her nature, that strong force of which all men who met her were at once aware, but which, until Dirk touched her, she had not understood and of which she had been only half-conscious.

He fastened the clasp of the necklace and pulled her back against him, sliding his hands into her bodice, cupping each breast. She watched his reflection, eyes languorous, while he bent to put his lips on her arched throat, then kissed her on the mouth, so hungrily that the cabin rocked.

While Dirk changed his clothes Lucy hovered about, not in the least embarrassed by his nakedness, handing him clean shirt and hose, helping him into his coat. She had automatically become his servant as well as Roxanna's, accepting it, with the same brisk practicality, as she did the fact that Roxanna slept with him. She had brushed his clothes, polished his boots and washed a bundle of dirty shirts. She tidied the cabin, made their bed and brought them food. When she saw that they desired privacy she tactfully withdrew.

Roxanna had never seen Dirk elegantly attired before, usually he wore only shirt and breeches, his feet bare. Now he was magnificent in a suit of cinnamon brocade, with a cassock coat which reached his knees, slit to the thigh on either side and trimmed with gold buttons. Under it was a waistcoat, lavishly braided, while the breeches fitted his slim flanks without a wrinkle and she could well believe that, as he said, he had a clever French tailor in Cayona. He wore his finery with a kind of careless arrogance. It served to emphasize his almost alarming masculinity.

'Oh, you are so handsome!' Roxanna breathed, a little wistfully. His spectacular good looks awed and depressed her. Surely, every woman who clapped eyes on him would love him to desperation? How could she ever hold him!

He frowned, made uncomfortable by the frank idolotry in her eyes, and picked up a black silk cloth, laying it about her shoulders, his hands resting with a brief, comforting pressure. She took her vizard from the table, having already explained its use to him, boasting a little of her life in London, wanting him to believe that there she had been someone of importance. He had pulled a suitably impressed face but in his eyes had been that lazy, indifferent mockery, as he listened. Now he gently took it out of her hand.

'You'll have no need for that kickshaw. We're not likely to meet any prancing fops tonight.'

In the stern-cabin Kate and Johnny were drinking. He seemed to burst from his satin coat with boisterous vitality, the diamonds on his fingers and flashing in his ears the symbol of his success in the 'Sweet trade'.

Kate was tidier than usual and wore a shirt and breeches of fine cloth. She and Roxanna exchanged a frosty stare and the young pickpockets's eyes did not miss the glitter of emeralds in the shadow of the black hood.

Lucy slipped her arm into Dan's, looking

up into his rugged face. He had allowed her to tidy him up. Lucy had taken her scissors to his unruly red hair and clipped his moustache. Roxanna could see that she was determined to make a respectable trader out of him. He seemed very sincere in his regard for the buxom, forthright maid. She had privately informed Roxanna that she did not intend to let him have his way with her until they were wed. Roxanna experienced a pang; even her servant would be a married woman whilst she was nothing but Dirk's whore. Her cheeks burned every time she imagined Nan Dob's scorn.

The day was dying fast. The great lanterns had been lit on deck and these were reflected in the glassy, chrysolite sea, and by a hundred points of light against the massive blackness of the island.

Roxanna paused, moved by the brilliant, haunting beauty of the night. The sky was a deep purple-blue, stabbed with stars; nothing could have been a greater contrast to dusk in England, where all was soft, muted, misted tones. Here even the darkness held an intensity, a violent, savage promise. The air was aromatic with spices, strong, rich and intoxicating, whispering of deep, secretive forests, lushy, treacherous swamps, and wide, verdant savannahs. It resembled in no way at all the twilight hours at home in her father's garden, where the bitter-sweet fragrance of herbs mingled with the stocks from Nan's border, the faint rustle of the fig and mulberry trees, the distant, ghostly hoot of an owl.

Suddenly, desperate homesickness overwhelmed her. She was terrified of what lay ahead. A premonition chilled the sweat sticking to her back, warning her of suffering on these ruthless, barbaric islands. She shuddered, certain that it would be unlucky to set foot on shore with this strong presentiment of evil.

CHAPTER 5

Flares, set in brackets on the stone walls of warehouses, cast a harsh glare on the backwash of humanity which teemed on the quay. Derelict mariners plucked at Johnny's sleeve with whining lies, while beggars crouched in the shadows holding out their withered hands, displaying malformities or leprous-sores. Children, naked, pot-bellied, raced among the legs of the adults, laughing and shrieking, but by far the majority of the rabble was made up of prostitutes, haggard, diseased slatterns who made a living on the waterfront.

The buccaneers leaped ashore from the longboats, bawling friendly ribaldry at the crowd.

Roxanna pressed close to Dirk as he guided her to where a coach stood, gilded and most comfortingly civilized, in the dusty roadway.

'Can't we have a clank of diddle before we get in the tumbler?' Johnny asked Dirk, mopping over his streaming face with a striped kerchief. 'Hell and damnation, but I never feel easy in that cursed house of Dubois. Let's go to Sarah Frisky's case!' Johnny gave a wide grin. Dirk loosened his rapier in its sheath, turned to give a brisk order to the coachman and they set off on foot down a narrow alley leading from the wharf.

Johnny halted before a tavern with a creaking sign over the warped door. He kicked it back and went into the murky interior. It was congested with a noisy crowd, and a babble of different tongues jarred the ear, together with shrill peals of laughter, the throbbing of a native drum and the staccato click of castenets. The air was foul with bad breath, sweat and tobacco smoke. Little children, wizened, half-starved dwarfs, thieved and pimped along with their elders.

A woman emerged carving her way through the mob. She wore a cerise satin gown strained across her vast breasts, the front daubed with food, great rusty sweat-stains under the armpits. Jewels glittered against her sallow skin, on thick arms and bare throat, a brassy blond wig was slightly askew on her head.

'Johnny!...Johnny, darlin'!' Her thundering voice rose above the tumult and she seized his arm in swollen fingers, loaded with rings. 'I'm right glad to see you, my bully! Come back weighed down with plunder, eh?'

Johnny beamed, expanding in what he obviously found to be most congenial surroundings. 'Well enough, Sarah, you greedy old bawd! How's trade with you?'

Her laughter rumbled up from deep in her obese belly. 'Brisk as ever! There's one commodity man will ever be after. And we shall be busier than usual now your lusty lads are back!'

She looked Roxanna over with an experienced eye.

'And where d'you get yourself that flash bunter?' she chuckled, giving him a nudge. 'When you tire of her, my blood, I'll give you a good price. She's pure white by her looks, and there's always demand for that!'

Both men roared with laughter at Roxanna's expression of outraged indignation.

A voice greeted them from over by the bar and a man advanced, jauntily weaving through the throng to halt at their table. He was of above average height with a swarthy complexion ravaged by smallpox, black hair and a hawk nose dominating a viciously sensual face. His clothes were splendid but soiled, and dirt lined his long, curved fingernails. With a bow, he introduced himself, his black eyes never leaving Roxanna.

'Sebastian Massey, at your service. Do you remember me, Comry?'

Johnny gave him a shrewd stare.

'Yes, I know you,' he ventured cautiously. 'You were in Davis' company, along with Dick Hammer.'

'Correct, cully,' Massey nodded, the

gold rings in his ears catching the light. 'Aye, those were days to remember!'

Massey had a reputation as a renegade and trouble-maker, brave enough but treacherous as a rattlesnake.

'Join us in the diddle,' he suggested and pushed forward the leather bottle. Dirk gave Massey a suspicious, warning look, darkening as the restless shifty eyes gloated on Roxanna while he wetted his heavy lips with the tip of his tongue.

'You didn't come here to pass the time of day, now did you, mate. What's your business?' demanded Johnny.

The other gave a lift of his lean shoulders under the dark blue velvet of his coat. 'I wanted to discover if you have anything planned for your next venture.'

He leaned over and dropped his voice confidentially. 'I'm off to meet Sawkins and Sharp at Nigger Bay. They are preparing for an island raid. You've heard of their success at Porto Bello? They came back loaded with booty!'

'Where are they heading?' asked Dirk, brusquely.

'The Santa Maria river,' responded Massey instantly, his fingers flexing on the table. 'And on to the town of Santa

Maria. There's a gold mine close by and they send caravans to Panama.'

'What of the treaty between England and Spain?' Dirk took a swallow of brandy.

'Pshaw!' Massey spat on the floor, disgusted with the authorities who might try to bring about peace and thus put a stop to the profitable pillaging of Spanish settlements. 'Devil fly off with their treaties!'

He talked on of the wealth of Santa Maria and even Dirk listened intently. An attack on a rich town promised more wealth than individual cruises by separate bands of marauders. And as the drink flowed, so they became more enthusiastic. Roxanna's heart sank, she wished violently that they had never come to this filthy hostelry, never met Massey with his disturbing plans that would take Dirk away from her.

Later, in the coach, Roxanna relaxed against the cushioned seat of the dark interior. She snuggled into the curve of Dirk's arm, his classic profile outlined against the window as they passed a flambeau blazing outside of a house. Soon the flares became fewer as they left the town behind them. The road followed the river, inclining slightly, and, on cach side, prosperous plantations flourished in the rich grass-lands.

The carriage jolted to a halt at the iron spike-topped gates of Lime Close, the plantation of Dubois, the merchant.

A negro came running, eyes and teeth white in the light of the rising moon. The great gates swung back and they rattled up a wide, curving drive. The house was impressive, built in an L shape, of two storeys with cellars beneath. A double flight of stone steps, with an intricate iron balustrade, led up to the first floor where, on a wide veranda, illumined by the light from the open door, Henri Dubois stood to welcome his guests.

He was a diminutive, middle-aged Frenchman, very modishly dressed, from his high red heels to the massive formal wig which he insisted on wearing although the sweat flowed down his face from under it. He showed at once a most flattering attention to Roxanna, bowing so low over her hand that his curls nearly swept the ground. Almost, she could have imagined this was some levée in a Paris salon, had it not been for the great hounds snarling and slavering at his heels, kept for his protection and to hunt down escaped slaves.

94

They were the largest mastiffs she had ever seen. Massive red-eyed beasts, their fangs bared at their master's visitors, before he spun round to shout at them:

'Back Vulcan! Down Pluto!' whereupon they slunk away to lie on the marble of the hall-floor, their tails thumping, noses across their paws, their blazing eyes still on the guests.

Roxanna felt Dirk's muscles tense beneath her hand. His face was set, his jaw tightly clamped as he watched the dogs.

Johnny and Dirk were greeted boisterously by three scarred, disreputable veterans of many a vicious skirmish. They were two sallow, black-eyed, quick and expressive Frenchmen and a huge, florid Dutchman, with heavy dewlaps and a fleshy, broad nose. Dubois introduced his other guests, neighbouring planters of English origin.

The buccaneers ogled Roxanna flagrantly, coming to kiss her hand, staring boldly down into her bosom, angling to put an arm round her. They appeared to know all about her. It was the first example she was to have of the very efficient grape-vine which existed among the quarrelsome, proud and yet, at times, violently loyal, Brethren. Her discomfiture deepened when she saw that they respected her not at all, treating her almost as they did the doxies which they could have for sixpence at anytime. Their attitude differed only in that she was of more value because she was white, noticeably unmarked by syphilis and had, as yet, belonged to only one man.

Dirk crisply intervened, his wide shoulders thrusting forward to hustle his confederates aside, his arm going about her in a proprietary manner which thrilled her. He led her to a carved walnut chair and fetched a goblet of wine, installing Lucy at her side. Dubois toasted the leaders of the *Hopewell*, wanting exact details of their trip. He spoke very good English with only a slight accent but his compatriots had few words of the language and Roxanna was delighted to hear Dirk break into French. Her respect increased by the minute when he switched to Dutch to address the blue-eyed, elderly Hollander.

He fitted perfectly into these surroundings, but Johnny was uneasy, perched on the extreme edge of a delicate chair which creaked under his weight. But, warmed by the heady wine, he soon loosened up, shouting at the hard-fisted, gaudily clad corsairs, bellowing with good-natured camaraderie as he tried to make himself understood by them. Kate's restless, calculating eyes were pricing the silver and costly hangings, while she sipped at the crystal glass in her lean, horny hand.

Dubois ushered Roxanna into the seat next to his at supper, all gratifying attentiveness.

The elegance and taste of Dubois's table was a revelation. She had not realized that the merchants lived in such luxury. Candles, in golden holders which had not long before graced a Castilian altar, shone on the snowy damask and lace cloth. Dubois had provided silver forks and knives for his female guests. The men used their daggers, and, disdaining the cutglass bowls provided, wiped greasy fingers down the fronts of their colourful coats. Dirk produced a fork for his own use from a slim case which he always carried in his pocket, and dried his narrow brown hands on the sparkling napery.

A different wine accompanied each dish until Roxanna's head began to spin and, looking across at Dirk, she could not quite focus. His eyes were warm and intimate as he smiled at her. He was drinking rum and lime-juice, the potation which, she had speedily learned, he liked the best.

The filibusters never stopped gesticulating and bragging while they champed lustily, wine slopping from their tankards as they raised them in the air in a dozen, obstreperous toasts. The two planters were more restrained, both in their early thirties, one beefy and corpulent, the other thin and lantern-jawed. Roxanna found their interest flattering and she gossiped spiritedly of the playhouse, London fashions and scandal. She could not resist flirting a little, employing a few of the coquettish tricks which Lydia had taught her so thoroughly.

The table had been speedily cleared and, with the wine circulating without restriction, glowing cheroots sending up fragrant smoke, the dice were rolling on the polished cedar.

'Will you play me?' Massey asked Dirk. He dragged out well-thumbed cards from his pocket.

'Aye, I'll play with you,' was Dirk's quiet answer, 'but we will use my pack!' He gave Massey an enigmatic glance, an expression which made Roxanna shiver and hope that he would never look at her like that.

Massey shrugged and managed to fetch a grin, watching keenly as Dirk's supple hands flickered through them with the ease born of long practice. But his smile faded, to be replaced by a furious mask, as he began to lose a lot of money. They played at putt, a game with which Roxanna was unfamiliar, although she had learned faro, basset and hazard. Dirk handled his cards with an indolence which covered a very watchful eye and sharp wit. She wondered briefly if he cheated; if he did not his luck was almost phenomenal.

The planter seated next to her became more bold as the rum fuddled his wits and he could see that Dirk was apparently engrossed in the cards. He rubbed his foot against Roxanna's under the table, he made play of brushing her arm as he reached across for the fruit, he cast sideways looks into her bodice. Ordinarily, she would not have given him a second glance, but an imp of perversity was urging her to try and make Dirk jealous, so she arched her brows and gave him a challenging smile. He leaned closer and blew his rancid breath into her face, then he jumped as if stung, sitting back in his chair as Dirk's voice cracked out:

'Roxanna! It's time for you to retire! Perhaps our host will be good enough to light you to our room!'

With an expression black as thunder he hooked a finger under his cravat and jerked it loose. Roxanna lowered her thick lashes, and in her eyes there was a little triumphant spark. She rose, Dubois with her, beckoned to Lucy, swept the company a deep curtsy and started for the door.

Dirk came round the table and she paused, expectantly. He held out his hand and there was a dangerous glint in his smoky-grey eyes. He placed a brilliant shining sunburst in her palm, the diamonds winking. He had just won it from Massey.

'I shall not be more than half-an-hour,' he told her. 'Then I will join you.'

Outside in the hall she turned to hug Lucy, transported with delight.

'He was jealous!' she breathed, and danced a few steps on the marble floor, heels tapping.

Lucy clucked reprovingly. 'Lud be careful do, Ma'am! He's no city fop for you to banter. He looked angry enough to kill you!'

Roxanna flourished the diamond brooch

under her maid's nose.

'But he gave me this! Hey-day, what care I if he *is* in a mighty dudgeon! That is how I like him!'

CHAPTER 6

Early the next morning, Johnny and Dirk borrowed horses and rode down to the harbour with Massey. Roxanna rolled over in the canopied bed to watch him dress and, when he had gone, turned into the silk pillow to dream again. She rose late and had a bath, the first since leaving England, luxuriating in a tub of scented water, her hair, newly washed, skewered on top of her head. Soft-footed black slaves brought in the buckets of water.

The bedroom was as lavish as everything else in the house. Rugs of soft subdued patterns were spread on the gleaming teak boards. A magnificent dressing-table with an oval mirror in a silver frame, matched the gilded dower-chest, elaborately decorated with painted panels depicting the nuptials of immortals on Olympus. The bed, which was fully seven feet wide, had come from the plundered residence of a Spanish governor. It was embossed with an intricate design of vine-leaves, while heavy amaranthine curtains draped the head and matched the coverlet.

From the garden, directly below the balcony window, the tinkling splash of a fountain helped to refresh the humid atmosphere. Insects hummed in a continual chorus, and harsh chatter of the parakeets came from the mangrove trees. Lucy helped her to bathe, then hurried off with Dan to view a tavern which was up for sale. Roxanna completed a very leisurely toilet and went down to eat with Dubois.

It was cool in the dining-room, the dark green shutters drawn against the glare. The two of them sat at one end of an oval table and were served speedily and silently by his disciplined staff. As they dawdled over the wine Roxanna learned a lot about Tortuga from this informed trader who had a finger in a great number of pies.

'Governor d'Ogeron did the most to cultivate this little island,' he supplied, reaching over to replenish her glass. 'He colonized it for the Compagnie des Indes in about sixteen sixty-five. He knew the

West Indies well, having been a planter in both Martinique and Jamaica, a salt trader in the Caicos, and, like most men here, "on the purchase" more than once!'

'A buccaneer?' Roxanna raised the goblet meditatively to her lips, wondering if he could fill in the details of Dirk's life which she was so very curious to discover.

Dubois nodded. 'This fact did not prevent the company advising him to use Tortuga as a base to cover settlement in Hispaniola. He carried out their orders with conviction and considerable ability. He even arranged for prostitutes to be rounded up in France and transported, in order to encourage these wild rogues to settle into domesticity. But, I am afraid, a good many of the ladies preferred to take up their old life on the waterfront. Sarah Frisky was one of them, I believe you met her last night. A very worthy woman and uncommonly astute. She owns many acres of grazing land over in Saint-Domingue, which she bought for a trifling sum and which have trebled their value since.'

'Did you know Edmund Raynal?' Roxanna asked abruptly. The pale green light wavered over her golden gown, tinting her skin till she seemed like some denizen of the water. Her almond-shaped eyes added to this impression, giving her the fey appearance of a naiad. Dubois considered her with pleased contemplation, resting his fine-drawn hands lightly on the carved arms of his chair.

'I did not meet your late husband,' he said with slow caution, 'but I have heard of him. He was a mighty rich man. Are you his heir?'

'He had no relations,' she replied, beginning to realize that she might be a woman of substance. She had been so preoccupied with her love affair that she had given the matter no thought. Now she remembered, all at once, that a wealthy woman could usually have whatever she wanted; and might marry the man she most desired.

She leaned forward, the thick auburn ringlets brushing her bare shoulders. Alert and interested, all her energies concentrated on this exciting knowledge.

'If I am his heir, and I imagine that I must be, what do you advise me to do?' Her voice was crisp and Dubois raised his quizzical brows in surprise, sensing that under her seductive and very feminine exterior, lay dormant a will which would make her a shrewd business woman, and give her the drive to run a plantation with a great deal of practical ability. He recognized the blood of merchant stock which beat strongly in both of their veins.

'My dearest lady, you must attend to it without delay,' he said firmly. 'His partner, Van Houel, is a man of repute. He will deal fairly with you. It would be a sound idea to write to him, explaining what has transpired, unless you intend to travel on to Jamaica at once,' he gave a subtle smile and added tactfully: 'Possibly you have not yet made future plans?'

Roxanna flashed him a quick glance. There was no doubt that he knew all about her liaison with Dirk.

'You can rest assured that I shall always be most happy to assist you in any way which may lie in my power,' he continued, and for an instant the cultured, polite veneer slipped and she glimpsed the real man beneath.

'Thank you, sir,' her voice was very cool and she quickly drew back, fluttering her fan between them. 'I may call upon your kind offer. Raynal grew sugar, did he not?'

When he turned to her again the libertine

had dissolved once more into the perfect host. 'We all do if we can. There is more money to be had from it than anything. Yet 'tis a tricky thing to produce the fine white sort for which there is such demand in Europe. Molasses, we can obtain, and crude brown sugar, but 'tis the Hollanders who possess the secret of making the other.'

For a while they discussed the plantations and their profits, then Dubois suddenly leaned nearer.

'What will you do, my dear, when Courtney leaves you to go "on the account" again?' he asked.

Roxanna stiffened and she levelled him a look of annoyance. 'What makes you so sure that he will?' she snapped, resentfully.

Dubois raised his shoulders and spread out his hands in a shrug. 'I have known him for many years, ever since he was running slaves from the Portuguese barracoons on the West African coast. He is a man with a very restless itch, and will never happily settle long in one place.'

His question perturbed her, although she tried not to show it, and when late afternoon came and still Dirk had not returned, she persuaded Dubois to have

Lucy and herself driven to the quay. There they learned from loitering sailors that Cormy and some of his men had rowed over to their ship. On deck were gathered many of Massey's crew, for a parley was in progress on the proposed trip with Sawkins.

In the state-cabin, the captains were drinking a toast to the enterprise. They greeted Dubois with a welcoming shout, needing his help to placate Governor de Pouancay, to bargain with him over commissions, supplies and ammunition. Dirk gave Roxanna a deep, warm smile. He was leaning with an arm across Johnny's shoulders, studying a chart spread out on the table.

'What is this map?' she asked, gazing at the carefully drawn contours which marked seas and land; cities indicated by a tiny fort, rivers by a red twisting line.

Dirk's hand came down flat on it. 'This is the Caribbean Sea and the coast of South America. Here is Tortuga,' his brown finger was placed squarely on a tiny blob. 'Here the Darien Strait, which Sawkins intends to cross, and here is Nigger Bay where we are to meet him.'

'When are you starting?' she whispered.

'Sawkins wants to be ready by March. We shall have to leave almost at once if we are to career the ship first,' Dirk frowned a little and did not look at her.

Later, in Dirk's cabin, Roxanna listened languidly to Lucy who was bursting with excitement.

'We have bought the hostelry, Ma'am,' she confided breathlessly, her face moist and flushed. ' 'Tis in a fine shambles at present but I can soon put that to rights. Lud, what a blessing that you taught me to read and add figures! Dan cannot even scrawl his own name! So all dealings with money will rest with me!' she added resolutely.

'When will you wed, Lucy?' Roxanna's eyes were wistfully dreamy as she climbed into bed.

Lucy beamed broadly, as she took out Roxanna's gown. 'Tomorrow, Ma'am, may it please you. Are you going to Nigger Bay with him?' She jerked her head in the direction of the door from beyond which they could distinctly hear Dirk's voice.

Roxanna heaved a slow, weary sigh, lower lip drooping, her expression gloomy. 'I don't know.' She lifted her arms and clasped her hands behind her head, staring up moodily at the painted cornucopia spewing forth a tumbled mass of fruit and flowers, with which some Castilian artist had ornamented the cabin ceiling.

'You know that you are most welcome to stay with Dan and me for as long as you want,' Lucy's tone was filled with concern as she paused in her tasks to look at her mistress.

Roxanna sat up and impulsively reached out to take her hand. 'Thank you, my dear. I may yet be forced to accept your kind offer. Oh, rat the troublesome fellow! I shan't rest until I can make him agree to take me!'

Dirk entered as Lucy was on her way out. He gave Roxanna one of those slow, unwinking stares which she was learning to recognize and dread. She lay still, watchfully alert.

He dragged off his sodden shirt, his face troubled. 'I don't like it!'

'The expedition?' Hope flared up in her that perhaps he might still be persuaded not to go.

'I don't trust Massey,' he muttered, as if to himself, beginning to pace the cabin restively. 'These island raids are not all that he supposes.'

109

It was the first time that he had given the slightest indication that he found his way of life distasteful. Roxanna had often wondered how he reconciled his obvious breeding, his taste for books and music, with the violence of his occupation. He sat on the bed to tug off his boots and shot her a sudden glare.

'What strumpetry have you been about today with Dubois? Did he offer you a good price for a night?'

Roxanna stared at him in speechless amazement. Then she became angry. He would not offer her marriage and yet he demanded her constancy. With eyes narrowed and hard with resentment, she bounced out of the bed.

'He was mighty civil to me,' she informed him. 'He offered to help and I dare swear he might even marry me!'

He gave a scornful bark of laughter, slinging his boots across the cabin. 'Marriage! Don't be foolish!'

She pattered round to stand squarely before him, her arms akimbo. She was wearing an apple-green gossamer nightgown which fell clear to her feet from a lace yoke trimmed with knots of ribbon. As she moved, the flimsy material undulated about her lissom curves. Dirk reached out an arm, catching her round her pliant waist. Roxanna wrenched herself free, eyes sparkling, crushing down her immediate reciprocation.

'And why shouldn't he marry me? I was courted by a lord in London!' Her chin lifted defiantly.

He was at once cool again, his remoteness shutting her away. 'Don't imagine that it worries me, Roxanna. When I am gone you may lie with whom you damned please but, for the moment, you are my mistress and it affects my honour to have another man paw at you.'

Her eyes were feline and vindictive as she watched him go to the window, his back to her, but the sight of the scars on his tanned torso drove out every feeling except pity.

He stood with his head back, staring out at the night, one arm along the window-ledge.

'Dirk, my heart...' Her voice was soft and he turned back to her. 'Leave this existence. I now own Raynal's plantation, you could come and live there with me.'

'No!' His voice cut like a lash and she winced. 'When I leave the sea it will be as my own master. I shall *never* pander to some woman because she holds the purse-string, or be forced into a marriage which I do not desire! The woman I choose as my wife will not be anything like you!'

She recoiled as if he had slapped her, then her head went into her hands, her shoulders shook and the tears trickled through her fingers. He stood looking down at her with a frown. She was like a lost child with her hair tumbled over her face, her loose gown touching her bare toes. Her utter dependence on him both irked and flattered him, and he suddenly sat down on the bed drawing her onto his knee.

'Listen, sweeting,' he urged solemnly. 'You must be sensible. Captain Brownrigg is lodging in the town, awaiting your orders. I have been discussing your future with him and he is perfectly willing to conduct you to Jamaica. I advise that you sell out your shares of the plantation and return to England. These violent islands are not for you!' He silenced her gently as she began to remonstrate. 'It is by far the best course. With your wealth and your beauty, and, believe me, you are the fairest creature I have ever seen, you could make a very good match!'

'I do not want to wed any but you,' she cried.

His eyes were sombre as his lips touched her hair briefly.

He stood up and removed the rest of his clothes, taking up a snuffer and going round the cabin putting out the candles. She saw his face, serious and set, as he leaned over the final flame before the cabin was plunged into darkness.

'I shall leave for Nigger Bay the day after tomorrow.' His voice was close to her, his breath warm on her cheek. 'I can't take you with me.'

'You are willing to leave me in a town like Cayona, or crossing these waters where we may well be set upon by more buccaneers or even Spanish ships?' she whispered slowly.

'I have told you what I have arranged with Brownrigg,' he sounded annoyed and bored. 'For the rest, I can organize an escort of the Brethren to see you safely to Jamaica.'

She twisted to grip him, her tears falling on to his naked chest.

'Let me come to Nigger Bay!' she pleaded urgently. 'That is all I ask...just to be with you for a while longer.'

For a moment, he made no reply and she sobbed unrestrainedly, wracked by the knowledge that he did not love her and could quite casually send her away from him forever. Till then, she had not really believed that it would happen.

'Very well,' his voice, very distinct in the stuffy gloom, was impatient. 'But know this, Roxanna. I shall have little time to spend with you. It will not be comfortable. We shall be camping on the beach, living very rough. There will be no opportunity for idleness!'

Ignoring the last part of his sentence, only aware that she had been granted a few more days in his company, she found his hand and covered it with kisses.

'Oh, darling, thank you! I will not complain, I promise! I would do anything for you. Indeed, I would be happy to work for you!'

'My love, you don't know what life is about.' There was laughter in his voice and he held her tightly in his arms. 'I doubt those pretty hands have ever touched anything dirtier than an embroidery needle, or the keys of your spinet. And remember, you contrary little witch, that it is only until we are ready to sail. Then back to Cayona you go!' he added emphatically.

Hot denials rose to her lips but she bit them back. It was of no use to argue the point now.

Roxanna was a witness at Lucy's wedding to Dan. She wore the magnificent gown which had been Roxanna's own bridal-dress, and they were married in a tiny, white-washed church near the harbour. A group of buccaneers fidgeted uncomfortably on the wooden pews, fully armed and longing for the ceremony to be over so that they might get down to the more serious business of drinking, the health of the bridal pair. At the wedding breakfast, ordered in an adjacent tavern, they relaxed, preparing for a carousel which would last well into the night.

Lucy wept when it was time for Roxanna to leave her. The two women hugged each other, poignantly realizing that they would be utterly alone, in completely new, at times terrifying surroundings. The last links with home were being severed.

'Oh, Ma'am, how'll you shift without me?' Lucy's eyes were red and puffy. They stood on the veranda in the deepening dusk. Behind them in the parlour the seamen were hurling jibes at two of their members who were wrestling, slippery with sweat, in the middle of the floor. Lucy gave an angry glance in at them. 'If Danny thinks I'm going to open my house to his ruffianly friends at all hours of the day and night, he has a surprise in store!'

She dabbed at her tears, turning back to Roxanna. 'There will be no one to dress your hair, or lace your busk...no one to wash out your clothes.'

'Pox on that!' Roxanna rejoined, a great lonely ache welling inside her. ' 'Tis you that I shall miss, dear Lucy!'

'You'll be alone among those great, rough barbarians,' Lucy was really concerned, her own happiness overshadowed. 'With no other female creature but that ill-born slut!' She had all the snobbish intolerance of the privileged servant and detested Kate. 'You watch her, Ma'am... she'd knife you as soon as look at you!'

Later that evening, when she got back to the *Hopewell*, Roxanna laboured on a letter to her father. She had not the smallest desire to communicate with him, but Captain Brownrigg had suggested it, wishing to save his employer from alarm should he hear of their interrupted journey from any other source. She sat at the table before the open window and chewed at her quill frowning in concentration. Then she jabbed it into the squat gold inkwell and began to scrawl with slow deliberation.

Her next letter, penned to Lydia, was less stilted; she grew eloquent as she described Dirk. He wandered across to stand behind her, reading over her shoulder, and his voice was filled with lazy amusement.

'God damn it, darling, you have made me sound a veritable Adonis!'

Her head was bent, seriously engrossed in her writing, and he placed his lips where the little tendrils of hair escaped from her braid, nibbling across the back of her neck, bare shoulders and ears. She leaned against him, giving a long-drawn, rapturous sigh, goose pimples rising all over her limbs.

'Oh, Dirk,' she half protested. 'How can I think when you do that!'

He laughed, and his teeth gently tugged at the pearl drop in her lobe. 'A charming little wench like you has no need to think.'

He drew her to her feet and she nuzzled under his chin, her mouth on the base of his throat where a pulse throbbed. His skin always tasted clean, slightly salty from his dangerous habit of a daily plunge into the sea from the ship's rail. Roxanna always waited anxiously for his return, not in the least comforted by the fact that he was careful to post a couple of men to watch out for sharks.

CHAPTER 7

At dawn Johnny ordered Rackham ashore to round up the crew. He returned with a boat-load of refractory, bedraggled rascals, reluctant to leave the stews of Cayona. Running before a stiff breeze, keeping close to the coast, it was not long before Nigger Bay was reached.

A longboat pulled out from the largest of the moored vessels and made swiftly towards the *Hopewell*. Johnny was at her side to greet the man who puffed up the rope ladder. He was thick-set, almost corpulent, and his fleshy face was covered with beads of sweat. His manner was overbearing as he swung on board and stood adjusting his velvet coat. In the wide sash which braced his paunch were two long pistols, while a cutlass knocked against his beefy thighs. His head was covered by a large black peruke, topped by a blue hat, both of which he removed to mop his glistening face and bald head.

'Death and Furies!' he cursed, rolling a pair of avaricious, cunning eyes over Johnny. ' 'Tis hot as Topheth's ovens!'

In the comparative coolness of the state-cabin, the visitor tossed his wig and hat onto the table and took a lengthy pull at the brandy bottle.

'Zounds!' he ejaculated, drying flabby lips on the lace at his wrist. 'That's better! Now then, who may you be, cully, and what's your lay?'

Johnny scanned his visitor's face; there was little about the man to inspire confidence.

'I am Captain Comry and want to join up with Sawkins,' Johnny was deliberately laconic.

'I've heard of you,' came the response, and he flung himself uninvited into a chair, stocky legs straight out in front of him. 'My name is Sharp, Bartholomew Sharp. You will find that I am the wits behind this expedition, tho' Sawkins has given himself the title of Admiral!'

His eyes darted round the lavish fittings of the cabin, resting on Johnny's officers who stood, a solid force behind their captain, apparently idly watching.

'So, you want to join us?' Sharp lurched forward suddenly. 'How many men do you muster?'

'Around a hundred.' Johnny relaxed and pushed over the bottle which Sharp took up and raised to his lips again.

'You had best come ashore and meet the others,' he grunted, and got to his feet.

Roxanna came in as he was picking up his hat. He paused and the crudeness of his leer was almost like a physical blow. Involuntarily, she edged closer to Dirk.

'Oh, ho,' Sharp was heavily jocular. 'What have we here?' He fingered his periwig uncertainly as if wondering whether to clap it on again. Then he bowed and grabbed at her hand, planting a damp, smacking kiss on it.

Johnny and Dirk exchanged a look over her head; the latter stepped closer, his hand resting lightly on the hilt of his rapier. 'This is my woman, Sharp. She stays with me until we sail.'

An affable smirk spread out across the broad features, and Sharp rubbed at a pulpy, purple-veined nose, 'I quite understand, my blood.' His raucous accents dropped to a murmur. ' 'Twill be a joy to have such an exquisite member of the fair sex with us!'

When Kate asked Johnny if she might go ashore with him to meet the other leaders he was furious, knocking aside her restraining hand.

'Do you think we want 'em jeering at us for not being able to move a step without a pack of jades at our heels?' his normally pleasant voice grated. 'You'll stay here with Mrs Roxanna!'

Roxanna was missing Lucy badly. Beside the loss of the unfailing good-natured presence, she was without her practical help. Like most women of her class she had never lifted a hand to dress her own hair and, finding it nearly impossible to lace her busk, she had to beg Johnny's assistance, when Dirk was busy on deck.

Now she leaned from the window, watching them pull for the shore across the still water to the palm-fringed shore. She gave a light-hearted wave, smiling fondly at Dirk, and turned back to the cabin with a contented little sigh. Kate sat on the table, scowling moodily. She crossed her slender legs and reached for a small pistol which lay among the muddle of charts, tankards and bottles.

Roxanna saw her and her eyes snapped. 'Put that down!' she blazed.

Kate raised a taunting eyebrow. 'And who do you think you're bloody well talking to! One of your damn' lackeys!'

'Put it down, I say!' Roxanna repeated, speaking through clenched teeth. 'It is Dirk's!'

'Stop your bawling, for God's sake!' Kate's reply was scathing. 'You are as jealous of that man as a pregnant wife.'

She held the firearm lightly in her thin, hard fingers. Suddenly all of her repressed loathing flooded Roxanna and she made a grab at it.

'Don't be a fool! You stupid stuck-up bitch!'

Kate gave her a sharp punch so that she stepped back on her skirt-hem and was pulled up short.

'How dare you call me names!' Roxanna landed her a savage box on the ears. Without a moment's hesitation Kate reached out and seized a fistful of curls. With a violent jerk she pulled Roxanna to the floor where she struggled like a wild cat, spitting and snarling oaths, hampered by a froth of restraining petticoats. Kate promptly knelt on her, fingers at her windpipe.

'You listen here to me, you fancy-priced whore!' Kate's pinched face swayed above her, eyes alight with detestation, the stench of her sweat offending Roxanna's nostrils. 'No one is going to take that tone with me again! I took my last order on that merchant ship, but never no more!...do you understand?'

Roxanna brought up her knee and kicked her in the groin. With a grunt of pain, Kate doubled over, letting her go. With heaving breasts, her chemise half torn off, skirt ripped, hair wildly disordered, Roxanna triumphantly snatched up the pistol and flounced over to her cabin.

'You have no need to sneer at my being jealous!' she shouted brazenly. 'You'd best look to Johnny! Did you note the way he eyed me when he laced my busk this morning? He could not keep his hands from wandering! He's so hot for me, I swear I could have him at a snap of my fingers!'

'Don't think you've got the better of me, you cow!' Kate hissed threateningly.

Feeling very pleased with herself, for she

had enjoyed the scrap, Roxanna wriggled round to undo her dress, slipping out of it and into her dressing-gown. She was very inclined to let Johnny lie with her, just to teach Kate a lesson, but she could not bring herself to be unfaithful to Dirk, even with his best friend. Musingly, she settled down before the mirror to repair the damage to her face and hair.

Then she found her way to the galley. It was exceptionally neat, the pans and dishes hanging on the walls, burnished as bright as any in Nan Dob's kitchen. Flour, salt, and maize were stored in labelled barrels, with kegs of brandy and rum beside them. A fowl, lately killed and ready for cooking, lay on the table, covered with a mesh to keep off the flies. She guessed that Dirk was the moving force behind all this.

There was no sign of Kate as she set a tray and carried it into the main-cabin. As she ate, curled up on the window-locker, she reflected on the miraculous chance which had brought Dirk and herself together. It seemed almost incredible that she had known him less than a week. She was quite adamant in her belief that they had been fated to meet; their destines irrevocably entwined and ordained by planetary intervention. Dirk scoffed at what he considered to be so much hocus-pocus, and she was alarmed at such blasphemy. Nan Dobs was a great believer in the power of horoscope and had given her a yellowing piece of paper marked with a circle and the signs of the Zodiac. This had been drawn up at Roxanna's birth and she often poured over it, mystified and enchanted.

Her former existence in London seemed as dim as a half-remembered dream and the lust for living, the rebellious impetuosity, suppressed at home, now took possession and became the major part of her. Every time Dirk made love to her she found a deeper delight, constantly amazed at the intense pleasure he gave her.

When the men returned they were in a riotous mood, and answered her eager questions readily, describing Sawkins and his men with hearty insults.

'Where is Kate?' Johnny demanded, collapsing at Roxanna's side, snatching up a bone from her plate. He had one arm about her, fingers smoothing the firm lines of her thigh through the thin satin. She shrugged and dimpled at him, hoping that Kate might see and be consumed with jealousy.

Soon she jauntily entered and went straight to twine her arms about Johnny's neck. Roxanna jumped to her feet glaring furiously at Kate's ears from where swung her own emerald ear-rings.

'What are you about with those?' she growled, eyes blazing. Kate looked over her shoulder with an insulting smile.

'They suit me well, don't you think? I had a fancy to borrow them for a while!'

With her lips drawn back in a snarl Roxanna was on her, reaching out to tear at the sparkling gems. Kate twisted and ducked.

'You lousy bitch!' Roxanna ground out and pounced, grabbing Kate by her hair. A barbarous, unbridled exaltation tore through her as she felt her nails lacerate the other's scalp. In an instant they were fighting, screaming abuse. Roxanna scratched Kate's cheek raw with her nails, whilst she was struggling to get her thumbs into her rival's eyes. Johnny sprang forward, grinning, to grapple with Kate who swiped at him furiously. Dirk took hold of Roxanna and gave her a violent shake, his eyes cold and angry.

126

'Stop this brawling! Do you have to behave like a fishwife? Any more of it and back you go apacking to Cayona!'

'Make that bloody thieving slut give me my ear-rings!' Roxanna yelled hysterically, in paroxysm of temper, 'or I'll tear her guts out!'

'You dirty little bitch!' growled Johnny, as he gave Kate's arm a twist. 'I'm not short of crop to buy you any gewgaws that you fancy without having to pinch 'em! Give 'em up!' he ordered.

'Take 'em, if you can!' Her voice was harsh with hate. 'She thinks herself my better! I'll settle her yet!' And she sank her teeth into his hand.

Johnny gave a wrathful bellow and fetched her a blow which knocked her across the cabin. He stood threateningly over her and, yanking out the emeralds with such force that a bright bead of blood appeared on either lobe, he tossed them to Roxanna.

She caught them eagerly but for all her triumph her scratches were beginning to smart, and her shins throbbed painfully. When Kate got to her feet her face was murderous, the right side already swelling and her eye closing up.

After that it was open warfare between them and, although they did not dare to fight, they vexed one another on every possible occasion. Roxanna knew that it was only fear of Johnny which prevented Kate from stabbing her.

In the cool dewy dawn a party was dispatched ashore to build rafts and the longboats were loaded with goods from the *Hopewell*. The sails were taken down to serve as tents, all tackle dismantled and the cannons carefully, and amidst much cursing from the boatswain, lowered onto the prepared rafts. The men had recovered their boisterous high spirits.

Dirk's tone was clipped, polite, but undeniably aggressive when he introduced Roxanna to Sawkins. The Admiral's men immediately dropped whatever they were doing as word spread like lightning that there was a woman in their midst. A flush crept up Roxanna's slender throat and bathed her cheeks as she met their interested stares.

Most of the men were stripped to the waist, wearing dirty faded calico pantaloons, heads and the backs of their necks protected against the rays, their sinewy, copper-tanned bodies glistened from their recent exertions. Sawkins drove them hard, and they toiled from dawn till afternoon, making the ships seaworthy. Now they welcomed a respite, taking swigs from battered canteens, running amused, curious and frankly calculating eyes over Roxanna; discussing her merits among themselves and questioning the new arrivals about her. There was hardly a man present who did not covet Courtney's gorgeous red-headed woman, and they let her know it in no uncertain manner.

But Sawkins was an exception. A wiry, grizzled man of around forty-five, he gave her one brief glance and then ignored her. Sharp, taking advantage of having already been introduced, was at once at her side, fawning and familiar. She tried to detach her fingers from his hot, clammy paw, casting a look of appeal to Dirk. It was sufficient for him to bring his hand warningly to his sword. Sharp stopped pestering her and, instead, began punctiliously to introduce the officers of the expedition.

Roxanna instinctively trusted Captain Peter Harris, a bluff Kentish sailor, dun-haired and ruddy-cheeked. He gave her a wide, friendly grin, delighted to

129

meet someone fresh from England. Basil Ringrose showed his gentle origin in the narrow lineament of his handsome features and his languid, delicate demeanour. He proffered his arm and conducted her to a more sheltered corner of the beach where the tall palms whispered in the slight breeze.

A large portion of the assembly had been brought by John Coxon. Ringrose pointed him out to Roxanna, making no attempt to disguise his disdain for the uncouth captain.

'Zounds, but he's an odious braggart!' His pale eyes were deceptively sleepy under heavy lids, while he ceaselessly waved a palmetto leaf to ward off the flies. 'And a perpetual thorn in our good admiral's side.'

Roxanna followed his direction and picked out Coxon with his short bowed legs and stocky body. Bizarre blue tattoo markings decorated his shaggy arms and chest and even with the distance of the heat-shimmering sand between them, she could hear him upbraiding his grumbling men as they strained at the winches to draw their stripped vessel up on to the shingle.

'And who are those men talking with Dirk?' she wanted to know.

'The short, fairish one is Edmund Cook, Sawkin's lieutenant. The thin, stooped fellow is Lionel Wafer, the camp surgeon,' Ringrose told her, swatting savagely at a mosquito which whined persistently round his lank, sunbleached hair.

The doctor interested her more than any of the rest. Dressed in a white linen shirt with sleeves rolled up, and dark blue breeches, he leaned lightly on the slender cane with the gold top which was the symbol of his calling.

In the tent which had been erected for them, she was pleased to find that the bed from Dirk's cabin had been set up and her trunk stood waiting. She had brought only one, storing the six other chests which had come with her from England at Lucy's tavern, together with her spinet. While she busied herself in making the tent tidy, Dirk went out to detail his men.

A seaman, retired from piracy, had built a shack for himself near the rutted track which wound inland through the jungle to Cayona. He had opened it as a tavern for his friends who chose Nigger Bay for their careening, knowing from experience that

131

what they most craved when the toil of the day was over, was liquor and girls. He kept both.

In the dusk of evening Dirk suggested a stroll on the beach. Outside, the moonlight turned everything to silver, a wide band of it lying across the flat lagoon.

The hulls of the beached ships loomed black, like stranded sea-monsters, while the damped-down fires glowed against the darkness of the forests. The peace and stillness lapped about her as, hand in hand, they paced slowly down to the water's edge. Dirk sat on a jutting rock and threw pebbles into the sea, watching them break the moonlit surface. His face, shadowed and dark, stabbed her with an ache of love and fear of being without him.

'How long shall we be here, beloved?' she asked.

'Two, three weeks, maybe.' He shrugged and turned to draw her close. For a moment she stiffened, then relaxed against him, bending to press her lips on his damp forehead, her fingers in his hair. She breathed in the completely personal smell of it which always roused her. It seemed to embody all the reasons why she loved him; his arresting appearance and powerful animal magnetism; the strange brooding sadness sometimes glimpsed in his eyes. The dominating strength, unexpected moods of gentle sweetness and the depth of character at which she could only guess.

'Three weeks! So short a time! I don't want to go home!' She forgot her promises, her vehement assertions that only to be near him would satisfy her.

He stood up and reached out to grip her by the elbows before bending to kiss her again on her protesting mouth. 'Don't waste time in quarrelling, sweeting. 'Tis a magic night! Be happy with what you have!'

She forced back the spate of angry words which would have precipitated an argument, while within her burned a dull resentment that he should be so unmoved by her, so intent on planning his life to exclude her.

Later, she lay wide awake while he slept beside her. She rolled on to her back and stared up into the darkness where the netting was slung over bamboo poles to keep off the mosquitos which relentlessly pursued them. She brooded on every aspect of their combustible relationship. The more she dwelt on it, the more it hurt her; it was like sucking on a nagging tooth.

Infuriated, she wanted to pummel the broad back which was turned to her, to shatter the deep, even breathing of his slumber, wishing that she had never met him, longing for the comfort of Nan Dobs, which she knew would never be hers again, yearning for home with a deep nostalgia. Then she suddenly grinned as she pictured Paulina's face if she could only parade Dirk before her envious eyes. That would put her nose out!

Dawn light was beginning to filter in through the tent-flap when Roxanna awoke. Dirk was already pulling on his clothes.

Roxanna sat up at once, determined to prove to him just how useful she could be. She stretched her arms over her head, yawning and shivering as the chill air struck her naked body. She quickly scrambled into her shift, one white petticoat, a red and green striped cotton skirt which reached to her ankles, and a blouse with low-neck and short puffed sleeves, and, leaving off her stockings, thrust bare feet into a pair of sensible leather shoes.

After splashing her face with cold water,

she carried the mirror to the light where Dirk promptly monopolized it to shave. Swearing, and dodging under his upraised arm, she powdered her face, rubbed rouge into her lips, then brushed her hair vigorously, leaving it loose and falling nearly to her waist.

Her reflection gratified her as she paused to tie the ribbons of her straw bon-grace under her chin, and to ease lower the round neck of her blouse. With a swirl of skirts foaming above her ankles she stepped out confidently into the dewy coolness of the pink dawn, and made her way across the beach to the cooking tent.

During the following days, Roxanna learned how to prepare meals on the open wood fire, and which was the best kindling stick to use. She tidied their tent, scrubbed at their garments in the ice-cold spring water which ran near the camp, beating them on the wide, flat stones. She went fishing with the cook who showed her how to run a line and the easiest way to catch a turtle.

At the far end of the camp several boucaning-pits had been made. These were beds of red-hot coals and wood, above which the long strips of raw beef, well

135

salted, were hung on frames of green rods. The racks were revolved periodically and grease poured over the smouldering embers to throw up a thick smoke.

At first Roxanna's hands quickly blistered and roughened under the unaccustomed work, but she found an odd pleasure in seeing this, feeling that she was proving her devotion for Dirk. When she noticed that, inevitably, she was becoming tanned, she was more worried. Like any lady of fashion she had taken great pride in her pale skin but when Dirk assured her that the honey colour became her well, she at once stopped bemoaning the fact that she was beginning to look like a gypsy.

One morning Dirk took her hunting. She had pleaded and cajoled, giving him no peace until he consented to take her along. She swung happily at his side as they took a winding path leading up into the foot-hills. Roxanna was entranced by the great trees covered in creepers and the bizarre blossoms, which threw off heavy, sickly odours. Parrots screamed at them from high in the branches. Many of the birds looked very familiar and she was sure that their like flitted in Nan's garden in the summer months.

Never had Roxanna known Dirk so at ease. He seemed quite a different person, as they penetrated the thick scrub. The questions bubbled from her lips and he explained everything she asked. His eyes glittered with a fervent enthusiasm and hunger for the soil, which astounded her.

They rested on a little plateau to eat their breakfast. Roxanna had brought food packed in a knapsack and laid out maize-bread, fruit, turtle-meat and yams, together with a canteen of rum and lime juice for him and a bottle of sack for herself.

Dirk lay on his back after they had eaten, looking up into the palm which towered above them.

'And tonight, darling,' he glanced over at her with indolent amusement. 'You shall sup on stewed kid, unless I've lost my skill with the musket.'

He shot all that was needed during the morning. At noon, they found a deep pool shaded by trees and peeled off their saturated garments to bathe in the clear spring water. Afterwards Roxanna sat on the mossy turf, shaking out her dripping hair to dry. She watched admiringly, as Dirk climbed onto a rock which hung over the pool and dived from it, his brown body cleaving effortlessly through the mirror-like surface. It was too hot to lie in the sun and she was almost asleep when he came at length to join her at the foot of a giant mahogany tree. He was cool to touch and the water ran from his hair. He stretched out at her side, turning to take her in his arms and in her nostrils was mingled the fresh, clean smell of his skin and the stinging fragrance of the flowers crushed beneath them.

When it grew cooler, towards the evening, they reached the edge of the camp. Roxanna hung back, reluctant to lose Dirk among his fellows, hating to leave that perfect day behind her. A presentiment warned her that it would be a long while before she was so completely happy again.

CHAPTER 8

'There is very little time left, so listen carefully,' Dirk's voice was grave. He spoke quietly and with deliberation. 'You will spend the night here. Tomorrow, a cart will come to take you to Cayona. Go to Lucy, and from there arrange to travel to Jamaica with Brownrigg.'

He gave Roxanna no chance to interrupt, speaking swiftly while she clenched her fists hard.

Dirk drew a leather purse from the pocket of his coat and tossed it onto the table. 'Here are a hundred pounds. That should be ample to see you safely to Jamaica. Be careful with whom you mix and trust no one but Lucy, Dan and Brownrigg.' He gave her a sharp, anxious glance, obviously perplexed by her stillness. 'Do as I say and no harm will come to you. Kate will be journeying with you as far as Cayona, but try not to quarrel with her.'

There was a long pause and she turned slowly to look at him, her hands limply in her lap, shoulders drooping.

'Shall I never see you again?' she whispered with a catch in her voice.

He came over and put his hands on her arms, drawing her up against him. At the familiar feel of his hard body, a sudden flood of smarting tears welled up.

'Who can tell what lies ahead for any of us?' he murmured, his lips against her forehead. 'Maybe one day we shall meet again.'

'But how...? When...?' she implored, clinging to him in desperation. 'Oh, let me wait for you in Cayona! Please...please... Dirk, darling!'

His eyes turned hard and uncompromising and he put her from him firmly. 'No, Roxanna! We have been through all this before! What you ask is impossible. I shall be away a long while, and I may be killed!'

She began to cry noisily. 'Oh, I can't bear it! I love you so!'

'You are young, you will soon forget me,' he began, but she would not hear of this, denying it violently. He caught her to him with a hungry, angry urgency which suggested a reluctance to leave her which he did not want to admit, even to himself. With a kind of lost abandon, she responded, spurred by the hope that he might yet be persuaded to let her wait for him, and by the longing to conceive his child. If this happened a part of him would remain with her for ever.

When he lifted his head his eyes were smoky and dark. For an instant, she was afraid that he was going to leave with the embrace incomplete.

'Please, Dirk,' she entreated, all pride stripped from her. With a hard stare in which there was impatience, desire and a hint of amusement, he flung his hat and sword on the bed.

Later, when he stirred and moved away from her clinging arms, she gave a strangled, incoherent cry. She watched as he moved swiftly about the shabby little room. At last he was ready and she sprang up, the anguished words wrung from her. 'Don't leave me!'

He caught her wrists and forced her to free him, his voice almost pleading, 'Roxanna, sweetheart, do not make it so deuced difficult! There is no other way, believe me. We can have no life together. It is best like this. One day, when you are older, you will understand!'

His lips brushed hers briefly, then he was gone. She stood staring disbelievingly after him. Then, with an agonized moan, she flung herself on the bed and sobbed heart-brokenly till she fell asleep, exhausted.

Darkness was settling over Nigger Bay, which was strangely quiet and peaceful. Lights sparkled in the lanterns on the ships riding the water, stocked and prepared, waiting only for the wind. Stivens' tavern was unnaturally silent; a baby crying, the shrilling of crickets, the twitterings and rustlings of the bats who lodged in the palm-thatch, were the only sounds. A negro and one old sailor were the sole occupants of the taproom, leaning on the bar in low, murmured conversation. In the bedrooms the coffee-coloured prostitutes yawned prodigiously, glad to rest now that the buccaneers had departed.

Roxanna opened her eyes which felt swollen and stiff, wanting nothing but to die, sodden with misery. Shudderingly afraid of the encroaching darkness, she dragged herself to the table and lit the candle. In the cracked mirror she saw that her eyes and cheeks were blotched with weeping, her lip-rouge smeared by grief and Dirk's kisses. She rubbed at the tears with the back of her hand, unable to marshal her thoughts.

Suddenly she lifted her head, listening intently, frozen and still, sure that someone was lurking outside the door. Instantly, came the hope that Dirk had returned, and at the same time, a cold dread lest it be Sharp sneaking in, or someone come to murder her for her money.

With her inside quaking, icy drops of sweat coming out all over her, she crept along the wall till she reached the door. Johnny had given her a dagger with a wickedly sharp blade as a parting gift. Roxanna gripped it in her right hand and, screwing up her failing courage, she jerked open the door.

A figure detached itself from the blackness, and wiry fingers were at her throat.

'One sound, you bloody bitch, and I'll throttle you!' The guttural tone was very familiar.

'Kate!' she spluttered, beginning to struggle. 'What the devil are you about? Let me go!'

Roxanna gave a violent kick at the legs pressing against her. The hands relaxed and Kate gave her a shove, closing the door softly. Roxanna massaged her neck and glared at her in the smoky light of the single candle. Kate's eyes were hostile and contemptuous.

'Trust you to hear me!' she snapped, dropping her knapsack to the floor. 'I am off to join Johnny, tho' he don't know it! He thought he could scour and leave me behind, the bastard! Well, he won't find it so easy to give me the slip!'

'Take me with you!' Roxanna demanded, her slanting eyes glowing like a tiger's, hungry and fierce.

Kate subjected her to a hard insulting stare and then gave a brash, vindictive laugh. 'What!' she jeered softly, in a way which roused the devil in Roxanna. 'Take you, you lily-livered ninny! Hell and furies, what a campaigner you'd make, to be sure!'

Roxanna bristled like a warring cat. 'I'll scream the rotten roof off this damned flea-trap if you try to go without me!'

At once Kate was upon her, knocking her back against the bed, where they sprawled. Roxanna twisted and brought up the dagger, driving it through Kate's clothes so that it pricked her ribs. She stiffened and drew back.

'Very well, then, come if you will. Indeed, I have a sudden notion that 'twill give me rare sport to see you after a hard day's marching in the heat or in the midst of a battle! Have you any men's clothes that you can wear?'

Before she had finished speaking, Roxanna was ransacking her baggage, searching for a pair of Dirk's breeches and a shirt which she knew he had left. She pulled

144

the soiled shirt over her head, senses tingling because the smell of his sweat still clung to it, rolling up the sleeves and hoisting the breeches, which were much too large, keeping them in place with a belt. Frantically, she raked through her possessions, trying to decide what to take, pulling open the neck of a canvas bag and thrusting in her jewellery, pots of cosmetic, her hair brush and bone-handled tooth-brush, before pulling the draw-string tight.

'Tie back your hair,' ordered Kate. 'If anyone sees us they are to take us for a pair of lads. Not that they would remain long deceived if they looked at you!' she added pithily. She jabbed a finger at the purse on the table. 'And bring that, we may need some crop!'

Trembling with excitement, fingers clamped about her dagger, Roxanna followed Kate down the stuffy corridor and out into the mysterious scrub which circled the beach.

At the edge of the lagoon they found a goatskin-covered coracle. They scrambled in and Kate pushed off. Carefully lifting the dripping paddle so that it did not splash, she guided the crude craft towards the towering black side of the *Hopewell.*

Kate was groping for a purchase.

'Here, grab this and climb up!' She thrust a wet rope at Roxanna, who got to her feet, made a wild grab and capsized the coracle.

The sea was icy, the shock taking her breath as she went under. She surfaced, her lungs filled with salt water, choking and gasping. Kate grabbed her by the hair and began to swear in a hoarse, furious whisper.

'Damn your eyes! D'you want to rouse the whole bloody fleet!'

She was clinging to a rope with her free hand and lugged Roxanna along until she too could hang on. They rested for a moment, breathing hard.

'Can you climb now?' Kate wanted to know. 'If you fall back into the sea I'll not come down for you!'

Roxanna swung her bag over her shoulder, humiliated that she had made a fool of herself, and braced her feet against the slippery hull, gripping with her bare toes and easing slowly up the rope. Kate reached down to seize her wrist, pulling her up until she found a footing on the broad, raised carving.

'Some careless bastard has left a gunnel

open!' Kate's voice was triumphant. 'In we go!'

There was silence except for the water dripping from them.

'There should be a glim somewhere,' Kate said briskly. 'Damn it, my flint will be wet...unless...' She was feeling along the wall and gave a satisfied grunt as she found the lantern. 'Ah, here is a flint and tinder too!'

'Dare we risk lighting it?' Roxanna's teeth were chattering so hard that she could scarcely speak.

'We shall break our damn necks getting into the hold if we don't!' came the retort, and a flame was blindingly bright as the wick in the candle caught. They were on the lower gun-deck, with tackle stacked, ready for use at a moment's notice, guns lashed just beyond the ports.

Kate heaved at a hatch in the floor, raised it and disappeared, taking the light with her. Roxanna hastily scrambled down after her, finding herself on the orlop-deck, home of provisions and the rats who scurried into the shadows, bright-eyed and bold, staring at the intruders. Another ladder took them down into the hold, where there was little but ballast and

147

bilge. A fetid odour, damp and foul, was stirred up as they waded through several inches of water. More dark shapes flitted away, emitting shrill squeaks. Roxanna's flesh crawled, but Kate's face held nothing but satisfaction.

Reluctantly, Roxanna crawled onto an oiled sailcloth, shivering. Kate hung the lantern on a nail and sat down with a pleased sigh, while Roxanna shot her a look charged with dislike.

'And how long must we remain in this mouldy corner? You may be used to such surroundings, but I certainly am not!' she remarked haughtily.

'God damn it!' exclaimed Kate. 'This is a palace to some of the kens I've padded in. Tho' I swear I've never kept sorrier company!' She threw Roxanna a glare, caustic enough to cripple her. 'You wouldn't have any notion of how some poor bastards live, would you? Too high and mighty to concern yourself, eh? You and your like would see a man starve for want of a groat!'

'That is untrue!' Roxanna was stung to retort. 'Any beggar who came to our kitchen door could get a crust. We often fed the children with broth.'

Kate gave a mirthless laugh. 'Broth!' she spat. 'Aye, I've had some of the "charity broth". Like grey water with grease floating on it! Fifty brats fed on one oxhead and household scraps!'

'That is not so at our house!' Roxanna snapped, remembering the good meat which had gone into Nan Dob's stews and her concern over the sickly, starved waifs who clustered on the door-step. 'You would have nothing to complain about if you came a-begging there!'

'Begging!' Kate bridled, caught on the raw. 'I shall never beg again!' She was silent for a moment, watching Roxanna, then: 'Ever been to the Whit?' she asked suddenly.

Roxanna shook her head, 'No, but I had friends who used to visit the highwaymen there.'

'Pah!' Kate's face twisted in a grimace. 'I've seen 'em, those mincing ladies, come to giggle at the bridle culls, imagining lying with 'em!'

Roxanna's eyes sharpened. It was difficult to believe that Kate was only seventeen. She felt a sudden curiosity about her background.

'What happened to your parents?' she

149

asked slowly. Kate shrugged her thin shoulders, her mouth lifting in a cynical grin.

'I never knew 'em. I was given to the parish-nurse to rear. A brandy-sodden old bawd who used us to beg as soon as we could toddle. When I was twelve the old dame had me ravished by her hulking brute of a son, God curse his memory, and sent me out as a whore. But I was not pretty enough for that and she found me more profitable on the buzz.'

'How did you get in the Whit?' For the first time compassion began to stir in Roxanna for this bitter, hard-eyed girl.

'Oh, someone babbled and I was took. It's a rare fine place, if your nose ain't too easily offended and you've plenty of cole for garnish!'

Roxanna recalled the rather imposing new façade of Newgate Jail, replacing the old building destroyed in the Great Fire. She was fast learning the thieves cant which was an integral part of Kate's vocabulary, but some of it still eluded her.

'What is garnish?'

'Bribes!' Kate explained. 'You have to pay for everything in there. For "easement of irons", that is to be allowed to wear light darbies instead of the heavy iron fetters; for decent peck and water that isn't brackish; for a bed and a sheet.'

Roxanna was puzzled. 'But, if you are in prison, how can you earn money for these things?'

'Oh, there are a hundred ways.' She warmed to her theme. 'You can pick the pockets of visitors, for example, and the queer culls make counterfeit money while they are inside.' Kate slid an insolent eye down Roxanna, one eyebrow raised. 'Why, you are asitting on as good a means of earning cole as a woman may have!'

Roxanna flushed, angry and offended. Kate threw back her curly head and gave a shout of laughter. 'Don't look so shocked! Many a wench gives herself to any likely cove just to get quick so that she can plead her belly and escape a casting!'

Roxanna awoke hours later in pitch-darkness. In her ears was a pounding, the sound made by the ship ploughing through a choppy sea. It was impossible to judge the passing of time in the stuffy darkness. Kate would not keep the candle alight for fear of using it up, so Roxanna sat sulkily, strained and watchful, never sure that Kate would not yield to her obvious longing to murder her.

Kate went on a reconnoitre, returning to say that it was time for them to go.

It took them only a few moments to reach the deck. No one noticed them and they paused to exchange an almost friendly grin before mounting the companion-way, two steps at a time. Roxanna could hear laughter, the chink of coins and the rattle of dice, while Dirk's voice sent a thrill coursing through her. With a wink, Kate rapped sharply on the door.

'What is it?' Johnny's voice was thick, bored and a little drunk.

'Please, Cap'n, 'tis the boy with the fresh bottles.' Kate imitated a boyish treble.

'Come in then, damn you! What kept you so long!'

Rackham had just played and all heads were bent eagerly over the table. No one glanced at them until Kate spoke again, her own accents ringing out clearly.

'Well, here's a pretty fetch! Have ye naught to do but get lappy?'

Johnny's head jerked up, to show a flabbergasted face. 'Kate!' he roared, eyes wide with incredulity. 'You damned little baggage!' He frowned, then grinned in delighted amusement, and she was snatched up in a bearhug. 'Naughty jade, am I not to be free of you then? Follow me round the world, would you?'

Roxanna felt her blood slowly freeze at the black expression on Dirk's face. He pushed back his chair and stood up, while she took a hesitant step towards him, stunned by the fury in his eyes.

She swallowed hard to control the sobs which were making her throat ache. 'Dirk, I had to come. Don't be angry. Aren't you pleased to see me?'

'You must be mad or a fool, or both!' He turned his back on her, shaking the dice and throwing them so violently that they bowled across the table. 'Beat that, Rackham, if you can!'

Johnny flung himself into his carved armchair, dragging Kate onto his knee. 'This may mean trouble with Sawkins, he swore that he would have no doxies on the trip.'

'Devil take that little weasel!' she snapped her fingers with extreme contempt. 'You'll not obey orders from him, my bully.'

'He is the bloody admiral.' The crease deepened between his eyebrows. 'We could be scragged for mutiny.'

Kate gave a harsh mocking laugh. 'I'd like to meet the swab that could cast you, Johnny. The nubbing-cheat ain't woven that would take your weight!'

'Stow it, damn you! You know 'tis bad luck to say that!' Johnny scowled angrily, as superstitious as Dirk was sceptical

Enviously, Roxanna watched Kate and Johnny drinking from the same mug, kissing and fondling. Her lips drooped in a pout and anger against Dirk mingled with the deep hurt and humiliation. Johnny noticed her glum expression and reached out an arm for her.

'Come, sweeting, here is a perch for you, too! In truth I did not think you possessed so much guts! Troublesome wenches, the pair of you!'

She was glad to slide onto his broad knee, comforted to have his bare brown arm, glittering with a thick pelt of crisp hair, cuddling her waist. Kate's eyes flashed warningly.

When everyone had retired to bed, she and Dirk were alone in the cabin, and silence settled thickly about them. He sat staring off into space, his long legs stretched out, but when Roxanna began to cry he leapt up with a swiftness which made her cringe.

'Zounds, stop snivelling!' He ordered. 'I'm not impressed by vapours and wailing!'

'Johnny is glad that Kate followed him,' she sobbed, reproachfully.

'Damn Kate!' He barked. 'And Johnny too! I don't care if they choose to play the fool! Kate is a hardy wench, she will be able to stand up to this life. It will kill you!'

He paced the cabin, then stopped dead in front of her and pulled his handkerchief from his pocket, tossing it over.

'Dry your tears! God damn it, Roxanna, do you never carry a clout?'

He fetched an exasperated sigh, and ran a worried hand over his hair. When he spoke again some of his fury had abated.

'My dear, you don't know what lies ahead of us. There will be days of marching through swamps stinking with fever, and in this heat! The brutality of plundering the towns will appal you! You will not last a week. And I shall have the added burden of having to look after you.'

'Why don't you tell me what is really

155

in your heart?' she accused. 'Say that you were glad to be finished with me!'

He frowned down at her, his handsome features sullen. 'That is true. I do not wish to be troubled with you further.'

'I knew it!' she wailed, tears starting afresh. 'Oh, you are so hateful! Cold and heartless! Oh, I wish that I'd never clapped eyes on you, Dirk Courtney!'

She longed to hit him, but there was a dangerous glow in the blackness of his pupils which restained her.

'I am not heartless!' he rejoined, hands thrust deep into his pockets, as he continued his restless pacing. 'What I did was for your own good!'

'I am sorry to be such a nuisance to you!' Her voice had a tart edge, his handkerchief screwed up into a soggy ball in her hot palm.

'You are not in the least sorry!' he replied acidly. And then added, half in good humour, half savagely: 'You know perfectly well that I can't send you back now! 'Tis a sorry mess. The devil only knows what Sawkins will say. We shall lose what little trust they have in us.'

'Tell him I came without your leave.' She felt suddenly genuinely sorry for the worry she was causing him.

He gave a twisted smile. 'Do you imagine they will believe that?'

'I won't be any trouble, I promise you,' she assured him, earnestly.

His eyebrows shot up as he scanned her face, with the slanting green eyes gazing adoringly from under sweeping black lashes, the high piquant cheek-bones, and short nose with delicate fine nostrils. Her wide mouth was slightly parted, the red lower lip glistening, reminding him of the eager passion of her response. All of her body was redolent with the promise of sexual gratification. Even her walk was provocative.

'Trouble!' he exclaimed. 'I imagine that you will be aplenty!'

She came nearer, pressing her breasts against him, certain that a few moments of violent union would wipe out the misunderstanding between them. His re-action was immediate, his arm crushed her to his chest and she closed her eyes, waiting for his kiss. But he gave her a little shake.

'Roxanna! What if you get with child!'

Her lids flew open wide. Often she had thought of this possibility, but he had never before mentioned it. His eyes had changed, dark as slate with a glow in them which excited her. She did not want to stop and think of anything.

'You don't seem to have been concerned about it till now.' Her tone sharpened.

'It was different before,' he was frowning again. 'You could have passed an infant off as Raynal's begetting, but there will be no such convenient measure here. I don't want a child of mine born in such circumstances!'

'Oh, you don't, eh?' There was a sour twist to her mouth. 'You've grown damned squeamish on a sudden! You were mighty hot for me when you thought I could take your love-child home and rear it! Could it be that you have grown weary of me? That you don't want me any more?'

His glance raked slowly down her with anger, contempt and desire. ' 'Sdeath, of course I want you! But I wouldn't see you come to harm. You should be flattered that I take so much heed of you! I shan't marry you if you do have a baby,' he warned her, as she twined her arms about his neck. 'And, whatever happens, don't say that I did not tell you so!'

CHAPTER 9

On a shimmering day in the first week of April the fleet dropped anchor at Golden Island. A boat pulled off from the *Hopewell* carrying Johnny, Dirk, the two women and a picked company of their toughest, most loyal men. Roxanna sat in the bows, her stomach churning, acutely nervous, anticipating a stormy interview with the Admiral. For a moment, she heartily wished that she was back in Cayona. One glance at Dirk's profile, however, as he stared at the shore, his supple body braced easily against the plunge and swell, pushed aside all doubts.

As the boat ground into the shingle he leapt out, wading through the surf, carrying Roxanna to set her on the firm damp sand. Instantly, a crowd gathered, and they edged through it, tight-lipped and grim, making to where Sawkins stood.

'Captain Comry to speak with the Admiral,' Johnny boomed, his beard jutting up aggressively. A deep scowl came swiftly to Sawkins' thin face as he swung round and saw the women.

'What is the meaning of this?' he demanded, glaring up at the two formidable young giants who faced him squarely. He was a small man, with an extremely tough, wiry physique, which had withstood the vicissitudes of jungle heat, hurricanes, pitched battles and a sojourn in a Spanish prison. 'Ye gave me your oath that these bitches would be left behind!'

Johnny gave a truculent glare, half-drawing his massive cutlass. 'I'll thank you to take a different tone with me, Sawkins!' he bellowed pugnaciously, while his officers shifted into position behind him.

Dirk dug his elbow sharply into his ribs, whispering an angry warning. 'Shut your mouth, you great dullard! The women stowed away without our knowledge!' Dirk's voice rang crisply over the sand.

A roar of laughter greeted this and he spun about, eyes glittering dangerously. ' 'Tis the truth, upon my honour.'

The men quietened to listen. Roxanna could feel the tension in Dirk as her arm pressed against his.

'God knows, I would not have had this wench with me for a great deal,' he continued, addressing the Admiral. 'But you know women, determined to get their way. So this one followed me, against my orders!'

Sawkins gave a snort, pulling at his drooping, grizzled moustache.

'I have a mind to believe you, Courtney,' he conceded at last. 'I know you to be a man of truth. But now, what is to be done with them?'

The expeditionary force had been joined at Golden Island by William Dampier who was renowned among the Brethren for his explorations in the South Seas. He came over to join the dissention and Roxanna watched him, distrusting his long features, the neat, almost Puritanic costume, the thin brown hair. His eyes were cool as they briefly met hers.

'They will be nothing but trouble,' he put in without hesitation. 'There is but one answer.' And he drew a swift, significant finger across his throat.

With an instantaneous movement, both Dirk's and Johnny's swords were out, and there was the scrape of steel as their officers followed suit.

Johnny thrust his tangled beard into Dampier's face, his face blazing with defiant challenge. 'If any man lays as much as a finger on either of them, I turn my lads loose!'

They found an ally in Massey, whose eyes sparked as he mentally stripped Roxanna of her tight-fitting breeches and shirt. Sharp, with a similar leer, ranged himself with them, too, raising his loud blustering voice in protest against Sawkins. Roxanna tried to conceal herself behind Dirk.

Sawkins silenced the clamour with a magnificent stream of invective, leaping on to a rock so that he might predominate the gathering. 'This is a damned peery lay. But as we are about to attack a mutual enemy, we can't afford to fight with you. The jades will have to come with us. But I warn you,' he added with great deliberation, 'if they do come, there will be no extra rests, and if they are any trouble we shall put a bullet through them!'

In the morning the company left Golden Island setting out in canoes and longboats. On reaching the shores of the Isthmus they were joined by a party of Indians who offered their services as guides. By them the information was confirmed that Santa Maria was garrisoned by four sections of musketeers and that whoever conquered it would be amply repaid for his trouble.

Leaving the boats high on the beach, Sawkins formed his straggly army into order. Sharp was put in charge of the advance party, moving off up the narrow track which disappeared into dense forest, his colours of red, green and white hanging limply in the humid air. Behind him came Sawkins and his men, with a third and fourth contingent under the command of Peter Harris. The men from the *Hopewell* were placed in the fifth and sixth company led by Coxon and Dampier, while Edmund Cook brought up the rear.

A hush crept over everyone as they penetrated deeper into the bush, awed by the oppressive sense of relentless growth which fashioned this lush, sickly-fragrant foliage. The vines concealed death among their leaves, snakes who lifted flat, darting heads, tongues flickering, wicked eyes watching the progress of the motley army. The wild, uncontrolled fertility brought forth huge, poisonous blossoms, matted undergrowth which tripped their feet. In subdued silence the ragged regiment trudged forward through the rich greenery, chaos of vivid creepers and remorseless sun.

The experienced campaigners ceased their bantering of the young fledglings, whom they liked to pulverize with their macabre humour. They sweated profusely, shirts already ripped off, wet rags bound round their unkept heads and shady palmetto hats on top. Each man carried a pack on his shoulders, containing his rations of bread, dried meat and a canteen of fresh water. Nearly all were festooned with weapons; a musket, a pistol and heavy cutlass, several knives, powder and shot.

Johnny muttered a terse oath at the dripping stillness and began to bawl a very lewd ballad. A gale of relieved laughter rose from their throats and they joined in, glad to have the human voice drown the weird rustlings and creakings of the wood.

At noon a halt was called. Roxanna, who had been too absorbed in her surroundings to notice much else, now found it very uncomfortably hot. She dropped her knapsack with a sigh and gnawed at the salted meat, too hungry to be fastidious, swilling it down with gulps of wine from Johnny's black-jack. Dirk was deep in conversation with Lionel Wafer, a disconcerting man, whose eyes mocked her continually. Kate, squatting on the sparse turf, was examining the filigree work on a silver-ornamented harquebus. Its owner, one of the most villainous men of the whole assembly, with a reputation for infamous brutality towards prisoners, leaned over her shoulder while they discussed its performance.

Roxanna wished that she possessed Kate's knowledge which enabled her to share comradeship with these men. They accepted her as one of themselves. She invited little attention, for with her rugged features and angular body she seemed as much the youth as any of the lads out on their first adventure. It was only when she looked at Johnny that her flinty eyes softened, the sudden warmth in her face betraying more tenderness than she would ever have admitted.

Johnny was seated with his broad back against the base of a tamarind, his booted feet braced against another, his hat, of woven palm fibres, pulled over his eyes. Roxanna knew that he was not asleep and went over to sit by him.

'How now, Johnny,' she wrinkled her nose at him. 'And what was so distressful about this morning's marching? Dirk was but trying to frighten me with his bugaboo tales!'

He pushed his hat back on his tawny locks, screwing up his eyes at the sun which could just be seen through the thick trees. 'I wonder if you will be so pert by this evening,' he conjectured dryly.

Sawkins could not afford the time to let them rest during the sweltering heat of the afternoon. It was imperative that they take the town by surprise, and the longer their journey took, the greater the risk of the Spanish garrison being warned.

The marauders had no energy left for singing. With mouths too dry even to spit, they tramped in silence occasionally bursting into surly blasphemy directed against their leaders.

Dirk relieved Roxanna of her pack, slinging it with his own, across his wide shoulders and she became oblivious to everything but the protesting discomforts of her body. The mosquitoes droned around their heads and Roxanna could feel her face beginning to swell with bites, streaked with her own blood where she had squashed them.

Dirk had advised her to wear thigh-length leather boots, to protect her legs from snake-bite. Her feet were very small and they had difficulty in finding a pair anywhere near her size. Now she could feel a hole being rubbed in the heel of her stocking. She plodded doggedly on, keeping her eyes on Dirk's straight back where the perspiration made dark patches on his shirt. For all the delicacy of her small-boned, slender appearance, she possessed a constitution which was resilient and extremely tough, and this stood her in good stead, together with a very stubborn will which was adamant in its determination to complete whatever project she had set her heart on.

It seemed as if they had been walking forever through the very ovens of Hell, before the admiral at last pitched camp for the night. His men sank down groaning, too tired even to curse, but he had them up again in an instant, profanities pouring from him as he stormed up and down their ranks, making them light fires, set the watches and refill their canteens at the stream.

Almost unconscious with exhaustion, Roxanna felt arms under her knees and shoulders and she was carried to the bank. Dirk pulled off her boots, putting her feet into the cool water and bathing her face and head, the refreshing droplets trickling down her neck. The crimson scarf, bound around his head to keep back his hair, was black and wet, his skin blotched with insect bites. 'If he says, *I told you so,* I shall just die!' She thought wearily.

He spread a blanket out on the grass of the clearing and lifted her onto it.

'I'm on first watch, but Johnny is nearby, so do not fear.' His kiss was sweet on her mouth and she drowsily watched the fires of dry brushwood blazing comfortingly. Against the gathering gloom she could make out Johnny's bulky form and see the glow of his pipe. As she slipped into the oblivion of sleep her brain was still repeating the nursery jingle which had haunted her during the gruelling afternoon.

'How many miles to Barley Bridge? Three score and ten. Can I get there by candlelight? Yes, if your legs be long.'

Four days later the buccaneers arrived at the settlement of the Indian Chief, King Golden Cap. The warriors who had travelled with them were of this tribe, and scouts had been sent ahead so that a feast was prepared in welcome. Roxanna slept,

168

drugged with exhaustion, for hours after their arrival, beyond caring what became of them. When she woke at last, she found that she was lying on a heap of soft skin and colourful woven blankets, under the awning of a hide tent. She was stiff, sore with sunburn, but that intense vitality which abounded in her had been restored by that deep, dreamless sleep. She got up, stripped off her filthy garments and washed thoroughly, although every inch of her skin seemed to possess its own little smart.

An Indian girl hovered in the tent entrance and it was obvious that she had been ordered to assist her. Roxanna guessed that Dirk had arranged this; it was like him to be so thoughtful. She smiled encouragingly and took the clean clothes held out to her. When she had put on the fringed, beaded, doeskin tunic and skirt, and thrust her feet into a pair of chamois-thonged sandals, she reached for her pack, and got out her hand-mirror. She pulled a wry mouth at her reflection.

After giving her tangled hair a vigorous brushing and applying cosmetics from her precious store, she stepped out of the tent, running into Johnny.

'Hell's curses, darling!' he complimented with a grin, the admiration in his eyes making her feel almost herself again. 'You make even those clothes look alluring!'

Roxanna slipped her arm through his, and they sauntered across to where fires smouldered. Whole deer and young suckling pigs were being roasted, slowly revolving on spits. The tattered men, sprawled on mats, drinking the potent native-distilled spirit, cheered on the warriors, fanning their hatred of the oppressive colonial authorities. The firelight flung grotesque shadows on their leaping, twirling forms, on the paint streaking their narrow faces and writhing brown bodies. They lunged with iron-tipped lances, giving blood-chilling yells, as the drums throbbed in thunderous pulse-stirring rhythm.

Dirk gave Roxanna a brief smile, looking up from the cards spread out on the earth, and she settled down beside him, legs curled under her, accepting a bowl of palmetto wine which Johnny had brought.

Bartholomew Sharp smirked conceitedly. There was that in his bumptious manner which riled her. His assumption that every woman on whom he deigned to cast his libidinous eye should be overjoyed at the honour, set her teeth on edge. But it gave her a triumphant feeling to see Dirk's face go sullen as Massey leaned attentively over her, whilst Sharp swaggered and boasted. Somehow, she found it almost impossible not to encourage any man who showed an interest in her.

'Mrs Roxanna, as graceful in her Indian garb as if out walking in Mulberry Gardens,' Sharp's heavy-jowled face was smooth and bland.

The mere mention of London woke responsive chords in her and she began to chatter vivaciously about life in the capital.

'Did you ever tread the stage, madam?' Massey edged closer to ask and she laughed gaily, flinging back her head, her slender throat arched.

'Nay, not I! But I have a very dear friend who is a player at the King's Theatre.'

'In truth, most perfect lady, you would grace any play!' Sharp was not to be outdone, his forehead damp from the heat of his wig, which had been stored away in his pack during the march, and was now worn for her benefit. He tried to take one of her hands in his. 'Those dainty feet and most fair ankles would trip right pleasantly, I am sure!'

The raiders were in an exuberant mood, the coarse wine loosening their tongues and dulling their senses. They quarrelled and argued over the gaming, and stared longingly at the forbidden bronze woman who flitted among them, serving the food.

Massey and Sharp were urging Roxanna to show them a coranto and she rose, half reluctant, but eager to display herself before Dirk. His expression was taciturn, and he sat, forearms resting in his knees, ignoring her. As she danced a few steps, a member of the Portugese contingent shouted encouragement and began to strum a guitar. She found the controlled measure of a set dance of no use, for he played a restless melody which wove itself insidiously into her blood.

The men grew quiet as they watched her sensuously twisting body. She directed the full meaning of her dance at Dirk, her lips curving in a smile of enticement and promise.

Johnny watched her covetously, his hand rubbing over his beard, lounging back on his elbows. Sharp was staring and pulling at his heavy lower lip, while Massey's face was a dark, salacious mask. The beat quickened and Roxanna stamped and gyrated, hair and skirt swirling out.

When the music stopped, she flung herself at Dirk's feet, throwing back her head to give him a challenging look, her breasts heaving. He stood up and reached out a hand to drag her to her feet. Her mouth, moist and parted, whispered his name, and his fingers bit into her wrists as he pulled her into his arms, hard.

In the shelter of the tent his ardour filled her with joy, but as he pressed her back on the rugs, Johnny called him. She had never heard him swear with such explosive ferocity as he rose and strode to the entrance.

Johnny sounded apologetic. 'Sorry, Dirk, but Sawkins is abellowing for you, wants your help with this damned jargon of Golden Cap. You can speak it can't you?'

Roxanna fumed, frustrated and furious, her blood pounding hotly. 'Damn this campaign!' she swore. 'Am I never to have him alone!' She was convinced that by the use of the erotic tricks which she was learning fast, she might have made him say that he loved her. She was asleep when he returned to fling himself down beside her, roll a blanket about him and sleep too.

When the refreshed and strengthened force set out again they were accompanied by the king and one hundred and fifty of his men.

For the first time Roxanna saw the crocodiles of which Dirk had warned her. They slid away from the leading canoe in which she was travelling, making the muddy brown water boil about their gnarled, horny hides. The bush teemed with waking bird-life, disturbed by the river-craft, rising with shrieks and the flap of jewel-bright wings. From the huge ceiba and sapodilla trees trailed creepers where Johnny pointed out massive coiled pythons that blended perfectly with their background.

There was a continual dripping of moisture and the flies attacked them voraciously until Roxanna was weary of swatting at them and sank back, annoyed and sweating in the bottom of the canoe, her freshly-washed shirt and breeches already soaked and foul. The river became so shallow that they were forced to wade, shoving the heavy boats before them and lifting them over fallen trees that blocked their way every few yards. They were soon plastered with mud, groaning and mutinous, while Johnny and Dirk drove them on with caustic invective, ridicule and threats.

Suddenly Roxanna started to scream, her shrill cries setting the men clutching at their muskets, spluttering nervous oaths. She stood, rooted to the spot, staring in appalled horror at the fat, yellowing leech which was hanging on her arm.

'Get it off!' she yelled at Dirk. 'Oh, God, get it off!'

He squelched over to her, mud to the top of his jackboots, and removed it, bidding her lick at the round, red hole left in her forearm. After this she kept every portion of her body covered, discovering that these creatures abounded in the water, avidly attacking the human flesh as did the mosquitoes, bugs, ticks and flies. And she began to loathe the jungle in spite of its lush magnificence, the nacreous, whirring wings of the tiny humming-birds, and the dappled butterflies which hovered over the wild orchids.

They camped on the mushy earth, dejectedly trying to scrape the sticky filth and grass-lice from the their bodies, clothes and weapons. The odour of the fetid muck even permeated through the food.

When the river party reached the rendezvous, Dirk tried to teach Roxanna how to use a pistol. She did her best to overcome her terror of the clumsy flintlock which threatened to explode and blow off her hand. His slashing sarcasm increased her nervousness, and at last he shrugged and told her to use her dagger in an emergency. She watched while he practised with his springy, slender poniard, sending it spinning through the air to stick in the trunk of a tree. It hit the wood with a twang, the ivory handle quivering and Roxanna shuddered. He was so expert that she wondered how many men he had slain with it.

Next morning they were joined by the remainder of the company. Sawkins was worried because guides had reported a platoon of enemy soldiers in the vicinity. He gave strict orders for absolute silence and, cautiously, nerves frayed and raw, the corsairs pushed on, some by water, the rest following a track along the bank, thick with rotting mangroves.

It was not until next day, as dawn

was beginning to turn the darkness to mysterious blue, that the straggly, savage-eyed army reached the edge of the bush, just beyond the walls of Santa Maria.

CHAPTER 10

The trees were full of rustlings, and the shrill waking call of birds. The scarlet and blue macaws were hurtling through the leaves, showering the cursing men with dew. Sawkins' army closed its ranks, shuffling and spitting nervously, clutching swords so that they would give no betraying clink, anticipatory grins on their bearded jowls.

'There she be,' whispered one of Coxon's men hoarsely, his red-rimmed eyes fixed on the walled town which was becoming more clearly visible as it grew lighter. 'Like a sleepin' wench waiting' ter be ravished.'

Excitement and terror were making Roxanna feel sick, sending the acrid bile up into her mouth. The stench of the men pressing close about her, their skins covered with layers of dirt, almost choked her. She looked up at Dirk; his face was drawn, jaw dark and unshaven, and his eyes were very bright and keen, his rapier unsheathed. They waited, hardly daring to let the breath slide through dry lips for fear of making a sound. All weariness was banished now that action was imminent.

Then, across the still air, came the réveillè from the fort, and the gates swung open to let a herdsman, driving cattle out to the pastures, pass through. Sawkins raised his arm, cutlass flashing in the first rays of the sun, and there was a general stampede as, roaring like devils, the corsairs followed him out into the clearing before the gate. The red and yellow uniforms of infantrymen were briefly visible, while a drum frantically beat to arms and, within seconds, a brisk musket fire was spattering down while the great iron-studded portals closed with a thud.

For an instant, they stumbled to a halt, then Sawkins had them in the shelter of the wall while an agile contingent began to scale it, getting a purchase on each other's shoulders. The first man on the parapet leapt over with fierce shout and others followed. Quickly, they dispatched the disorganized postern-keepers and were straining at the windlass which, groaningly, opened the gates for their confederates, who poured across in a headlong charge, raising a hideous clamour.

Somewhere a church bell set up a warning, the newly wakened citizens rushing in panic-stricken alarm, firing frenzied, wide shots from upper windows, while the men struggled into their clothes and, seizing weapons, ran from the houses to repel the invaders. Shrieks, yells of pain, the barking of dogs, were punctuated by the sharp staccato of continual firing and the hum of poison-barbed arrows from Golden Cap's bowmen.

Roxanna, borne along by the first impetuous rush, had a jumbled impression of an open square with white houses on each side, and a tangle of men, slashing, hacking and thrusting at any one who got in their way. In the pandemonium she lost sight of Dirk, and, clawing at the combatants locked in vicious deadly struggles, she fought to get free, searching the mob for someone who would protect her. She saw Johnny's head appear for an instant in the melée. He was impervious to everything, his teeth bared in a terrible grin as he brought his heavy sabre down across the arm of a youth, severing it at the elbow. The boy stared in uncomprehending horror, watching the blood spurt from the severed arteries before he began to screech.

With the breath tearing harshly in her throat, her legs trembling like jelly, Roxanna broke through the throng. She skidded to a halt, catching sight of Massey, her cry arrested on her lips. He was tearing the pike from a halberdier whose cuirass sent off sparks in the sunlight. She saw him turn the weapon and thrust it deep into the man's belly, his face contorted as he gave it a violent twist. The soldier screamed on a continual high-pitched note, collapsing to his knees, still impaled. With his booted foot braced against his victim, Massey wrenched the bloody pike free and vaulted over the prostrate form, running off down a side-turning. The man lay, groping with frantic fingers, attempting to push back the pinkish viscera which slithered from his wound.

Roxanna turned and almost fell into the arms of a Spanish musketeer who swung up his firearm, murderous rage on his dark, aquiline features. With a reflex action she ducked, hearing the weapon whistle down in a ruthless blow which missed her by a fraction.

Acting on impulse without conscious thought or effort, she plunged her dagger into the gap exposed beneath his raised arm, where his back and breast-plate joined. He twisted with a yelp of pain and astonishment as she dragged her knife free. With one hand he grabbed her by the hair and, with the other, hit at her again. As the heavy butt glanced off her forehead she went momentarily out of her mind. Blindly, she struck at him repeatedly, a roaring in her ears mingling with her own sobbing breaths and his harsh, incomprehensible curses. His fingers seized her by the throat and, almost demented, she tore at his hands, her eyes seeming to burst from their sockets. The pounding in her head became unbearable and she lost consciousness, the world spinning dizzily while his body crushed her down on to the blood-stained roadway.

For several minutes Roxanna lay senseless and it was a while longer before she came conscious enough to remember where she was and what had happened. She tried to sit up but found that she was pinned down by the soldier's weight.

She lifted one hand with a great effort and saw that it was darkly sticky. For a horrified instant she thought that it was her own blood and that she must be seriously wounded, then realized that it was from him.

Very slowly, nausea sweeping over her in waves, she slipped from under the dead man and, crouching low, mopped at the beads of cold sweat on her face. Bemused, she frowned down at her bloody hands, groped for the hilt of her dagger and, with the ground seeming to heave under her, staggered through the press of fighting men.

She found herself in a clearing, and crawled behind a barricade where, dropping her head down between her knees, she was violently sick. After a while she felt better, and worry about Dirk began to force itself through the haze, filling her with an urgent desire to survive and an equal determination that he should live also. The thought that Dirk might be lying somewhere wounded drove her to her feet, running back into the fray to seek him.

Sprawling bodies, limp or awkwardly huddled, lay in every alley and street. The wails of children, the agonized screams of men meeting a sudden death, and the howling of women paying the traditional price of the conquered, resounded about her. The fight had thinned to a few isolated skirmishes, the soldiers defeated, and the victorious buccaneers already started on an orgy of pillage and rape. Sawkins and his officers were doing their best, with foul vituperation, their fists, and biting irony, to restrain them until the town could be systematically searched, but it was well nigh impossible to control over three hundred berserk, unprincipled desperadoes.

Now and then a bullet, whining suddenly from a window, told of a continued measure of resistance, but the square seemed suddenly as deserted as at siesta time. A yellow mongrel sidled along the wall, pausing to sniff at the pool of blood pumping from a decapitated corpse, whose head had been stuck on top of a spear by some grisly-minded wag. At that moment a tall figure loped into view, grimed and haggard but instantly recognizable.

'Dirk! I'm here!' Her voice cracked with relief and hysteria.

'Are you hurt? My God, you are covered in blood!' His arms were about her.

'I don't think I am hurt. I had a knock on the head,' she croaked. 'The rest is from...' She stopped, beginning to sob uncontrollably. 'Merciful heaven! I killed a man!'

Dirk took her by the shoulders and shook her roughly. 'You have killed? Well, so have I!' he snapped tersely. 'There will be few of us in this town by evening who have not taken life. Now, pull yourself together!'

His brisk tirade did her good. She walked with him across the square and down a street which ran parallel. The victors were engaged in looting and there were crashes and bumps, the outraged voices of men trying to protect their homes. Dirk did not stop until they arrived at a spacious dwelling built in white stone by a master architect with an eye for beauty and proportion of design.

'The governor's residence,' Dirk informed her. 'Our dear admiral has taken it over as headquarters.'

From a paved courtyard, surrounded by well-kept gardens, they entered the

184

lofty imposing apartments which were in a fever of activity. Blood-stained raiders were tramping ruthlessly through the house, searching out terrified servants, intent on extracting every shred of plunder. Messengers pelted in seeking Sawkins, carrying news from the captain busily sacking another quarter of the town, and in the drawing-room, the surgeons were dealing with the wounded.

'Are there any dead?' Dirk questioned Wafer, seating himself astride a chair, folding his arms across the back watching the skilful fingers of the doctor as he sutured a gash in the leg of a grey-faced freebooter.

'No fatal casualties reported as yet.' Wafer neatly bandaged the dirty, hairy calf. He turned to Roxanna, and commenced to examine the lump on her forehead. She could feel her face growing hot at his humorous scrutiny.

While she sat still under his ministration Roxanna looked about her. The walls were hung with a rich arras and paintings in massive gilded frames. Wrought-iron, branching girandoles hung from the ornately decorated ceiling. In niches stood statues and delicately-fashioned urns. Every

185

feature of the room declared that the governor was a man of artistic appreciation and a collector of beautiful objects.

But now this sanctuary had been invaded by insensate boors who spat onto the valuable Persian carpets, scuffing the marble flooring with muddied boots.

Dirk was already familiar with the layout of the house, as he had been among the party who seized it. He conducted Roxanna up the staircase, along cool, airy corridors, to a bedroom.

'I have commandeered this room.' He closed the door behind them. 'Get to bed and try to sleep.'

She could feel panic beginning to overwhelm her again as he turned to go.

'Can't you stay with me?'

There flashed over his face that look of impatient, chill contempt which she knew meant that he considered she was being unreasonable.

'My dear, there is much for me to do. We leaders will be hard put to it to stop our men from an orgy of destruction which will undo any vantage we have gained. When they find the drink I expect we shall be fighting them almost as hard as the citizens, to thrash some sense into their thick skulls! You will be perfectly safe here. Lock the door and don't open it until I return.'

Roxanna's head ached with a fierce persistency, a stupefied inertia making her limbs feel weighted. 'I don't understand, Dirk. Where are the people who lived here?'

He shrugged, eager to be off. 'The place was all but empty when we took it. No doubt the governor made off into the jungle.'

He mitigated his clipped accents with a sudden grin, kissed her lightly and was gone through the door in a couple of strides. Weariness surged through her in increasingly insistent waves and she pulled off her clothes and crawled between the silk sheets of the bed.

But every time she closed her lids, which felt as if the eyeballs had been rubbed in grit, she saw the musketeer looming over her and then his dead face and the scarlet on her hands. She tossed feverishly, trying to think of anything but that, frantically conjuring up pictures of home, struggling to visualize Nan Dobs. But she found that her recollections were hazy, she could no

187

longer remember clearly the features of any of her relatives.

When at last she slept her dreams were filled with crawling horror from which she was roused by Dirk hammering on the door. The room was dark but she fumbled to let him in, blinking in stupefaction at the candle he carried, falling back across the bed, at once returning to a deep torpor. Only now, deeply comforted by his slumbering presence, her rest was healing and restorative.

She awoke at noon next day. Resolutely she shut the experiences of the battle away in a dim recess of her mind. She got up, pattering across the room, filled with a determination to find suitable clothes. In a dressing-room gowns lined the walls and the tallboy was stuffed full of feminine garments. A pierglass flung back her reflection, and she quickly went through the drawers looking for a dressing-gown.

The corridor outside was deserted, and she tiptoed along it on bare feet. From below came the occasional voice, heavy footfalls, scraping of chairs and she glided over the carpeting, pausing at the head of the stairs. The disapproving stares of the family portraits on either side were a little disconcerting; the men in starched ruffs and sombre colours; their ladies prim in wide farthingales. Roxanna cocked a snook at them and ran lightly down.

A man was lounging back easily, cleaning his musket with an oily rag. He eyed her, whistling softly between tobacco-stained teeth, bearded and sinewy and with a sly, cruel expression on his once-handsome features. She recognized him as one of Sawkins' bodyguards.

'Where is the kitchen, sirrah?' she asked with icy hauteur. He gave a grin and shoved back the hat, decked with plumes, which crowned his bedraggled locks. From five feet away his odour reached her, rank and breathcatching.

'What do you want the kitchen for?' he enquired with a most offensive slow wink. 'Goin' ter do some cookin'?'

She treated him to a look scathing enough to blight him, but his grin deepened.

'I want hot water and slaves!' she curtly ordered.

'I can't leave me post, just like that!' he expostulated lazily, adding: 'Not even fer Courtney's flash blowsè. Wait a bit, I'll call me matelot, he'll help ye.'

He raised his voice in a bellow which echoed across the hall to be answered by a youth whose head appeared round the door of the drawing-room. He came over to them at a leisurely pace. His mate at once pounced on the black bottle protruding from the torn-down pocket of a coat so magnificent that it could have been only recently stolen. He knocked down the protesting hand with a grunt and took a long swig.

Laconically, he made known Roxanna's request and the lad scratched at his lice, exasperating her by his dull stupidity. She tapped a pettish foot.

'Come now!' she urged. 'Tell me where all the slaves are gone! To be sure there were servants aplenty in this house!'

She set off down another passage and he trotted beside her.

In the kitchen were gathered a dozen or so scoundrels, keeping the petrified servants on the run. They turned to stare as Roxanna swept in, her russet hair tumbling down her back, face imperious and a challenge in the cat-like eyes.

'Ah, here's Courtney's lovely darling!' One of Sharp's bullies paused in chewing at a roasted capon to speak. He rubbed gravy-soaked fingers down the side of his baggy pantaloons. His face was flushed with wine and the arrogance of the conqueror. His comrades raised their tankards in greeting, slopping liquid on to the knife-dented boards of the table. Roxanna tossed them a disdainful stare, at once letting them know that she was not in the least afraid of them, secure in the knowledge that while Dirk lived they would not dare to molest her.

'Where is Lieutenant Courtney?' She walked across to stand directly before the speaker.

He eased over on the trestle, patting the space beside him. She refused the invitation, knowing that she must firmly squash all attempts at familiarity. He pulled a rueful face at this chill reception, his mates scoffing at his discomfort.

'I last seen 'im in the square checking the prisoners,' he replied, and she remembered that it was the buccaneer custom to herd the wealthier citizens into the church. She stiffened as he added with a sly grin. 'You'd best keep an eye on 'im, love, with all these Spanish wenches about!'

191

CHAPTER 11

Thoughtfully, Roxanna popped the shining soap bubbles which floated on the scented water in which she was soaking. A young Creole slave-girl hovered nervously, waiting to obey her slightest whim. She had found this terrified little creature being mercilessly ravished by four of Sawkins' hellions. Roxanna did not understand a word of Spanish but when the girl crawled over, clasping her round the legs, begging for protection, her meaning was clear enough.

The Creole held out a soft, fleecy towel which Roxanna wrapped round her, stepping out to puddle the carpet with the imprints of wet feet. She smiled and the small dark face responded in pathetic gratitude. She had been the servant of one of the governor's daughters and she dexterously dried her new mistress's dripping tresses.

Roxanna sat on a tabouret and peered at her reflection. Her face and neck were tanned to a warm honey; so were her hands and arms to the elbow where the deeper shade blended into pale cream. She stood up, dropping the enveloping towel and viewing the whole of her body critically, running her hands down the sleek length of thigh, sucking in her belly to whittle the slender waist and lift taut the line of her breasts.

She was so deeply preoccupied that she failed to hear a step outside and looked up, startled, in the mirror, as the door opened. It was Dirk. He paused for an instant, then slowly closed it, leaning back, crossing his arms on his chest and there was a gleam in his eyes which set her trembling as he perused her body. She half-turned, with a deliberately languid movement, and took up her robe, negligently shrugging her shoulders into it, sneaking a glance at him.

She noticed at once that he had changed from the filthy garments he had been wearing on the march. A fawn leather jerkin, laced up the front with thongs, covered a full-sleeved cambric shirt thrown open at his brown throat. Amber breeches were tucked into the tops of suede boots. He was looking so remarkably handsome that she could not wait to have him. She snapped her fingers to dismiss the gaping slave. He came towards her and she returned his kiss with abandon. His mouth tasted of rum. As she stared up into his eyes, there was a peculiar frightening light in them.

During the brief, violent mating which followed, she was constantly aware of an undercurrent of savagery and a nervous tension in him which she had never before experienced. When the storm was spent, he lay heavily against her, his head on her breasts. Reluctant Roxanna opened her eyes, she was drowsy and satisfied, but there was a nagging worry which ruffled her serenity. She drew a sigh which disturbed him. He rolled away from her and turned on his back, fingers laced behind his head, staring up into the draped, silk canopy.

'My darling...' Her voice was low and warm. 'I love you so much.'

She leaned over him, brooding with deep tenderness, bending to brush his eyelids with her lips, tasting the sweat which beaded his face. He gave her a keen, unfathomable stare, then sat up, straightening his clothes.

It was only then that she indignantly

recalled that he had not spoken for the whole time he had been with her, treating her like a drab to be used and left.

'Dirk!' she shot him an annoyed glare, jumping to her feet. 'You always seem in a mighty hurry to leave me after you've had your way!'

He glanced over his shoulder at her, pausing to pick up his sword-belt from beside the bed. 'There is a meeting below. I must attend it.'

She was already flinging on a shift.

'Wait for me! I'm coming too!'

She loathed letting him out of her sight. He shrugged, pulled the stool under him and watched her somberly as she dressed. The stolen gowns were of costly material, if not entirely to her taste. They fitted her reasonably well, possibly a shade too tight in the bust and too ample at the waist.

She had chosen a dress of purple velvet, instinctively conscious of the provocative contrast this colour made to her skin, green eyes and fiery hair.

'It's a most fortunate chance that the Spanish lady was of a size with me,' she commented, watching him uneasily while she rolled the ends of her damp hair into fat ringlets. 'I could not have worn that old frippery any longer.'

Trying to calm the increasing apprehension which she felt, she slid emeralds into her ears. Dirk's expression grew even more sardonic as he felt in his pocket and tossed a crystal phial over to her. She took out the stopper and drew a long, ecstatic sniff. The perfume was heavenly musky, titillating the senses with its brash odour.

'Umm...' She closed her eyes in sheer enjoyment of the erotic fragrance. 'Where did you get it, Dirk?'

'We frisked the bordel next to the soldiers quarters,' came the pithy reply. 'I took it from one of the whores!'

The sneer was pointed, unmistakably intended to goad, and she searched his eyes with worried concern, unable to understand this turbulent, angry mood. Going across to him, she put her arms about his shoulders and he leaned his head back against her breasts.

'Darling, what is troubling you?' she whispered gently and at once regretted it.

'I'm drunk!' he blazed. 'We have been drinking all day, between rounding up petrified citizens and putting them to the torture to discover where they have hid their valuables!' There was a look of unutterable disgust on his face. 'D'you know the best way to make a woman tell you where her money is hidden? Take her child and press your dagger to its eyes, while it yells in terror. Threaten to blind it if she remains obstinate. And if it's a man you are dealing with, set your most brutish churl to raping his daughter.'

Suddenly he seized her, pulling her roughly against him between his legs, the hard thigh muscles gripping her like a vice. 'And you...what does any of this mean to you? You are content as long as your lusts are satisfied! You wanton, rapacious little bitch!' He released her so violently that she stumbled back. 'Now, let us to our gallant comrades who are snarling like a pack of curs over a bone!'

The Governor's house was the finest in Santa Maria and constructed around a wide courtyard. In the centre, a fountain sprayed a jet of water up into the sizzling air. The upper storey was supported on pillars which formed a portico, shaded and cool. The lower rooms had doors leading on to this and it was here that Dirk and Roxanna found the captains. They lolled in cane chairs, tankards and blackjacks on a table, wine-jars on the pavement.

Sitting on the floor, their backs against the wall, were several of the Admiral's picked men. Among them Roxanna recognized the ones she had discovered mauling her Creole. They grinned at her sheepishly, remembering her rage when she had burst in on them, so furious that she had ranted till she was breathlesss, swearing with a newly-acquired fluency. They had slunk back as this glittering-eyed termagant had lashed them with her trenchant tongue, amazed when she picked up a heavy candlestick and clubbed their ringleader. She had arrived too late to prevent the damage being done but it seemed that they had developed a very healthy respect for her temper.

Sawkins screwed round in his chair and scowled. Although seemingly untiring, he was strained and cantankerous. He had rampaged through the town seeing that pickets were posted, and, amidst surly objections, flatly forbidden unnecessary torturing of prisoners, putting to 'the question' only those from whom money could be extorted.

Down in the plaza there was bedlam, as, by the light of great bonfires, the raiders celebrated. Glutted with conquest, their noisy revels set the priests and the wealthier women and children, who were sheltered in the church, trembling and crossing themselves. They were convinced that the buccaneers were in league with the devil. This superstitious awe greatly assisted their attacks, for they were invariably outnumbered, relying on their superiority of arms, their ferocity and their devilish reputations to make up for man-power.

Sawkins was tired and in a bad mood. 'We are frisking this damned place inside out, but the fact of the matter is, there don't seem to be the crop we expected. Those yellow-bellied dogs down in the town may think all is well, but we came here for more than unlimited booze. The devil of it is that we missed, by about four days, three hundred pounds in gold! They were warned to expect us and we've only unearthed a bare twenty pounds.'

Captain Dampier, face mournful, hunched his shoulders under a dusty black broadcloth coat. 'The accursed governor escaped to Panama, taking that money with him and warning them too!'

'There's nothing to be gained by moaning,' Johnny's voice came from a canvas hammock slung between two pillars.

'We'll get a fat ransom for the place.'

'Rest easy now, Admiral,' Sharp slouched forward on his chair, hands clasped between sturdy knees, small, crafty eyes missing nothing. His besmirched red coat was open, sweat glistening on his fleshy chest. 'There's wine and wenches aplenty here, and the crop trickling in!'

Sawkins took immediate exception. 'We did not travel miles of damned jungle to swill bub and fumble some mort's petticoats! We came for riches and, by God, we don't go back without them! We must push on to Panama!'

'Panama!' John Coxon seemed to wake abruptly from the comatose state to which over-generous celebration had reduced his wits. He gave vent to a filthy curse. 'I value my men and my life too much to venture that! You must be touched!'

The other captains were silent, and Sawkins ran an eye over them while he began to talk, describing in detail the wealth that might be theirs if they dared Panama. The avaricious looks which settled over the unsavoury countenances of his scarred, ruffianly officers, were a confirmation that his words were swaying them in his favour. But Coxon was wary.

200

'Look'ee, Sawkins, me and my men want to go back to Golden Island. No damned marching agin Panama for us! We should be killed, they keep a bloody great garrison there and well you know it!' His voice rang under the arches of the pergola. An audacious fighter, renowned for his brash onslaughts, and tip-and-run raids, he was unused to facing an organized army. 'It was only a piece of luck that saved us at Porto Bello!'

In the background someone snickered. Coxon swung about, fist clamped onto his sword-hilt, but the faces that stared back at him were bland and expressionless. Sawkins did not move, only his stubby fingers beat a light tattoo on the arm of his chair while his lips curled in a thin smile, faintly insulting as if he were dealing with an obstinate child.

'Cool off there, cully,' he remarked in a very quiet voice. 'Now then, has anyone else an idea to offer?'

Several had suggestions, which they hoped would give them fat pickings and very little fighting, but Sawkins listened with a dubious expression.

The Admiral let them talk themselves out, then, sinking his voice confidentially, spoke rapidly. 'Look here, mates, there ain't much to be got out of cruising in the South Seas. What we could get in one stroke at Panama would take us months to accumulate picking up prizes at sea. I know the risks, but Satan blind me, buccaneering ain't a safe trade!'

They stirred restlessly, more than half-convinced. But Coxon swore heatedly and swayed up on his feet, shouting Sawkins down with sheer force of lung-power.

'Listen to him prate! Ye poor dunderheads! Don't be taken in by his promises!'

Sawkins rose to face him. His voice was level. 'Coxon, I am growing aweary of your belly-weathering!'

'Hell and damnation!' Coxon exploded into cursing fury. 'You can do without me and my crew too! Go to Panama on your bloody own and see how you fare!'

He glared about, swung on his heel and marched off with drunken dignity.

Jeers, cat-calls and offensive comments followed him from Sawkins' scornful supporters and the Admiral sat down, craggy face dark as thunder-clouds.

'The misbegotten, treacherous rat!' he ground out.

'Send a couple of men to nab him and

cut his throat!' Kate briskly suggested.

Voices were raised in agreement, while Sawkins' henchmen licked their lips like hungry alley-cats as they waited his order. But he shook his greying head.

'His men would desert without him to lead them!'

Dirk had been sitting, relaxed and quite silent during the whole of the time they had been there, a brandy glass clasped lightly in both hands, his long limbs crossed, negligently before him. Without moving, his deep voice carried across the tumult to address Sawkins.

'There is only one way out of the dilemma,' he said, imperturably. 'We all know that Coxon is green-sick with jealousy of you. He wants to be Admiral, so why not let him? 'Tis but a title, he has not the wit to command. We shall still make decisions in council and he will be forced to submit to the general vote!'

This began a wrangle which lasted a full hour and resulted in Sawkins agreeing. Coxon was recalled and was childishly pleased to accept the position.

Roxanna could feel the sun blistering her shoulders through her grenadine wrap. The dazzle of the street made her eyes smart, its sandy surface churned up by the hoofs of Dirk's stallion, the yellow dust rising in a choking cloud. She sat uncomfortable on the pommel of the saddle, and she could feel the easy movements of Dirk's body behind her as they rode, his hands resting on the reins with an assured touch. There was an unnatural hush in the town which spoke of disruption, sorrow and death.

That morning she had awakened to find Dirk already up, standing by the window and shaving. It gave her a great deal of pleasure to watch him, while he drew the cut-throat razor over his lean jaw with sure swipes. Zila, her slave, padded about, bringing more hot water and later, a breakfast tray. He sat on the side of the bed, whilst he and Roxanna shared this meal of fruit, fine white bread and eggs boiled in their shells. Roxanna poured him black coffee. The sharp scent of the oranges reminded her keenly of the King's Playhouse where the fops spat pips at the actors or pelted them with orange peel if they disapproved of the performance. She told Dirk about this, wanting to make him laugh. The heavy, sombre mood still hung about him and

204

she hated to see the look of self-accusation in his eyes. There were so many things in England that she badly wanted him to know about; her dearest ambition that one day they should return there together. But they would have to be married first, and this desirable state of affairs seemed no nearer being accomplished than when in Cayona.

He never told her that he loved her, try as she might to seduce him into an admission. He assured her that she had the most perfect breasts, the loveliest legs, and the most glorious hair he had ever seen. His voice sent thrills down her spine when he spoke of the fascinating curves of her belly, the delightful hollows of her back, the satiny feel of her skin. The things he said were often outrageous, and delighted her immeasurably, but he never, even in their most intimate moments, said 'I love you.'

She was uneasy because he was spending so much time down in the town and asked him, her eyes hard, if he ever joined in the raping. To which he replied, his voice teasing, that he had never found it necessary to resort to rape. After that she insisted that he take her with him on his next visit to the church where he was making an inventory of plunder. He tried to persuade her against this, but she would not listen, more than half-convinced that he had some Spanish woman whom he was eager to meet.

Now they rode through the hot street where a few dazed survivors turned to stare at them. The wind was heavy with heat; the flowers seemed to exhale it instead of perfume, it made Roxanna sleepy and sick and painfully tired. From behind closed shutters a baby cried, and a buzzing cloud of flies rose from a corpse as they passed.

'I must see that it is collected and removed for burial,' Dirk remarked. 'Or we shall have a pestilence here.'

In a whirl of dust, pounding hooves and glittering arms, a search party clattered past them on their way to hunt for refugees hiding in the bush. Turning down a road with walled gardens on either side they glimpsed fountains, and spacious terraces through the grilled gates surmounted by family crests and came to the church-dominated market square.

Drunks sprawled in the gutters, and women sat despondently with them. The female population which Sawkins allowed his men to use as they would, were slaves, indentured servants and prostitutes. The ladies of quality who could command a high ransom were not touched. It was the women of the tradesmen and artisans who suffered the most in the hands of the raiders, for unlike the others, who were used to men and the traffic in sex, their ravishment filled them with disgust and shame.

Sawkins found it hard to discipline his subordinate vandals, but he had insisted that all valuables be brought in for a fair division. Coxon followed this sagacious course and slowly, the coffers stacked in the church were being filled with booty. A crowd of marauders, lounging in the purpled shade of a wall, were trying to trip one of their mates who was staggering along under the weight of the ironbound chest on his shoulder. A woman danced listlessly, clicking castanets, sounds of a quarrel came from a wine-shop. Three free-booters were forcing rum down the throat of a girl who strained away from them with trembling supplication while they roared with drunken laughter.

Dirk dismounted at the church and

lifted Roxanna, his hands firm and hard under her armpits. She started up the steps savouring in advance the delicious coolness of the great dim structure but, at that moment, a party of citizens appeared round the corner, herded along by guards who were using long hide whips with deadly effect. A cart, drawn by a shaggy grey mule, rolled forward with them and, as they drew level, Roxanna's breath escaped in a horrified gasp to see that it was nearly full of bodies, piled anyhow, limbs sticking out at grotesque angles.

Roxanna blanched and cowered back against the porch, sick in the stomach. She clutched blindly at Dirk's arm and his eyes were cold as he saw her utter revulsion.

'I warned you not to come!'

CHAPTER 12

Roxanna never asked to accompany Dirk again, preferring to remain in the comparative shelter of the house. Ruthlessly, she went through every cupboard in the bedrooms, taking anything which caught her fancy. Zila, who was a clever seamstress, made alteration to the clothes, and Roxanna gloried in being able to trail a skirt again. She enjoyed the luxury of this great house, where the floors were of gleaming mahogany, and cooled by the cunning design of rooms which led from one another, divided only by ornate iron grills. The days passed in torpid somnolence as they waited for the ransoms to arrive from Panama. Dirk was kept fully occupied; with his fluent command of languages he was invaluable. Roxanna was resentful, wanting him by her always, living for the nights when he was there with his passion, his odd, contemptuous smile. His very presence always made her feel lightheaded.

Sharp and Massey took shameless advantage of Dirk's absence to court her, and, being quite unable to resist male flattery, she allowed them to visit her. She knew that they were dangerous, but this added a spice to the game. Usually she contrived to meet them together, but one afternoon, so hot that even the crickets had ceased chirping, Massey came alone. He was very spruce in stolen finery with much gold braid which flashed in the checkered sunlight. His black hair was oiled, his cheeks were carefully shaved, leaving a thin line of moustache on his upper lip. His inky eyes lingered on her with an assured insolence which made her bridle. He gave a brief, ironical bow and settled himself beside her on the stone bench.

'A pesky hot afternoon,' he commented. 'You are bored, most beautiful lady?'

In spite of the softness of his tone, it held a sleepy menace which made her wonder if the sentry were about, and also if he would hear her if she were to scream. Massey produced a lute from under his cape.

'There you are!' He put it into her eager hands. 'Now you must sing me a love song.'

Roxanna gave him a wide, happy smile, as she delightedly ran her fingers over the delicate instrument, and began to pick out a tune, her low, melodious voice singing the words of a sentimental ballad taught her by her music-master.

Massey watched her closely. Her lashes made twin black semi-circles as she kept her eyes fixed on her fingers moving across the strings.

'Don't I get a reward for bringing it?' he

murmured, edging nearer. His breath was unpleasant, sickly-sweet with wine. She turned to look at him and his lips almost brushed hers, but she drew away. He rapped out an oath and pulled her roughly to him. At once she froze at his effrontery.

'Hands off, sirrah! D'you think I am some cheap bawdy-case strumpet to be handled by you!'

Baulked, he released her, leaning back on his elbows, scowling his chagrin.

'You are the fairest doxy in all Santa Maria,' he ventured, with suave earnestness. 'There's not a wench here or, I trow, in all New Spain, as can come anywhere near you!'

'Say you so?' She found herself relenting under this blandishment. 'I expect that you have inspected them passing close!'

He lowered his heavy eyelids like a dangerous panther. ' 'Slife, if the lady a man has set his heart on will not be kind, what can a fellow do, but seek consolation in other arms?'

Roxanna gave a shrug which betrayed her indifference so clearly that his mouth tightened. He was unaccustomed to wait for any woman and his hand closed on her wrist.

'You've never even let me kiss you!' he said, huskily. 'Sharp boasts that you have given him your lips.'

'Oh, does he!' She snatched her hand away, her voice tart. 'He is a damned liar!'

'I am happy that it is not true,' Massey insinuated an arm along the ledge behind her. 'I never did believe that you would tolerate a braggart like him. You are a rare lass. Real quality. I can see that with half an eye!'

Suddenly, she felt him stiffen and glanced up to see Dirk striding towards them under the arched roof of the patio. She hoped that she did not look as guilty as she felt and hastily composed her features into an expression of flat unconcern. Without a word, Dirk went straight to the table, poured himself a drink, drained it with one swift toss and refilled it. He looked grimed, strained and tired. Great wet arcs spread out from under the arms of his shirt and up from his belt.

Massey rose, reaching for his hat. Dirk met his black, baleful eyes in a brief, antagonistic stare, then Massey bowed curtly to Roxanna and swung off through the iron gate. Roxanna continued to pluck out a tune, simulating an abstracted thoughtfulness, refusing to look at Dirk.

'I advise you not to lie with Massey!' His voice suddenly cracked across the tinkling melody. 'He is not a very savoury fellow. You would probably pick up the pox at the first coupling and I have no fancy to catch it!'

She placed the lute on the stone seat, all of her delight in it completely ruined and paced towards him, dark red skirt whispering on the marble pavement, her temper beginning to rise.

'I don't want him!' She tried to keep her voice steady.

'I know that you don't!' There was simmering anger in his eyes which paralysed her. 'But you would have him sniffing round you like a dog after a bitch, because it tickles your vanity.' He reached out and gripped her shoulders in his large, strong hands, shaking her till her spine cracked. 'You slut! You'll never get me crawling at your feet, I promise you!'

'Dirk!' Her voice rose to a terrified scream. For a moment she thought he was going to kill her and remembered Lucy's warning not to provoke him. 'I was but passing the time. It drags so with you away all day...'

Disgustedly, he flung her from him, and she fell back against the table with the breath knocked out of her. He stood over her, big and menacing.

'The only thing you can do to amuse yourself is to behave like a harlot!' His voice was taut and hard.

Roxanna drew herself up, all the resentment, the secret shame which she felt at her concubinage, welling in a surge of rebellious rancour.

'Why should I not act like one?' she shouted. 'It is you who make me a whore! Why don't you wed me? There is nothing to prevent you!'

There were bright tears in her eyes and her words ended on an imploring note. He was standing, very tall and lithe, his feet set slightly apart. The angry bitterness, the brooding intensity of him, reached her with the force of a physical contact. She longed to put her arms round him, draw down his head and kiss him until they both forgot their quarrel.

His eyes went down over her with scornful slowness. His lip curled. 'Marry you! I can't!'

'Why?' she demanded, her head back to

glare up into his face.

He half-turned away, spreading wide his hands in a gesture of apology and explanation. 'My father was a nobleman, back in England at the time of the Civil War. He had extensive property and was a baron in his own right. And the family could be traced back in direct line to the Conquest. So you see, I cannot wed you.'

Roxanna flushed scarlet and then went pale.

'So!' she hissed vindictively through lips so stiff with rage that she could hardly speak. 'You, an outcast, a slave, a buccaneer, will not wed me because my father was only a merchant while yours was a damned feudal Lord. I've only red blood in my veins and not blue and that's not good enough for you!'

He turned with reluctance and looked down at her and there was compassion in his gaze. 'That is the way of it.'

With a penetrating stare she searched his face. 'And if you were son of a nobody, would you marry me then?' she cried.

'No!' said Dirk brutally. 'No, I would not! There is too much of the whore in you to make a man a good wife!'

Roxanna drew in her breath on a sob,

her hand flying to her mouth, 'Oh, how I hate you!' she ground out.

'You would have the truth!' he rapped out, exasperated.

She was beyond reason, stabbing about in her mind for words that might hurt him, wanting to cry with the pain of her bitter humiliation. She tore across the gallery, her skirts caught up in one hand. His voice followed her.

'The ransoms have arrived. We leave for Panama in the morning!'

She stopped dead in her tracks, appalled at the thought of more marching, fighting, suffering and discomfort. And for what? For a man who did not love her, who despised her and had no intention of marrying her!

There was a Chinese urn in a niche in the wall. Roxanna snatched it up and hurled it with all her force onto the floor where it smashed into fragments. She stamped her heel on to some of the pieces and stormed off.

Just after dawn the disorderly army gathered in the market place. The men leaned on their muskets, chewing their quids, yarning and pinching the girls for the last time. The officers thundered up and down on the backs of leggy bays, rounding up the stragglers, thumping sense into the befuddled heads of the drunks. Roxanna was still in a raging temper. She stood in the ranks, jostled by Comry's men with Kate breathing down the back of her neck. Sullenly, she glared at the cotton breeches and shirt which had replaced the fine gowns, and she started to curse with a steady flow of profanity.

Dirk and Johnny were among the last to join them and, within minutes, the order to march was given. With packs bulging with loot, the Indians shouldering heavy, padlocked chests, the corsairs streamed back into the bush. The townsfolk watched in silent apathy, the scrunch of sand under booted feet, a woman's sudden sobbing, the yapping of a dog, were the only sounds to break the depressing silence.

The guards, posted on the banks, reported that a ship had been found deserted. Coxon at once took possession of this with his own men and the rest followed in the canoes paddling down the dirty, smelling, sluggish river. Within hours they reached the sea.

Days passed in deadly monotony until it seemed that they would never reach

Panama. It became as a dream city, a mirage created by their own exhausted minds. The sun burned without relief until nightfall when they were chilled with sudden sharp cold. Many were smitten with jungle-fever, recurrent in those who had lived for long in the Indies.

Roxanna was seasick and huddled miserably in Johnny's piroque. Dirk wrapped her up in his boat-cloak and shielded her as well as he could from sunstroke. Johnny showed a concern which infuriated Kate and would have gratified her had she been well enough to appreciate it. But at last, one dusk, Panama Bay was sighted. A party, led by Sharp, went ahead to the first of the little group of Islands which dotted the sea. The watch, kept to give warning to the city, was effectively silenced. Coxon's ship dropped anchor, the canoes beached and the men staggered ashore, legs buckling under them.

Dirk went to see Sharp. He had captured a bark, and was only too eager to agree to Dirk's suggestion that Roxanna should travel in it. Depleted as she was by sickness and exhaustion, further journeying by canoe was out of the question.

Johnny was very much opposed to the

idea, and argued hotly on the waters' edge next morning.

'I don't like it, Dirk, be hanged if I do!' He squinted across to where the bark waited, tugging at her cables, sails dazzling against sea and sky, which were a sharp, smarting blue. ' 'Twill be the first time in years we've sailed apart. It would be a cursed jade that's at bottom of it! You are getting mawkish over that wench, my lad! You'll be wedding her next!'

Dirk shook his head, smiled and lifted Roxanna into the boat which would take them over to join Captain Sharp.

Roxanna and Dirk missed the battle in the Bay of Panama, for Sharp insisted on attacking Pearl Island, remained there for a night, and joined up with his comrades next day, bringing with him a haul of fine pearls. Sharp was not very popular with those who had fought. Ugly rumours spread that he had deliberately lingered to avoid the fighting. But there was so much dissention among the leaders, who were unable to agree whether to attack Panama at once, that his malingering was overlooked. Coxon had a furious quarrel with Sawkins and the result was that he departed with his men and Sawkins was made admiral again.

One of the first things Sawkins did when he was re-elected admiral, was to dispatch the women over to the galleon *Most Blessed Trinity,* which had been turned into a hospital.

The forecastle of the ship was still smouldering, and Basil Ringrose, who had come with them, told them that the Spanish soldiers had fired it before surrendering. John Snelgrave, Dr Wafer's assistant, came up from below decks to greet them. He stared at them almost without comprehending, breathing in deep lungfuls of fresh air.

An incredibly foul stench took Roxanna's breath as she followed him back through the hatchway. The floor of the long, low-roofed deck was packed with men. Lionel Wafer, red to the elbows, was striving to do his work by the light of half a dozen smoking rush lamps. He gave Roxanna a glance which still held a glimmer of his old ironic humour, although he looked weary enough to drop. Ever since the battle he and his helpers had laboured over the wounded freebooters. Without rest they had heaved them in turn on to the table, subjected them to a hurried examination and dressed, stitched, or amputated ceaselessly.

Now, by the fitful glare of the lantern swinging on a hook above his head, Wafer reminded Roxanna of a print she had once seen of Satan. His breeches and shirt were dyed darkly with perspiration and blood, his lank hair tied back from his gaunt face. These impressions imprinted themselves on Roxanna with the strong charnel-house stink, odours of blood, sweat and the overall smell of fear, pain and death. Then she forgot it all in the upsurge of compassion which gripped her.

As she helped Wafer, she did not remember that the men tremblingly waiting the crude ministrations were brutal ravaging buccaneers. All the warmth of her affectionate disposition went out to them. She comforted those who wept like children as Snelgrave sutured lacerated flesh, and cracked jokes with others, who grinned stubbornly, while their faces turned grey, teeth biting into their lips rather than cry out in pain.

That night Roxanna, Kate, and Ringrose kept watch to enable the exhausted surgeons to rest. Although she was so tired that her leg muscles ached and her temples throbbed, Roxanna was ashamed to complain in the face of so much suffering. Every so often they patrolled between the rows of groaning, or ominously still forms. It became very quiet in the small hours, and Ringrose grew garrulous, telling Roxanna about the planter's daughter in Virginia whom he hoped to marry when he had made enough money.

He even recited some poems which he had written to this paragon. They had formed a romantic attachment when he had visited America during the previous year, and he attributed every virtue to this peerless young lady. Roxanna privately thought she sounded rather a bore. But she listened sympathetically enough, leaving him at last to attend the wants of a lad whose leg Wafer had amputated.

He was called Jeremy, one of Johnny's crew. She had assisted Wafer when he used his surgeon's saw on the jellied mass of splintered bone and smashed flesh. Strapped to the table, already unconscious through loss of blood, the boy had been passive under the operation, quickly accomplished and rounded off by the application of searing irons dipped

222

in hot pitch and applied to the stump. Whether he would recover was a point on which the doctors could only shrug and conjecture.

Now, he was beginning to swim back up through the layer of consciousness to the torturing reality of his own agonized flesh. Roxanna leaned over him as he whimpered. Taking up a cloth she mopped the sweat which trickled across his face, running back into his hair. His self-absorbed suffering seemed to become something almost tangible. In her highstrung state every movement he made, every shuddering, indrawn, pain-laden breath, seemed to travel through her fingers which rested on his brow, up along the nerves of her arm, deep into her heart and brain. 'Easy there, darling,' she murmured, and taking up a pannikin of water she raised his head with her arm supporting him, while his lips groped for the rim. A part of her mind remained cool and alert, and at the same time it seemed that she was under his skin, experiencing all his pain, the racking agony of his right thigh which seemed to be in a bath of flame. Protesting, blubbering, aware of her at one moment and in delirium the next, he had at last reeled off into unconsciousness.

For three weeks the work was neverending and Roxanna crawled on to her bed, whenever Wafer gave her permission, so tired that she slept without bothering to undress. She was so busy that she was only abstractly aware that she had not seen Dirk. For once her appearance did not matter; all that she had time for was a hasty splash of cold water over her face in the morning and a brush passed through the snarls in her unkept hair. And yet, in spite of the back-breaking toil, she knew a deep inner contentment, rejoicing with Wafer if one of the bad cases showed an improvement; recalling prayers to repeat for those who were dying, trying to relieve their burden of guilt and fear.

But when the word was brought across one day that Johnny and Dirk would be coming aboard that evening, she was at once all worried concern about her looks, rushing to the mirror in the great-cabin, giving a horrified squeal at the sight of her hair which straggled in greasy twists about her shoulders, suddenly aware of the lice which pricked at her skin under her filthy shirt and breeches. She tore off to the galley for hot water and had a very thorough wash.

Wafer winked when she ran down to fix dressings late in the afternoon wearing a velvet skirt and a cream silk blouse. The men who were sufficiently recovered to be propped up, grinned their approval.

When Dirk's tall, upright figure appeared over the ship's side, she caught her breath on a sob, running towards him, hair flying. In his arms she was both laughing and crying, swept off her feet and crushed against him. Johnny gave her a resounding kiss and hugged Kate to him, and when the excited greetings were done they went straight to the state-cabin where they settled into chairs and the women demanded to hear all the news.

Edmund Cook, Sawkins' right-hand man, who had been put in charge of the *Trinity*, was just as hungry for information.

'What is to happen?' he questioned Dirk and Johnny, drawing his heavy fair brows together in bewilderment. 'Are we to attack Panama?'

Johnny shook his head vigorously, tilting

up a decanter of brandy to swallow a lusty swig. 'I reckon Sawkins has missed his chance there. Devil knows why he hesitated, he was so hot for it!'

Cook blew out his cheeks, his leathery face chapfallen as he seated himself, cutlass rattling against the table-leg.

'And another piece of news,' interposed Johnny, leaning forward, elbows resting on his knees. 'Sharp went off in his bark to search for those fellows who deserted at Pearl Island and he captured a ship bearing, in her hold, the pay for the Spanish garrison. A sum amounting to fifty-one thousand pieces of eight!'

Cook gave a long, low whistle, his eyes sparkling, and Kate clapped gleeful hands.

As she listened to the men talking Roxanna watched Dirk adoringly, every expression that passed over his attractive features, every gesture of his fine-drawn, slender hands. And when he drew her close to him on the padded window-locker, with his slow, warm smile, leaning over to brush his lips across her cheek, she was wildly happy.

Several of Cook's men had wandered in to hear their report and they joined in the general amusement at Dirk's account of the letter Sawkins had received from the Governor of Panama.

'The Governor asked us why we had come to the Spanish Seas,' he began. 'Sawkins dictated a reply to the effect that we had come to the assistance of King Golden Cap. The Admiral added that if the Governor would give us his word not to persecute the Indians further, together with a present of five hundred pieces of eight per man, and double that for each captain, we would go our way and trouble them no more!'

A howl of delighted laughter greeted this grim sally.

Much later, when they were in bed, Dirk told Roxanna that he had to go on an inland expedition with Sawkins.

His voice was cool and steady but she guessed that it would be dangerous.

'Why does he want to take you?' She wanted to know, rudely shocked from the warm, sensual aftermath of love-making. Dirk's rough eagerness, which had brooked no delay, had amply rewarded her for the trouble she had taken in making herself look pretty.

'As you know, I speak the native

227

dialects, and am damned useful to him.' Dirk's tone was deliberately casual, but she rolled over on to her stomach propping herself on her elbows, her breasts nestled against his shoulder, searching his face anxiously. 'Is Johnny going with you?'

He shook his dark head and smiled gently, taking one of her hands and pressing it against his lips. 'No, I want him here to look after you.'

Roxanna, with her intense receptive sense to any change of mood in him, was aware of the deepening delight, of a tenderness absent until then.

'I like Johnny,' she remarked.

'Do not like him too much!' he rejoined shortly, and she was startled by the sudden grate in his voice. His arms came about her, hurting her ribs, and he put one hand under her chin to hold her face steady while he looked deep into her eyes. 'If I find that you have played me false, I will kill you! D'you understand?'

'Of course!' Her answer was low. 'I love only you. Nothing can alter that.'

And she smiled, strangely pleased, seeing behind his sternness a need for her which, before, he had always emphatically denied.

CHAPTER 13

The thought of Dirk's danger intruded into whatever task occupied Roxanna next day. Whether she was busy scrubbing out the hospital quarters, dressing wounds or preparing meals, every so often she would come alive to his peril and her heart would take a plunge. Silently, she prayed for his safety, accomplishing her work automatically. And when Johnny swung aboard in the evening in the company of Massey, she welcomed them as she did anything which would divert her thoughts.

By the next night, Roxanna's worry had mounted to fever-pitch. Repeatedly she asked Johnny if he thought Dirk was safe. He always replied that, knowing Dirk so well, he was completely confident in his ability to survive. When she heard Massey down in the waist she rushed eagerly to him, and he gave her a delighted grin which went flat when he realized that her interest was only a frantic desire for news of her lover.

Johnny got out the cards and dice-box, and Roxanna watched dully, her mind clouded with dismal forebodings. The strength of the wine made her drowsy. When Johnny grew weary of play he lay full length along the locker, his head pillowed in Kate's lap while she leaned lovingly over him, her fingers in his thick curls. Her face was watchful, lynx-keen, as she noted the look in Massey's eyes when he bent his head close to Roxanna's. Mesmerized, Roxanna looked into those black pupils in which she could see her own image. She had no will to refuse when he guided her out on to the quarter deck.

At once, the cool night air cleared the wine-fumes from her brain. She watched Massey uneasily. He pressed closer to her, his arm clipping her waist, and he began to talk, words tumbling out in a rush. Promise of presents, lewd endearments, protestations of love. He was panting excitedly and she tried to wriggle free, but he would not release her.

She turned on him with a harridan's tongue, her burning scorn almost stopping him. Then, with a snarl of anger, he brought his mouth down on hers with such force that her teeth cut into her lips.

With a strength enforced by disgust and panic, she jerked free, and pelted across the deck but, in the dim light, she tripped over a coil of rope and went sprawling.

Massey pounced, kneeling over her, blotting out the sky with his shoulders. With all his weight pinning her down, knocking the breath from her body, he pushed his leg between hers and began to tug at her clothes. She fought him like a tigress, teeth snapping in an effort to bite, before he gave her a clout which sent the stars whirling sickeningly.

But suddenly Massey's weight was hauled from her. For a blasting instant she met the full vehemence of Dirk's outraged fury before he swung Massey about, and sent a blow crashing into his astonished face.

At the hubbub, Johnny came tearing from the state-cabin, and excited voices sprang up from every part of the ship as men gathered to watch.

Shivering with fright, trying to drag her torn shirt together, Roxanna crept closer. Johnny flung her such a searing glance that she halted. She had always imagined that he was more than a little in love with her and that whatever she did he would support her. Now he deliberately turned his back on her.

Dirk and Massey were circling slowly. Dirk's nose was streaming blood and Massey's right eye was cut, swelling more with every second. Dirk seized him by the throat and drove his fist against his jaw with a resounding crack. Massey went down like a felled ox and Dirk flexed his fingers, massaging the grazed knuckles, staring unseeing before him as he turned on his heel.

Massey lay dazed, then slowly sat up, his pulped and bloody face contorted in a grimace. Roxanna saw the gleam as he pulled out his knife, and tried to rush forward, giving a scream as it flashed towards Dirk's back. He swerved aside so that it just missed him and men grabbed Massey roughly. He had drawn steel in a fight with bare hands and had transgressed a buccaneer law.

'Dirk, oh, Dirk!' Roxanna wailed, struggling with Johnny.

'Be still, you damned troublesome bitch,' he growled threateningly. 'Hold your bawling!'

The sanguinary audience was shouting at Dirk to kill Massey.

'Go on, Courtney,' they urged. 'Hit him while we hold him down!'

Dirk gave Massey a long stare, when he struggled in the grip of two hefty seamen, then his eyes went to Roxanna and she shrank at the light in them.

'He is not to blame.' His voice had a chill bite.

'She'd be the better for a belting!' advised Johnny sternly scowling at Roxanna. 'And, as for that rat, report him to Sawkins!'

'Sawkins is dead!' Dirk curtly informed them. 'He was killed at dawn as we attacked Pueblo Nuevo! The Spanish were warned, we found the river blocked and the streets barricaded. It was while we were charging these that Sawkins was shot!'

Then he moved, in two strides looming over Roxanna.

'Get inside!'

He followed close behind her and in the main-cabin she swung round, on the defensive. There was an air of recklessness about him with a strong streak of sadism underlying it which petrified Roxanna.

'Do you recall what I told you before I left?' he ground, his unshaven jaw set. She nodded, unable to speak for the dryness in her throat. 'You have broken faith with

233

me,' he accused. 'Harlot!'

The injustice of his accusation doused her fear, her own hot temper beginning to burst into flame.

'I was trying to fight him off!' she declared flatly. 'My God, I've been near mad with worry about you. I didn't want him to make love to me!'

'Liar!' He snarled out the word. 'You have always encouraged him.'

'Darling, don't say that,' she began, taking a hesitant step towards him. 'I love you. You must believe that!'

He gave a grunt of harsh laughter, his face twisting unpleasantly. 'Love! There is no love in your vain little heart, only lust which any man can satisfy!'

Roxanna drew in a sharp breath. Something evil and dangerous glittered in her narrowed green eyes.

'You are vile!' she shouted, and spat full in his face.

He moved like lightning and his blow sent her sprawling. In all their numerous quarrels he had never before struck her and, for a moment, she was stunned, her ears ringing. Then, with a snarl she was up and on him like a demented creature. Kicking and clawing, blind and deaf with rage, she possessed a strength which momentarily halted him. The suppressed frustrations because he did not love her, the smouldering resentment at his refusal to wed her, the shame and hardship she had endured because of him, made her almost mad. She would have killed him in that moment had it been possible. She shrieked invective at the top of her voice, cursing him, calling him every filthy name she knew, repeatedly yelling that she hated him.

He shook her till her teeth rattled, trying to bring her to her senses, his face raw and bleeding where her nails had raked him.

'Roxanna! Have done!'

She suddenly stood stock-still, her eyes wild. Then she swung up her fist and smashed it into his face.

His eyes went dark, mouth contorted in an ugly line. He caught her savagely by both wrists, then groped behind him and snatched up a length of rawhide which lay on the locker. Roxanna twisted, struck out with her feet, sobbing with pain but indomitable in her fury, fighting like a wildcat while he beat her.

Johnny intervened, his tawny eyes alarmed. 'Enough, Dirk!' he said tersely. 'You'll kill her! Let be. She's been punished enough!'

Abruptly, Dirk let go, his expression changing to one of self-loathing. Gasping for breath, Roxanna stared at him. With an inscrutable look in his sea grey eyes, he moved towards her bending to kiss her on the mouth, in a way which somehow added to her degradation and yet thrilled her. She stopped sobbing, lying heavily in his arms. In a corner of her brain grew the dreadful certainty that, by her actions, she had forfeited any hope of gaining his love and respect.

The sunlight came through the diamond-paned window of the cabin, making bright patches on the discarded clothing lying by the bed. Roxanna stirred, disturbed by the brightness. She reached out across the bed, her arm found Dirk and she snuggled closer.

As she grew more fully awake, her bruises began to ache, every muscle felt stiff. She looked at the sleeping Dirk, he seemed somehow much younger and defenceless, and she had a sudden yearning for his child. Pressing her hands over her flat belly, she tried to imagine it full, rounded and pregnant, and longed to see a small, dark head in the crook of her arm, to guide a hungry little mouth to her breast.

When she smoothed back his tumbled hair, Dirk turned into her warmth, pulling her against him with a drowsy grunt, while she sucked in a quick breath. It seemed impossible that she could ever become satiated by his lithe, bronzed body, his combination of selfish strength and knowledge of how to give her the deepest pleasure.

Roxanna dressed carefully, craning over her shoulder to see in the mirror, suddenly afraid that the swollen weals on her skin would mark her for life. She scowled at the slumbering man, smoothing the imprints of his fingers on her upper arms. In the great cabin there was no sign of Kate or Johnny, and the wild disorder of it offended her. She started to tidy up, piling the platters from the evening's meal on to a tray, kicking open the door and carrying it to the galley. This was as deserted as the rest of the ship, and the fire had not been lit. She swore profanely and knelt before it, raking at the cinders. As the flames sluggishly licked around the logs, she set a black iron pot to boil, then looked up, hot and dusty, to see Wafer leaning on the door, watching her.

'I shall be needing you below shortly,' he informed her briskly. 'Where is Kate?'

'How the devil should I know!' she stormed, thoroughly nettled after the tussle with the stove.

Wafer moved, lazily and easily, an amused grin on his pleasant mouth. 'There is no need to be snapping like a turtle,' he said, and seated himself on a corner of the table, swinging his cane. Then an eyebrow went up quizzically. 'And how is it with you after your beating?'

She threw him a cross glance. 'How did you know of it?'

' 'Tis news all over the camp,' he remarked, dark eyes twinkling.

Roxanna ladled water from the pot where the bubbles were beginning to rise and scowled at him over the steam. 'This damned ship is worse than any market place for gossip,' she grumbled.

She began to swill the pewter plates and tankards in a wooden bowl, scouring them with a handful of sand. 'And I am not coming to attend your precious patients today!' Her tone was acrid.

'My dear, you are in the devil of a pet

this morning.' Wafer paused, watching her skilful, neat movements. 'I have just come from young Jeremy. I think he is going to live, Roxanna.'

She stood still, hands flat on the bottom of the bowl, up to the forearms in sleazy water. 'That is very good news,' she said slowly.

Thoughtfully, she dried her fingers and began to polish the glasses with a cloth. Wafer cocked an eye at her.

'But he is still in need of a great deal of care. Some of those wonderful sack-possets of yours.'

She gave him a sharp look. 'Lionel, I vow that honeyed tongue of yours would wheedle blood from a stone... Well, you must needs get me fresh milk to make 'em. This is as sour as my sister Paulina!'

Searching through the provisions, she clucked with disgust at the weevils running in the flour, the rat-droppings in the cupboards. There were fat white maggots in the only piece of beef; the cheese had fungus furring it; the butter tasted rancid. Roxanna was exasperated by the slovenly methods of the cook. She waged constant warfare with him, reviling him violently although he was a Portuguese half-breed and could understand little of what she said. He would grin at her, completely unmoved, nonchalantly lounging back against the table, cleaning his teeth with the point of his dagger, examining the morsel extracted before wiping it on his greasy breeches.

With an oath Roxanna tossed meat and cheese from the window.

'Fugh! This galley would sorely vex my dear old Nan. She'd throw a fit at the sight of it!'

'And at the sight of you, Dirk's mistress.' Wafer gave her a shrewd, sympathetic glance.

' 'Tis a pretty fetch,' she conceded, busying herself in collecting the articles to put on a tray for their breakfast. 'But, God help me, I dote on the fellow!'

Although she made her tone light, she could not disguise the little lines of bitterness and disillusion about her young mouth and eyes.

'You have done wondrous well for those poor lads,' Wafer's deep voice was kind and sincere. She looked up with a quick grateful smile. 'They fairly worship you and, believe me, they are not men whose loyalties are easily captured. Rest assured that Dirk shall come to hear of it!'

It meant a great deal to Roxanna to have a little praise and to be appreciated. In her heady relationship with Dirk, this was one of the factors which she most missed.

Wafer strolled along at her side as they made their way to the main-cabin. 'Can I offer you a measure of advice?' he said. 'Smooth Dirk over. Forget your pride. He'll make life devilish difficult for you else. And keep those very charming cat's eyes off other men!'

Roxanna sobered immediately, then gave a toss of her hair and opened the cabin door, adroitly balancing the tray on one knee.

Dirk was sitting up in bed, his skin very brown against the pillows, his swarth features sulky. His nose was swollen and Roxanna had grievously marked his face with her nails. Johnny lolled on the coverlet.

'Hello, there, sweeting,' he boomed, giving her a smile which indicated that she was once more in favour. He reached out to pinch her as she leaned over to set the tray on the bed. 'Oh, what lovely peck! I'm so hungry I could eat a mule.' He stared, teasingly into her face. 'And how are the bruises?'

Roxanna refused to smile. She was very piqued by the way in which both Wafer and Johnny considered her invidious position humorous. But Dirk was not laughing.

'Why did you rouse me, Johnny?' he growled.

Johnny snatched up a piece of black rye bread. 'Kate and me went ashore after you took Roxanna off to bed. Ten thousand demons, but you should've been there! Because he led your party safely down the river from Pueblo, Sharp reckoned to be elected admiral on the spot. There was a great row, knives out, pistols smoking and all! But in spite of it, that bastard managed to get voted in, you know what a crafty swine he is. He promised the lads two thousand pounds each if they would serve him!'

'Ha! And how many fell for that gerrymander?' Dirk heaved up into a sitting position.

'Sixty have deserted and gone to find Coxon,' Johnny shrugged. 'We've had little option but to join him. Dampier has remained, tho' he hates Sharp, but he don't fancy crossing the Isthmus in the rainy season!'

Roxanna said nothing. Whoever became leader, or wherever they went, it could only mean an extension of work and discomfort. She stared moodily out of the wide window, and then she became conscious that Dirk was watching her. She turned her head, suddenly vigilant, and gave him a tremulous, tentative smile.

But there was no answering warmth in the strange grey depths of his eyes, so beautifully pale against his dark skin, only a hard, bright stare which seemed to bore right through her.

CHAPTER 14

Roxanna's mournful supposition with regard to their continual restless wanderings proved only too correct, for none of Sharp's promises were realized. He was not a successful admiral, possessing no real authority and a complete lack of any organizing ability. June found them on the Isle of Gorgana, which offered a

243

safe anchorage where they half-heartedly prepared for an attack on the town of Arica.

On one hot afternoon, Roxanna was resting on the sand, staring up into a palm tree, listening sleepily to the pounds of the surf. From where she lay the *Trinity* was just visible, a helpless hulk on the beach where it was being careened. Little groups of men lounged in the shade, resting after a morning of grilling toil. There was a sullen restlessness seething in them; every time Sharp passed, they looked up with a slinking bravado and mutinous grumblings. But these troubles were small in comparison to the major worry hammering at Roxanna's mind. She suspected that she had conceived, and had spent the past week counting off the days on her fingers and making alarmed calculations.

She had been so confident that this would not happen, following several courses which both Lucy and Lydia had advised. Sitting up and coughing violently after love-making, to Dirk's amusement, and doing her best to keep every thought of babies from her mind while they embraced. It was true that at times she had neglected to put these precautions into operation.

When she first realized her condition she was secretly delighted, partly because she had managed to persuade herself that once she presented Dirk with an infant he would marry her and partly due to an essentially primordial urge to bear a child for the man she loved. But he had been so coldly scathing when she confided her hopes to him on the previous day, that she had been shocked and afraid.

Since the night when he had discovered her with Massey his moods were unpredictable, either taciturn or wild. He joined in drinking bouts with Johnny, returning to her with a violence which at times disgusted her. Gone forever seemed to be the half-tender, half-amused attitude which he had once had towards her.

She had never been so much in love with him.

If they were separated for an hour she began to fret, never happier than when she could sit and watch him when he was at council with the captains, or drinking and gaming. His quick, impulsive gestures, the jerk of his head to toss back a lock of hair from his forehead, the movements of his artistic, beautiful hands, thrilled her immeasurably. Meeting the unwinking eyes under the curved black brows she would shiver in frightened, delighted anticipation, remembering the last time he had made love to her, hating and loving him in the same breath.

Kate was sprawled on the soft sand. Roxanna looked at her speculatively. She was the one person who might be able to get her out of this predicament. Roxanna shrank at the thought of asking her help, fully aware of the enjoyment Kate would get from her embarrassment. A feeling of trapped desperation swept her as she remembered Dirk's taunting reminders of her promises that she could well deal with any such eventuality.

She prodded Kate, giving herself no time to reconsider, in a harsh voice jerking out an account of her symptoms. Kate listened without comment, then sat up lazily.

'Why come to me?' she drawled. 'I'm no midwife!'

'D'you take me for a flat?' Roxanna spoke through a tightly-clenched jaw. 'I know well enough that you can aid me if you will.'

Kate leaned forward, one side of her face twisted into a cynical grin. She held out her right hand, palm upwards, rubbing her thin fingers together significantly.

'Garnish,' she demanded.

'What d'you mean?' Roxanna retorted.

'Chummage!' Kate's face was diabolically amused. 'Money, you dolt. You get nothing in this world without you pay for it.'

Roxanna scrambled to her feet and looked down with blasting indignation at Kate.

'How much do you want?' Her voice was cutting.

'I am not short of cole,' Kate mused. 'Johnny has aplenty and I've won some at cards from your fine bully. But I've always had a mind to have some emeralds, just like yours!'

'And what do I get in return?' Roxanna snapped.

'A potion which has been proved to be mighty effective.' A faint smile tugged at Kate's mouth, making Roxanna suspect that she had it in mind to mix her a draft of poison instead. 'I got it from a bawd in the Whit. It should bring you on, if you're not more'n three months gone.'

Roxanna pulled the ear-rings from her lobes, slamming them down into the greedy palm. Kate kept her side of the bargain, running off to her tent to fetch a powder which she mixed carefully. Roxanna drank it down in a tankard of hot brandy. All night long she was kept awake by grinding cramps in her belly and a violent purging. Kate's medicine worked, and she knew both relief and disappointment.

When the *Trinity* was ready, the whole company crowded aboard her, abandoning the other ships. It was the beginning of a chaotic, haphazard journey, with constant rows breaking out, Sharp being totally unable to discipline either his men or himself.

No attempt was made on Arica although it was still discussed at great length. To appease the malcontents who were apt to mouth ugly comments on his lack of success, Sharp raided a small settlement for the purpose of re-stocking with food and water. Roxanna was thankful that she was allowed to remain on board. All they brought back was a very little gold, some fruit and olive oil, which Roxanna immediately demanded for cooking.

She did not have to work so hard as when the *Trinity* was a hospital ship, and had almost automatically taken over the cooking and general management of stores. She had plenty of help, including Jeremy who obviously adored her, certain that she had saved his life. He was learning to hobble about with the aid of a crutch and acted as a kind of bodyguard and general assistant. Had it not been for Dirk's perversity, she could have been contented enough with her lot during the lazy days when they drifted down the South Sea coasts.

On Christmas morning the *Trinity* dropped anchor at the tiny island of Juan Fernandez. The corsair leaders gathered in the state-cabin for a festive meal. Late afternoon found them still at table, the air thick with cheroot smoke, bad breath and perspiration, the bottles passing freely around.

Roxanna had been with child again for four months. She had told no one of her condition, afraid that if Dirk found out, she would be intimidated into taking action which she knew that she would regret. She wanted her baby passionately, and thought of it all the time. Her figure was still trim and Dirk had not remarked on her missed periods or the fullness of her breasts as she had half-expected him to do. He seemed abstracted and sullenly remote. She managed to conceal the bouts of sickness which came on her without warning, but she had an uneasy feeling that Kate's inquisitive eyes had noticed a change in her.

Roxanna lay on the window-locker, wearing a jade skirt and a white blouse, her legs and feet bare. She dreamed and wiped the sweat away, remote from the roars of laughter, the bawdy jests and songs, remembering Christmas spent at home. Suddenly she opened her eyes and turned to Johnny who filled an armchair with his bulk nearby.

'D'you recall Yuletide in England, Johnny?'

'Aye, that I do. When I was a lad, our farmhouse was always full, and then the table in our mother's great kitchen was loaded with peck.' He gave a noisy sigh, blowing out his cheeks. 'To think on it makes me wonder why on earth I became a prig when I could've been seated there at this very minute with a plump little country wife.'

Kate gave him a nudge. 'Johnny, you're getting mawkish. Pass that clank and let me fill it for you. Christmas was like any

250

other day for me when I was a chit. I was hungry and got beat as usual. Our highflown madam here had it a sight different, I'll warrant,' she added, spitefully, going on to tell of Christmas in Newgate.

'I spent one winter in the Whit. And on Christmas Eve the hangman brought up the heads of some queer culls he'd cast a day earlier. He passed through the taproom with 'em in a dust bucket and took 'em away to his kitchen to pickle 'em, in bay salt, so as the birds wouldn't be apecking the eyes out when they were set on spikes on Tower Bridge. Faugh! The stench was awful, even for the Whit!'

Sickness rose into Roxanna's mouth, and she gave Kate a glare, sure that she had told that gruesome tale to bring on her nausea.

Johnny roared and slapped his thigh in grisly mirth. Roxanna tried not to think of the row of heads always to be seen on the Bridge. In a high wind one was often blown down into the street below.

'We used to visit the squire,' mused Johnny, his rugged face softening. 'To sing him carols and have a beaker of hot sack.'

Dirk was silent and Roxanna watched him from the corner of her eye, realizing that he had never known any of the simple pleasures of which Johnny spoke. He was seated in his chair with the relaxed, easy grace which gave her so much delight to look at, his fingers laced about his wine glass, elbows on the padded arms.

A sudden sharp fear lanced her as she felt herself being subject to a close, disagreeable scrutiny. She shifted her gaze from Dirk to Sharp and there met the full force of lust on his bloated face. There was a kind of panting eagerness about the way in which his tongue came out to lick over his lower lip.

On the previous evening, Dirk had spoken to her of the Admiral, coming in late and watching her as she sat brushing her hair. He had looked her over slowly and then flung himself on to the bed with a sarcastic burst of laughter.

'Sharp has just offered me a deal of money for you!'

She closed her eyes, sick and faint, all the colour draining from her face. When she had looked across at him, pride had made her take a firm hold on herself.

'I was a fool,' he said thickly. 'I refused him.'

His voice had sounded faint and far away, while everything had merged and gone dark. She had gripped his leather jerkin with fingers that shook, nearly pulling him off balance, burying her face against him, sobs of relief and misery tearing at her.

His muscles had tensed under her hands and there had been a flash of bewilderment and angry tenderness in his eyes. Then he had shaken off her grip and turned his back on her.

The shoulders turned stubbornly to her were very wide under the soft, buff covering, tapering to a tightly-belted waist. As she saw the candlelight glimmering on his long black curls which covered the collar of his shirt, she had longed to break through the barrier which he deliberately created to shut her out, to tell him how desperately, madly and eternally she loved him.

Roxanna was considerably relieved when Sharp's attention was diverted to Massey, who had begun a riproaring argument that rattled back and forth about the table. He sprang to his feet, the stool crashing over behind him.

'No, blast you, Sharp!' he shouted, eyes furious and drunken. 'You are only finding an excuse to linger here to avoid more fighting! My men will not take further orders from you.' Massey thrust his sweating face close to the Admiral's. 'We have all had a bellyfull of your lies!'

'Massey, you seem to have forgotten that I am your captain.' Sharp said, ominously.

'I did not vote for you.' Massey's fist descended with a thud into the table. 'You only got elected by lies. Where are all the rich spoils you promised us, eh, Captain Sharp?'

'You mutinous scum!'

Sharp stood with a swift movement. There was a blinding flash and Massey gave a strangled scream, falling across the table, his fingers clawing at the wound in his chest, his blood mingling with the spilled wine.

Sharp stood over him, the pistol still smoking. He glared round balefully.

'Does anyone else share our friend's views?' he demanded. 'I can see that I've been too lenient with you rogues. 'Tis time for a few changes.' He pointed with a dirty, jewelled hand at Massey's body.

'Get that garbage out of here.'

In silence two of them carried out the corpse. Sharp suddenly rounded on Dirk, savage and tyrannical. 'Last night, Courtney, I made you a fair offer for yon piece-of-arse. You turned it down. Gad's Curse, you men have got to learn to take my orders. Your doxy ain't so grand that she's too good for me to have a lick at! Now, I take her with captain's privilege and you'll get damn all for her.'

No one moved. Sharp slouched back in his chair, his features twisted in a grotesque mask of conceit, triumph and rapacity.

Slowly Dirk sat upright, his face supremely haughty.

'I'll see you in hell first!'

Sharp's face purpled to the ears. 'You saw what happened to Massey!'

Dirk was on his feet in a bound.

'Lay one hand on Roxanna and I'll have your life!'

Sharp made a move for his pistol but Dirk's hand came down in a way which made him gasp at the pain of a sprained wrist, and Johnny hurtled from his chair to fling his arms about him, pinioning him firmly. Dirk took the pistol and thrust it against Sharp's back, while excited pandemonium broke loose.

Swearing vengeance and protesting violently, Sharp was roughly hustled into the hold and there, chained securely. Johnny grinned at Dirk and nodded across to where Roxanna stood leaning on the quarter-deck rail.

'So Sharp had a mind to debauch her. 'Tis true she's still a tidy little armful and don't show it yet, but another month will round out her belly a deal more!' He gave Dirk an affectionate poke in the ribs.

Dirk's eyes narrowed, and then suddenly widened. He tossed Johnny a curt, annoyed glance and bounded up the companionway with long strides. Roxanna saw him coming and knew at once that her secret was out.

'Why didn't you tell me?' he demanded roughly. The clamour of the dissenting men seemed suddenly miles away; they were as isolated as if on a mountain top. She groped for the carved rail for support.

'I feared that it would displease you,' she faltered.

'Why should it if it is my child?' His voice was frigid and hard.

Her fingers locked behind her in a fierce impatience, huge, oblique eyes bright and defensive, like a cat guarding its young. 'You made your views most plain on the last occasion,' she flashed spiritedly.

'I can't be sure that it is of my begetting,' his expression was surly, perplexed. 'How do I know that 'tis not Massey's or any other's.'

Roxanna felt so faint that she had to shut her eyes, blotting out the cruel, handsome face that she loved so well. Helplessly, she longed for Nan Dobs who petted and cosseted her charges when they were ill, who was so very proud when they bore children. But there could be no such rejoicing at the birth of this baby, only shame because it was a bastard.

All the secret pride she had felt in bearing him a child changed to a heaviness so that she hated him and it. She stole a glance up at him, saw the set of his mouth, the nervous flickering of jaw muscles under the smooth, sunburnt skin.

'There is no way in which I can convince you,' she whispered, her face white and shrunken. 'I can only repeat that I love you, God help me. This infant is yours and I think, in your heart, you know that I speak truly.'

The infuriated bawlings in the waist rose

to a crescendo and Johnny shouted to Dirk to join him. Roxanna crept into the cabin which she shared with Dirk and threw herself on the bed where grief engulfed her. She was beyond caring who was elected leader or where they went; Dirk was angry with her and as far as she was concerned the sun had gone out and the world was black.

Surprisingly enough, the changeable buccaneers selected a man from the crew; John Watling, a middle-aged, sober sea-farer. He enforced strict discipline to which the headstrong, unpredictable followers did not object. Revelling was forbidden, everything about the ship was kept neat and orderly.

Women, he found particularly odious, and considered the two on board nothing less than wanton Jezebels. Roxanna knew that he was on the watch for any excuse to despatch them. But she was assured by the strong contingent of men who were loyal to Dirk and Johnny, and by the friends she had made during her devoted nursing of the wounded. Jeremy in particular did his utmost to help her, swinging along on his crutch, admiration in his every glance. When the news of her pregnancy leaked out he treated her with a fussy concern which both amused and irritated her. When Dirk had been more than usually off-hand with her, these little attentions were balm to her wounded self-esteem.

CHAPTER 15

Lionel Wafer was inflexible in his determination that Roxanna should not go with Dirk when Arica was raided. In vain she badgered, stormed and argued: 'But I must be with Dirk! He may be killed or hurt!'

Wafer's usually amused face was stern as they stood in the waist, jostled by tense men who strapped on their weapons, while exchanging boasts, gloomy predictions or obscene ribaldries before scrambling down into the longboats.

'D'you want to drop that babe before time!' he snapped bluntly, and this gave Roxanna pause, so that she reluctantly watched Dirk swinging over the rail and remained behind with the doctor. She could not shake off a sense of foreboding and grumbled continually to him.

'Dirk is not well.' She voiced her worry as they tramped into the galley to find a drink. 'He has that recurring fever on him. And 'tis Friday too! Any fool knows that bad luck will follow anything done on this day, from the crowning of a king to turning a mattress. I should know, I was born on it!'

'Watling would not hold with such heathenish tarradiddle,' Wafer eyed her humorously, as he began his preparations to deal with the wounded who were bound to be brought back.

She helped him; putting the heavy iron pot on the stove, rolling strips of linen into bandages and laying out the stock of herbs. These had increased, for Wafer spent all of his spare time, when ashore, on treks into the bush with Indian guides who pointed out the most suitable plants.

The ship was very quiet after the flurry of departure, only a skeleton crew remained aboard.

Roxanna listened for every sound, very edgy. 'If Dirk is killed,' she thought frantically, 'I don't want to go on living.' Even the baby, whose birth she was anticipating with an impatient longing,

260

could never compensate her.

Wafer was fully aware of her agitation. He lit his stubby clay pipe, rolled up his sleeves and came across to the table to assist her.

'Dirk has been in many a skirmish, you know,' he remarked, his bony supple fingers ripping at a length of white cambric. 'If you had gone with him he would have had the worry of looking after you.'

'I know that.' She left her chair and took to a worried pacing. 'But he is sick. Did you note his colour this morning, I've never seen a man so yellow! Did that damned Watling have to take him?'

'Watling needs every man,' Wafer replied soberly. 'There aren't many of us left.'

Jeremy, acting under Roxanna's urgent prompting, was watching the shore through a telescope. A dozen times she ran up the companion-way to peek through it and scan the beach for signs of the buccaneers. The hours dragged interminably and it was not until evening that she heard Wafer's feet pounding down the ladder to the galley.

'They are coming.' He sounded tense, strongly-cut features set. 'I saw them break through the trees and make for the boats.

The Spaniards are after them and it looks as if they've had a bad time!'

Before he had finished she was pelting on deck to watch their army tumbling into the water amidst the rattle of Spanish gunfire. Her relief was almost agonizing as she picked out Dirk's familiar outline in the stern of the foremost boat. Down in the waist, to greet him, her joy turned to horror as he heaved himself over the side and she saw blood soaking his shirt. His movements were unnaturally slow and clumsy, his face drawn and drained of colour under the tan.

'Dirk! Oh, my darling!' He swayed unsteadily, looking down at her with baffled anger, screwing up his eyes in the effort to focus and marshal his wits. Johnny climbed up the rope ladder after him and Roxanna rounded on him.

'What the devil has happened?'

'He stopped a ball in the shoulder. Best get him to Wafer without delay. We've had damned bad luck and Watling is dead!'

It was on the tip of Roxanna's tongue to retort that it was a good job too! But in time she remembered that it was unlucky to speak ill of the dead. She had enough trouble without inviting more! Wafer came at once to Dirk and put Ringrose and Kate in charge of the rest. Doctor Snelgrave had been left behind in Arica, in a church with the wounded which had subsequently been recaptured by the Spaniards. They could ill afford to lose a surgeon.

'Come on, lad,' Johnny was helping Dirk to stand.

Roxanna watched him with growing alarm as he mounted the companion-way, hanging on to the rail with his uninjured arm, his step slow and heavy, frighteningly unlike him. When he was at the top, she raced to the galley, snatching up a kettle which was just on the boil, a pewter basin and a bundle of linen. In the main cabin she found Dirk slumped in a chair, legs stretched out in front of him, head leaning against the back, his eyes half closed. She dumped the things on to the table and turned to Wafer.

'What can I do?' she wanted to know.

'Get his shirt off, for a start,' Wafer ordered, clicking open his case of instruments, his calm, methodical manner steadying her.

Roxanna unfastened the buttons, trying to ease Dirk's left arm out of the sleeve. He opened his eyes, which were dark and lack-lustre, and tried to sit up, scowling with pain and the effort of concentration. She was able to pull the shirt up from his belt, away from his back and down over his damaged shoulder. She heard him swear beneath his breath and saw that he was running with sweat, while blood trickled brightly from the jagged lips of the bullet wound. She mopped him over with a towel, soaked a cloth in warm water and gently bathed his injury. He gave her a wry, dazed smile.

'Here's a pretty fetch, eh?' he muttered, wincing as she unwittingly put a little pressure on his arm. Her voice broke with hysterical rage.

'I knew something like this would happen today. Christ, why weren't you careful!'

'It's the fever.' His speech was slurred and he fell back, utterly spent.

It was getting rapidly darker and Johnny lit the candles in a silver candelabra, standing it close by one on the table to throw light for Wafer. He wasted no time, taking up his long forceps, and humming tunelessly to himself.

Dirk went rigid as the instrument probed the wound seeking for the ball. He gripped the arms of the chair until his knuckles turned white, his teeth clamped together. Roxanna watched in numb helplessness as agony contorted his features and he groaned. She reached across to wipe the perspiration which flowed down his face, dripping off his chin. Wafer cursed as the forceps grated against the lead-shot but skidded away from it.

'The deuced thing is well lodged in the muscle.' He grunted, dropping the instrument on the table and taking up a smaller one. 'Have a drink and then we'll try again!'

Roxanna held the brandy to Dirk's lips and he took a deep swallow. The wound was bleeding freely and she mopped it up as it ran out. The bloody swabs accumulated in the wooden bucket and Johnny set to work tearing up some more.

'He's going to bleed to death!' she muttered as she passed him.

'Nay, not he!' Johnny's voice was gruffly assuring. 'Look at the size of him, lass. He can afford to lose a lot!'

Dirk's strength was dwindling and as the steel entered his tormented flesh again his breath rushed out on a yelp as he shrank back. Johnny took hold of him, bronzed face set and, though he writhed, did not loosen his grip until Wafer had clamped firmly round the ball and triumphantly drawn it out.

'Got it!' he cried, with immense satisfaction. 'Now, Roxanna, bandage him up and get him to bed. Johnny will help you. I must away to the others!'

She bound the wound, thoroughly alarmed at the blood which seeped relentlessly through the linen. He was so very quiet, his head tipped back, body limp. He suddenly began to shiver uncontrollably.

'Damned cold,' he complained, his teeth chattering.

'We must put him to bed, Johnny,' Roxanna leaned over him, attempting to hold his wandering attention. 'Dirk, can you walk? Try to get up, darling!'

Her words penetrated the fog of pain and fever and he sluggishly, automatically, dragged up onto his feet, weaving like someone drunk. Johnny eased Dirk's left arm up over his own hulking shoulders and they made a stumbling progress to the next cabin. Roxanna ran on ahead to open the door, light a candle and throw back the bedclothes. Dirk sat heavily on the edge of the bed, then slowly swung his legs up and lay down, still shuddering

266

violently, while he poured sweat.

Roxanna pulled off his boots and stockings, which were stained and soaked, and had a peculiar, sharp odour which was not usual for him. She unbuckled his belt, peeled down his breeches, then tucked the blankets up under his chin. He lay prone, occasionally groaning, his breathing rasping and difficult.

'He's not going to die, is he, Johnny?' She felt stupid with fatigue, every bone in her body seemed to ache and there was a gnawing pain in the small of her back. She drove an impatient fist into the palm of her other hand. 'Oh, God, if only I had my recipe book with me! There's a cure for every fever under the sun in it!'

His illness resembled the ague which Nan Dobs treated so successfully, but Roxanna could not remember what should be given. She bitterly supposed that in any case the ingredients needed would not be available and fell to cursing in weary frustration. Never had she longed for Nan and her sage council with such hopeless desperation.

'Stay with him, Johnny,' she begged. 'I'll go seek Lionel's advice.'

As she passed through the state-room

267

she swept up the bucket and took it into the galley, covering the stained rags with cold water to soak until she could wash them. Wafer, Kate and Ringrose were working on the wounded survivors. From those who had returned, more or less unscathed, she pieced together the events which had led to their defeat.

One section of the raiders had attacked the town, another the fort and these two forces had been prevented from amalgamating as had been planned. Meanwhile, the citizens had reorganized and attacked the guards set over prisoners, killing them. The corsairs were forced to retreat. Their ranks were kept closed and orderly until Watling was shot down. Then, leaderless, they began to flounder. Of the hundred men who set out that morning, only sixty returned.

Wafer briskly rapped out instructions to keep Dirk as hot as possible and encourage the sweating all that she could. He rattled off the ingredients for a potion which she would find in the medicine chest and must mix and administer without delay. Back in the galley, Roxanna hurriedly added the powdered herbs to boiling water. The names came back to her from lessons in Nan's still-room. Virginia snake-root, cardus seeds and marigold flower, green walnuts, hartshorn and poppy. She found them all there, a tribute to Wafer's earnest application to his calling.

As she watched the brew begin to simmer, she remembered other cures in which Nan placed considerable faith. Her father was always given rusks soaked in port wine for the ague; there were none on board but she dipped some pieces of crust in sack, hoping that it might serve as well. Another remedy, thought to be marvellously effective, sent her speeding to the forecastle, after glancing at the medicine to see that it was not bubbling too fiercely. She poked her head round the door of the crew's quarters. They were resting, unusually subdued, voices a mournful, pessimistic monotone.

'I'll give a gold piece to the first man to find me a spider and its cobweb!' she promised.

'Dead or alive, Ma'am?' one enormous ruffian asked her.

'Dead!' she replied firmly.

Within a short time he appeared at the galley door with a little crumpled ball of cobweb. Roxanna gingerly placed her prize on the table. The spider was supposed to be rolled into a pill and swallowed by the patient, but she had a shrewd idea that Dirk would object to this, having no faith in her superstitions and nostrums. The cobweb was to check bleeding, and she resolved to place it against the wound next time she changed the dressing.

The water in the skillet had boiled down, but not quite sufficiently. While she waited she set to work preparing a caudle to strengthen Dirk, heating a pint of milk, adding white wine, the yokes of three eggs and pinch of cinnamon. She took a sip before pouring it into a pewter posset pot. The potion was ready and that went into a tankard which was placed on a tray with the caudle, spider, cobweb and wine-soaked bread. With all these aids she was more confident that she could keep death at bay and make Dirk well again.

Johnny was busy replacing the blankets which Dirk kept throwing off. He was tossing and muttering, breathing jerkily. Johnny had opened a window and at once she slammed the horned-panes shut, fastening them close.

'Damn you for a snabbling pimp, Johnny!' she stormed. 'D'you want to witness his finny? You know death comes in at an open window when a person is sick! And besides he must be kept warm!'

'Warm!' repeated Johnny, as he ran a hand over his streaming face. ' 'Tis like an oven in here already and stinks worse'n the Whit!'

'Get out then, if it doesn't suit you!' She was bending solicitiously over Dirk. Somehow she had to get the medicine down him.

Dirk grumbled and swore continually as she put an arm under his head and heaved. His body was slippery and in the heat of the close, airless cabin wet patches appeared on her blouse, at the armpits and under her breasts. She hauled him into a sitting position and braced his back against her shoulder, reaching over to stuff another pillow behind. When she took up the tankard he turned his face aside, but Johnny seized his head and Roxanna poured the medicine into his mouth. He swallowed it and she followed this up with the sack-posset. He flung up an arm and almost knocked it out of her hand, but he was as weak as a baby and Johnny easily controlled him. She spooned the bread between his protesting lips, not stopping until that too was all gone. Then they laid him down and she piled four extra blankets on him.

She stripped to her petticoat and shift, fastening her heavy hair into a knot at the back of her head. With her discarded blouse she wiped her underarms and chest, lifting the neckline of her shift and blowing down it.

'You go and help Lionel, Johnny,' she said quietly.

Although bone-weary she collected up the tray and carried it out into the great cabin. On returning she found that Dirk had just vomited on to the floor. He lay there looking at her as she came in, his expression miserable and humiliated. She knew well enough that illness shamed him. Then his eyes rolled shut and he slid back into unconsciousness.

Roxanna began to cry with helpless frustration as she mopped up the vomit with a towel. All of her carefully prepared medicine was wasted; only the spider in the linen bag slung around his neck could help his fever now. She wrung out a cloth in cold water and laid it on his forehead. He had stopped shivering, but his skin was burning to touch. She crept away to the galley to wash the towel, his shirt and the blooded bandages.

Fresh water was too precious to waste, so Jeremy drew her up buckets of sea water. This made it impossible to work up a lather and made the washing stiff, but at least it was clean and would soon dry on the decks under the hot sun. She made a hurried job of it, afraid to leave Dirk for very long, straining her ears all the while for any sound. When she returned to the cabin he was half out of bed, begging for water.

She held the mug to his lips and he drank it down in greedy gulps. She saw that the blood had soaked through the dressing and brought fresh linen to change it. He made no protest as she did this, although she was terrified that it might hurt him. When he wanted to get up she pushed him firmly back and brought in the chamber pot, doing all that she could to save him any unnecessary movements.

At last, when he seemed to be sleeping, she lay down on the bed beside him. As she relaxed she felt the baby kicking, a curiously comforting sensation. Within minutes she was fast asleep.

An odd sound woke her with a start.

Dawn was just beginning to filter into the cabin and she saw that Dirk was standing by the bedside, unaware of her or his surroundings in the toils of delirium, his eyes starting with fear.

'The dogs!' he whispered. 'I've got to get away! Listen to them baying!'

Slowly, Roxanna backed away, easing herself from the bed, never taking her eyes from him. He looked mad and she was terrified. Then he stumbled and crashed against the bed where he lay sobbing convulsively, his hands digging into the mattress, shoulders heaving. He wept with deep racking sobs which seemed to come up from his belly and lungs; the effect was terrible and heartrending.

Roxanna snatched up a blanket and covered him for, sweating as he was, she was afraid that he would worsen the chill.

'Dirk, my dearest love.' She was on her knees beside him, her arms going round him, her fear swallowed up in pity. 'What's the matter? We are on the *Trinity*. There are no dogs here!'

With frantic annoyance she saw that the wound was bleeding, broken open by his struggles. She tried to get him back on to the bed but he was over twelve inches taller than her and several stone heavier and she could not budge him. Swearing aloud and weeping, she left him, running out to where Johnny slept. Roxanna pounded on his arm and he shot up, his hand flying to the hilt of the broadsword which was beside him. She rapidly explained as he dragged on his breeches.

It did not take Johnny many seconds to heave Dirk across the bed and Roxanne heaped the blankets over him. Johnny poured himself a drink and looked at her.

'A clank of diddle for you, sweetheart?' he offered, and she took the tankard gratefully. As the light grew stronger she caught sight of herself in the mirror. She groaned, putting up a hand to her hair.

'What a sight!' she commented ruefully. 'One look at me would be enough to fright the poor wretch more than any pack of hounds!'

Johnny shifted over to sit her on the bed. He took one of her hot, sticky hands in his and raised it to his lips, kissing the fingers reflectively. 'I vow and declare you are the prettiest thing I've seen in ages!'

She shot a significant glance down at her swollen stomach, 'Even with the baby-lay?' she asked dubiously.

He tipped her chin with one stubby finger and kissed her lingeringly on the lips. 'Even with that!' he assured her. 'You know well enough I would have been its Pa if I'd had my way!'

She sighed. 'I shall never understand men. You were in an almighty passion because you believed I was going to lie with Massey, and yet you have never stopped trying to make love to me yourself!'

'That was different.' His eyes were guileless, and the colour of ale with the sun shining through it. 'If you went to bed with me you wouldn't run rusty on Dirk. Me and him are mates. We share everything. I shouldn't mind if he wanted the use of Kate for a night.'

Roxanna, essentially warm-hearted, could never do anything but like Johnny. It satisfied her vanity to know that he wanted her. She often gave Kate a little secretive, superior smile which she knew goaded her beyond words.

'Dear Johnny.' Her voice was soft and

she patted his shoulder. 'You are a great comfort to me.'

'I'd be an even greater if you'd let me!' he said, earnestly.

Two days later Dirk seemed so much better that she dared to open the window a crack. She had been busy all morning, tidying the cabin, changing the sheets and washing him. Dirk lay and watched her, still too weak to move, but the fever had subsided and Wafer was pleased with the healthy appearance of the wound. Roxanna sang softly and came over to brush his tangled locks, pushing in the waves with the palm of her hand, rolling the ends rounds her finger in much the same manner as she did her own curls. During his illness she had served him as devotedly as she knew how, performing the most unpleasant tasks without hesitation or disgust.

'Darling,' she said suddenly, pausing to look down at him. 'Were you dreaming of dogs during your fever?'

He passed the tip of his tongue over his lips. 'Did I speak of them? Aye, that fancy usually haunts me.'

His voice was low and she wished that

she had not mentioned the subject as it seemed to distress him. He began to speak again.

'My father was killed by Raynal's hounds whilst trying to escape from slavery. When they carried his body back to the plantation, his throat and most of his face had been torn away.'

Roxanna remained perfectly still, then she groped for his slender, hard hand. And Dirk talked uncontrollably, in a harsh spate of words. He told her about his mother, a half-Dutch, half-Irish immigrant, who had been an indentured servant in Raynal's household, and his father, a Royalist nobleman, deported when Oliver Cromwell ruled England after the defeat and execution of Charles I. Lord Courtney had lost everything he possessed in fighting for his king; his lands in Cornwall, his manor house, all of his rights and, at last, his freedom, when he was sold into slavery.

A stiff-necked fighter, the last of his line, who seethed with resentment at his humiliation, he passed this feeling on to his son. Raynal was a Parliamentary supporter and lost no opportunity to degrade the Cavalier in every conceivable way. Dirk's mother had been his only solace. Because she was of humble birth he would not wed her, until forced to do so to prevent her child being born into bastardy.

When the boy was ten years old, this beloved father made his desperate bid for freedom and Dirk saw the dogs tear him down. Raynal's hatred spread to him and although, being the child of a servant, his duties should have been confined to the house, he was often set to work in the fields under the overseer's whip. Raynal had already earned his reputation as the most brutal owner in the Indies and imposed severe punishments on his slaves. For insolence to either himself or his overseers, flogging; the loss of a hand for striking a master; the loss of an ear for theft; if a slave escaped he was hunted down by the pack of half-wild hounds. Roxanna remembered the great, slavering beasts Dubois kept near him.

Dirk's voice was halting now. 'No matter what he did to me, I always remembered that my ancestors were high-born and that my father had fought for the king. When I grew older, he had me taught to read and write and made into a clerk.'

'Had he repented of his treatment?' she

asked, her eyes searching his face.

'Don't you remember that he liked striplings?' he said and, at Roxanna's horrified gasp of understanding, continued, 'That is what prompted the flogging I received, because I was so abusive in my refusal of him.'

Roxanna understood, all at once, his inexplicable moods. It had turned him into a ruthless, selfish adventurer. The man that she idolized.

His voice trailed off in the middle of a sentence, and she saw that he slept. Roxanna stayed beside him, so proud that he had confided in her, that scalding tears rose in her eyes.

CHAPTER 16

Captain Sharp, elected Admiral again, did not sail from the vicinity of Arica at once. In a fit of bravado very typical of him, he cruised up and down the bay, tantalizing the inhabitants. At last they were forced to sail further afield in search of provisions. In April they landed on the Island of Plata, pitching camp on the beach.

One morning, shortly after, Roxanna walked across the sand to where a cluster of men were gathered. She was within a month of her delivery and moved carefully, her shoulders back to balance the ungainly bulk of advanced pregnancy. The only thing which vexed her about her condition was the loss of her figure, feeling a dowdy frump with her skirt hanging inches short in front, her blouse pulled out over her thickened waist. But she was very proud to be carrying Dirk's child, and contentment radiated from her, giving her skin a velvety bloom, and making her thick hair even more lustrous. Her eyes darted restlessly over the throng, looking for Dirk. She found him standing with Johnny, an arm flung about his friend's shoulders.

He was fully recovered from his wound and she was delighted to find that he was grateful to her for the way in which she had nursed him. Also, he was interested in the child. Sometimes, as they lay in bed, his hand would come to rest gently on her belly to feel the strong, thrusting movements of the tiny limbs stirring within her and there would be a kind of awe in his voice as he asked, 'Is that the little one?'

It filled Roxanna with a dizzy confidence that once it was born he would marry her. Now she watched him with pleasure, noting how distinguished he looked, the forceful manner in which he gestured when he was making a point and the way his eyes flashed with an enthusiasm when he spoke.

Sharp came towards his men. Since he had been in charge, there had been the usual outbreaks of near mutiny and ugly remarks that the only thing in which he excelled was a retreat.

'We want to go back to Tortuga,' Dampier's voice was openly antagonistic. 'For nearly a year we have been cruising these damned islands and we are aweary of it!'

His supporters shouted their agreement. 'So that's the lay, is it?' Sharp remarked. 'And how many of ye have a mind to that?'

'Around thirty,' Dampier announced crisply.

'Not all of my lads, then,' Sharp raised his voice and pulled up his stocky figure, strutting a little. 'Some of ye have still guts enough to go sailing with me.'

He could see that the major part of the company, either through avarice, or a thirst for adventure, would be remaining. He tossed Dampier a smug glance, legs astraddle, thumbs hooked in his belt. Dampier lifted his thin shoulders in a distasteful shrug.

'There are always gullible dupes who heed the cock who crows the loudest,' he said disparagingly. 'I suggest that we put it to the vote. The majority keep the ship and the rest take the canoes and go their own way.'

Those who elected to leave the Pacific included Wafer and Dirk.

Roxanna was flabbergasted to see Johnny staying with Sharp. He looked at her a little shamefacedly.

'That's the way of it, lass, Kate and me are going to bide. Truth to tell, the roaming itch is still with me.'

Dirk's features betrayed misgivings. 'Don't trust Sharp. There never has been any solid foundation to his promises.'

'Pah! Away with this melancholy, lad!' Johnny beamed on them both. 'I'll be with you in a few months to drink your bub and lie with your wenches! Don't fret your bowels out about me!'

Dirk shook his head doubtfully, a worried frown creasing his eyes.

'Ten thousand devils! I can watch out for myself!' Johnny's bluff heartiness rang a little false in Roxanna's ears. 'If Sharp gets up to any tricks I'll take my chive to his gizzard!' His voice went roaring across the beach so that several men looked round with grins on their bearded, tanned faces. 'And if it weren't for that jade of yours being brought to bed, you'd have been with me too!'

'I had hoped we might buy a plantation between us!' Dirk said morosely.

Johnny gave a quick grunt of mirth. 'Can you imagine me a gager planter, rich and pot-bellied, wedded by a gown-man to some plump trull and getting a mause of brats on her? Hell no! This is my life!' He made an expansive gesture with his arms. 'That treacherous whore, the sea, and a good ship riding her. We'll meet again in some ken, fear not!'

Their hands shot out and gripped fiercely.

'And you, darling,' he said, hugging a sobbing Roxanna, 'mind you call that brat of yours after me!' He lowered his voice to whisper, his lips against her ear. 'I wish I had enjoyed the begetting of it!'

His face swam through a mist of scalding tears and she raised her mouth for his kiss. Both she and Dirk stared from the canoe as long as they could see the glint of sunlight on Johnny's yellow hair, the flaunting crimson of his shirt as he raised his arm in farewell.

This was the beginning of a journey which burned it self forever into Roxanna's memory. For twelve days they crept up the coast, beaten by torrential rain. They arrived at their destination, aching with the damp, their sodden rags plastered to hungry bodies. Dampier dispatched a scout to discover if the Gulf of San Migual, into which flowed the river which he meant to follow, was free of the enemy. His man returned with the alarming news that it was alive with Spanish warships and that the local Indians had been browbeaten into assisting their oppressors.

Dampier gave his orders, his narrow lips set.

'The gulf is out of the question. We shall have to sink the boats and make across the Isthmus on foot.' A unanimous groan arose to interrupt him, but he added, ' 'Tis our only chance.'

Their silence was eloquent. Apprehensive, barbate faces already hollowed-cheeked from the near-starvation rations of the past days. The Isthmus was one hundred miles of swamp and dense jungle. Dampier's voice was unrelenting.

'Before we start, I make it plain that if anyone falls behind we shall be forced to kill him. We can't risk a member of our party coming into Spanish hands and betraying our course under torture.'

His eyes rested uncompromisingly on Roxanna. She made no reply, but her heart gave a lurch as she saw Dirk and the doctor raise alarmed eyebrows and Wafer's mouth turn down at the corners in a wry grimace.

The weather was capricious giving them a day of sapping heat followed by another of driving rain squalls. Whichever it was, the fetid bush dripped continually, rotting what remained of their tatters and making them ache with fever.

Miraculously, none of their band fell out and, one morning, as they groaned and sweated to the breasts of a hill they looked down into a verdant valley where blue smoke columned up from a cluster of native huts.

The flat of Dampier's sword beat back those who would have rushed the encampment at once. Methodically, he ordered pistols to be primed and energy flowed back into his gaunt, limping scarecrows at the prospect of food. The Indians scattered in terror when these men burst upon them, yelling like demons, their beards and tangled hair matted with filth, rags flapping about their sinewy limbs, their eyes sunken and completely ferocious. The raiders were in luck as there were but a few left to protect the women and children, while the large section went hunting.

Dirk and Wafer trudged back to the shelter of trees where Roxanna had been left with Jeremy and those men who were too weakened to fight. They shouldered the improvised litter on which they had carried her for many days. She knew that they were worn out and sometimes protested that it would be better to kill her than struggle on further, but Dirk would turn to soothe her, promising her that he would never leave her.

For a few hours, Dampier allowed them to rest and eat but he had no intention of remaining until the hunters returned. When they set off again they were invigorated and refreshed and had guides to help.

At last, when reaching the top of a rise, they saw, in the far distance, the deeply blue water of the Caribbean Sea. Joyfully the buccaneers raised a cheer, shouting and thumping one another on their naked, sun-scorched shoulders, already boasting of what they would do when they reached Tortuga.

On the other side of the hill lay another village, where they borrowed piroques, and paddled down the Conception River to the sea. The mouth of the river was not far from an old pirate haunt known as La Sounds Key. To their unbounded delight, they found members of the Brethren already camping there, one Captain Tristain and his bullies. Boisterous confusion reigned as eager questions were asked.

Roxanna rested under the shade of a huge tree, unable to believe that she was really safe at last. She was numb, shaken and ready to weep, the baby a leaden, suddenly intolerable burden. Through a haze of exhaustion she watched the men, seeing how their tiredness dropped away as they found themselves heroes.

Captain Tristian's frigate was not large,

but he crowded aboard Dampier's bedraggled army and they set sail for Golden Island. Jim Rackham nearly fell over the rail in his enthusiasm, when Dirk and his little party scrambled up the *Hopewell's* towering side.

Their shipmates clustered excitedly about them, and the returning marauders were only too ready to give wildly exaggerated descriptions of their prowess in battle.

While Dirk and Rackham talked, Roxanna ordered water and a tub to be brought to Dirk's cabin, and, within minutes, was soaking luxuriously. Nan Dobs never allowed expectant mothers to indulge in hot baths so near the time of birth, but she chose to forget this. Dirk was some time in joining her and when he did, his hair was dripping and he wore a towel knotted round his hips. He sat on the side of the bed and regarded her as she scrubbed away at the accumulated layers of dirt. She was nervous under his disconcerting stare, wondering if he was in an amiable mood; on the journey common suffering had brought them close, now she sensed his withdrawal.

'Has all been well here, during your absence?' she asked, at last.

He stood up and stretched, rubbing his chin through the stubble. 'Aye, Rackham has managed passing fair. Several of the crew have settled down with the native women and don't wish to return.'

Roxanna was freshly impressed by his handsome proportions, admiring him as he took a razor from his pack, poured hot water into a silver basin and, scowling at his tanned reflection, began to scrape away at his beard.

'And you...?' she questioned, hesitantly. 'What do you plan?'

He grimaced under the blade, screwing up his eyes in concentration, cursing softly as he nicked his chin. 'I shall buy a plantation, my dear. I've had a bellyful of roaming, and have developed a mighty taste for security.'

Her voice was little more than a whisper. 'And what of me?'

He dabbed at his face with a towel, lean cheeks smooth once again. He looked down at her, hands on his hips, his magnificent frame brown and toughened.

'You can stay with me, if it is your wish,' he said slowly, adding hastily when delight and relief lit up her weary eyes; 'For a while at least! And do not imagine that

I intend to wed you. Not even for the baby!'

Roxanna felt too tired and despondent to restrain the tears, as she stepped from the tub and commenced to rub herself dry. She longed for her old nurse, yearning to be comforted and made much of. If only she had remained in London she might have been married to someone of importance by now, instead of being big with a bastard child! But, catching a glimpse of Dirk as he dressed for supper, she knew that she could never do without him.

She sniffed, dashed off the tears with the back of her hand and went over to the mirror. It was the first time in weeks that she had been able to take a full-length view of herself and an utterly horrified expression crossed her face. Her eyes stared out from muddy circles set in a thin, drawn face, her skin was tanned and roughened, the whole framed in dirty, tangled curls. With mounting concern, she scanned her body with the stretched belly, heavy breasts, sunburned arms and shoulders. Aghast, she dragged the towel about her again.

Dirk offered his help in the difficult task of freeing her long hair of lice, repeatedly rinsing it and going through the locks with a fine comb until he was satisfied that every plump louse was squashed and each minute egg destroyed. He assured her that the salt sea water had done the same for him, and as he leaned over her his black hair shone healthily and she caught the disturbing fragrance of it.

Creams and lotions from her precious, dwindled store, restored her skin to something of its former suppleness. She touched her lips and cheeks with rouge, spitting on her tiny brush and smoothing her thick lashes with upward strokes. There were no clothes that would meet across her ungainly girth, so she slid on Dirk's dressing-robe, a maroon and gold striped damask garment which trailed behind her, the sleeves flopping far down over her hands. But she rolled them back and pulled the neck open into a deep V between her breasts clasping her emerald necklace about her throat.

Dirk's expression, when she joined him in the main cabin for supper, gave her ample reward for her efforts. His officers rose to a man and bowed as she entered. In the rosy illuminations of the many candles her skin had a peach-soft bloom, and the dignity of posture which pregnancy gave her, made her seem like some ancient pagan goddess of fertility. They loved her for her undaunted courage, her compassion to their wounded and for her determination to stand by her man. They could forgive a woman many faults if she had the glamour and allure which Roxanna possessed in an almost unfair measure.

She basked in their approbation, glancing at Dirk who was seated, gracious and easy, in his chair at her side. His singular charm made her catch her breath with the force of her longing to lie with him again. Not for ages had he looked so handsome. He wore a faultlessly tailored black velvet coat, elaborate with silver thread, and his linen sparkled in the candlelight. His nobility of bearing gave him unquestioned authority so that these men accepted him without demur as their new captain. His eyes, heavy-lidded and smoky, seldom left her, and in them she read the headiest compliment of all, his desire for her which sent a tingle all through her body.

Early in the morning of their first day at sea, Roxanna was awakened by a dull ache in her back, which fanned out across her abdomen and then faded away. Within minutes the sensation was repeated. She prodded Dirk frantically in the back. He grumbled, reluctant to wake, but, when she told him, he was up and out of bed in an instant.

'Have you started your pains?' His face was alert with anxious realization, and there was the sound of compassionate remorse in his voice. 'Oh, my darling, I had hoped to get you back to Cayona before this happened!'

He had put tremendous pressure on his men to get the ship stocked and ready, they had only lingered at Golden Island for two days. She was inordinately pleased at his concern. His face was so worried that she almost laughed, but a pain stabbed sharply and she gasped instead. At once his arms were about her, his expression humble and contrite. 'Shall I fetch Lionel?'

Roxanna told him that the doctor would know little of childbirth, as this was a strictly female prerogative, always left to the offices of a midwife. But Dirk fretted and fumed so very gratifyingly that, to please him, she agreed to allow Wafer to examine her.

She was amazed to discover that he was far more conversant with the procedure of a confinement than she had suspected, having delivered more than one infant during the course of his chequered medical career. He was unexpectedly gentle and considerate as his cool fingers prodded and probed. He straightened up and told her that the child would not be born for some hours and that she would do better if occupied during this time.

Roxanna got up, washed her face, combed out her hair, pulled on Dirk's dressing-gown and busied herself in tearing up sheeting into makeshift diapers. When Dirk and Rackham had completed their immediate duties about the ship, they joined the doctor and Roxanna in the main cabin and settled down to play cards. She found it increasingly difficult to concentrate, curled at Dirk's side on the locker, her head resting on his shoulder, his arm round her. At last the quality of her pains altered, coming close behind one another, fierce and hard.

'Darling,' she murmured to Dirk. 'I think it is time that I took to my bed!'

She went into the cabin and he followed her. His face betrayed alarm.

'Stay with me,' she said, glad to lie down. It seemed right to her that their baby should be born on the bed where she had first made love with Dirk. The pains were coming faster, every one sharper than the last.

Dirk took the cabin in a bound to shout for Wafer when, in a rush of amniotic fluid, the child's head began to appear. The doctor came in calmly, rolling up his shirt sleeves, despatching Dirk for hot water.

'Now, then, my girl,' Wafer's unruffled voice cut in through the pain, 'your babe has beautiful black hair, I can see it. Be a good lass and in a few moments you shall hold it in your arms!'

Dirk set down the bowl and the kettle and, following Wafer's instructions, sat on the bed and took Roxanna's right thigh across his knee. She lay on her side, facing him, her back to Wafer, and she smiled up into Dirk's tense face. The thought which dominated all else was the joyful knowledge that her longed-for baby was almost born. She was hardly aware that she was naked from the waist down and about to be delivered by a man.

'Hold on to Dirk's hands, sweetheart.' Wafer's voice was forthright and practical.

'And push like the very devil when you get the next pain!'

Her fingers obediently closed about Dirk's. She saw the dark hairs gleaming on their backs, clearly aware of every little detail. For a second she rested, listening to the ordinary, daily sounds coming in at the open window, the voices and footsteps from on deck, the eternal whisper of the sea. Glancing round, she met Wafer's broad, confident wink, then looked deep into Dirk's eyes as a wave of pain washed over her. She strained on his hands and closed her eyes, her teeth locked together. She heard her own throaty, expulsive grunts. Exhausted, she suddenly gave up pushing.

'Don't stop!' Wafer barked. 'The head is born!'

But, almost before the words were uttered, Roxanna was carried along by another convulsive wave and he received the baby boy into his hands. Roxanna wonderingly looked round to see her son. His thin, mottled limbs shuddered with the tremendous effort of breathing and his little chest arched as the cabin resounded to his shrill, squalling cries. She had not been prepared for the rush of violent love which poured through her with the thrilling exultation of achievement. Wafer cut the natal cord.

'Give him to me!' Her voice was husky and demanding. Wafer picked him up and wrapped a blanket about him before putting him in her arms. She grinned at Dirk, her eyes sparkling with rapturous tears.

'Why, darling, he is the image of you!'

Dirk was looking down at the baby, his expression moody and wistful, although he smiled faintly.

The child was long and skinny, his face red and wrinkled and his elongated skull crowned with a fuzz of black hair. He had stopped crying and was looking about him, blinking his dark blue eyes. Roxanna thought that she had never seen anything more perfect.

'Mind that you leave his right hand unwashed,' she instructed seriously. 'Then he will be sure to gain riches. Oh, and what time is it? I must know so that I can have his horoscope accurately drawn!'

Wafer paused, smiled and nodded, although she knew that he had as little faith in these things as Dirk. With a lift of his sardonic eyebrows he held the child out to Dirk. 'You can have little doubt now who fathered him!'

Dirk gazed thoughtfully into the tiny, screwed-up face, and then he leaned over to brush his lips across Roxanna's, with almost the kiss which a husband gives his beloved wife of many years. An expression of pure joy transfigured her features as she looked up at him. Wafer laid the child on the bed and turned his attention to Roxanna, making sure that the afterbirth came away properly. Dirk swabbed the blood from Roxanna's loins and helped her into a clean shift. Their child began to roar lustily as Wafer washed him, beating at the air with angry, futile fists.

Dirk lifted Roxanna effortlessly to let Wafer spread the bed with fresh sheets. She snuggled against him, wide awake and excited, but once back under the blankets, sudden tiredness swept over her. Just before she surrendered to sleep, a warm bundle was tucked into the crook of her arm. Enchanted, she touched the soft, tender cheek with her forefinger, breathing in the smell of his damp hair, smiling when he gave a little sneeze.

Dirk bent over her, making sure that she was comfortable and she reached out to rest her hand fleetingly against his face. He gripped it in his own, turning it gently and placing a kiss in the palm. Then nothing could hold her back from slumber, and she sank beneath it, as into a great, soft, feather mattress.

CHAPTER 17

An hour or so after the birth of her baby, Roxanna was awakened by Dirk's presence in the cabin and by a shuffling outside the door. He opened it at the tentative knock, and she heard a hurried, muttered conflab. He came back to her with a grin.

'Do you feel well enough to receive some visitors?' he asked.

Still dazed with sleep, she yawned, stretched and demanded her hair-brush and a mirror. Sitting up she tugged at the tangles until her hair was tidy, and then settled back against the lace-frilled pillows. Some dozen or so of her companions on the campaign came sliding in. Grinning, half-embarrassed, weapons held tight to stop them clanking, they advanced towards the centre of the floor. Men, whom she had seen behaving like bloodthirsty madmen in the din of battle, now had an unaccustomed gentleness across their villainous faces as they tiptoed and whispered. Their spokesman, a colossal broken-nosed rascal, his black beard plaited into a score of tiny braids, was nudged forward by his matelots.

He crept to the bedside on splayed bare feet, and cleared his throat, twisting his shapeless hat in his big, leathery hands. 'With yer leave, Ma'am,' he began showing yellow-brown teeth in a smirk. 'Me an' the lads would like to offer ye our congratulations on having such a bonny son. Ain't that so, boys?'

Unshaven faces earnest, shaggy heads nodding in agreement, they winked and glared, smiling with such pride on Roxanna and her infant it was almost as if they were responsible. 'Aye, that's the lay o' it, Jude!' they rumbled.

Jude, obviously uneasy in this rôle he had been nominated to play, scratched about under the scarf covering his greasy, unkept locks. His companions frowned and gazed solemnly, reprovingly, at him. He turned red, scowled, fingered his beard and then leaned over Roxanna and spoke in a hoarse undertone.

'Ye proved yerself a real matelot on the march, and the lads'll never forget 'ow ye nursed 'em. We'd like ter give yer this, fer the little 'un!' He produced a heavy, solid silver cup, encrusted with precious stones all round the rim. It flashed, sending out dazzling rays of colour in the late afternoon sunlight, as he dumped it into her lap. Roxanna was deeply touched. She gave them a radiant smile, and held out the baby for Jude to see. He chortled and thrust a dirt-seamed finger at the infant's tightly closed fist. At once the small fingers opened and then curled about his massive one. Jude beamed delightedly at his cronies.

'Look 'ee 'ere. See 'ow the little devil grips me!' he bellowed, startling the child, who set up an infuriated screaming which scared Jude far more than a battery of Spanish gunfire. He backed away, pulling at his bulbous nose, and apologizing profusely to Roxanna.

During all this, Dirk, had remained standing, steadying himself against the galleon's slow roll, a twitch of a smile on his full lips. Now, he took the child and held him to his shoulder, his narrow hands rubbing the small back in long, soothing strokes. The cries stopped, and the interested buccaneers crowded round till Roxanna was afraid that they might breathe too freely on her son and contaminate him. Dirk produced several flagons of rum and sent them off to 'wet' the baby's head.

For two days the child yelled hungrily and Dirk paced the cabin, rocking him. He handled him with such confidence that Roxanna had a sudden suspicious pang, wondering if it was the first time he had been a father.

On the morning of the third day, she awoke to find her breasts hard and swollen and then the child fed, suckling noisily, the milk dribbling from the corners of his greedy mouth. He roared instant protest at being interrupted when she held him up and patted his back until he belched, bringing up a curdled mouthful.

Dirk came in when he had sucked himself into a stupor, bloated with milk. He dropped into a chair by the bed, his jackbooted feet thrust out and shouted with laughter at the baby's engorged expression.

'Strewth! If he don't look like a paunchy old man who has filled his guts with port and chicken pie! Greedy little rascal! Now, perhaps, we'll get some sleep tonight!'

Next day Dirk strode in with a frown drawing his black brows together. 'Have you any more clothes for the babe? Every time I lift him he's soaked!'

Roxanna stirred crossly. 'Alack!' she said. 'There are garments aplenty in my boxes at Cayona!'

'Well, that is of little use to us now!' Dirk was curt and Roxanna sat up, flinging back the clothes. She stood up, her legs like string, feeling the birth-blood flow from her, warm and sticky, on to the pad of linen between her thighs.

'What the devil are you about!' Dirk barked, his arm going round her. She shrugged off his help.

'Someone has to do the damned washing.'

In the great cabin there was chaos. Diapers soaked in a bucket, a sordid bundle of sheets, stained from the birth, on the floor.

'Hell and Furies!' She exclaimed, weakness making her fractious. She pushed up her sleeves and set to work. Shortly, all was ready to be spread on the decks to dry. With her head spinning, Roxanna went back to bed.

The infant did not stir until, at last, Roxanna woke him herself to relieve the painful surging pressure in her breasts. Wafer strolled in as she was feeding him. 'Damn me!' he remarked with evident satisfaction that things were going so well. 'He's in the land of plenty!'

That evening when Dirk came to bed she sat up, her eyes anxious.

'Are you pleased with him, Dirk?'

His stare was sharp and calculating. 'Of course I am, sweetheart. He is a wonderful babe.' Roxanna was tense and edgy. Suddenly the words burst out:

'Then why don't you give him your name?'

He tossed her a quick, impatient glance. 'Marry you, d'you mean? You know that I can't.'

'Why?' She was on her knees on the bed, the tears making her green eyes bright, a flush beginning to spread up from her throat to her cheeks. He put out his hands and gently pushed her back against the pillows.

'Darling, don't excite yourself! You will spoil the milk and give our young man the colic!'

'I don't care!' Savagely she knocked

his hand aside, wanting to slap his face. But she remembered the violence of his temper and restrained the impulse. His cool exterior infuriated her. 'It seems to matter not a jot to you that he is a bastard!' she accused, bitterly.

'Indeed it does!' His eyes flashed and hardened under the slur. 'Even so, I would not make an unwise match just to legitimize him. My father married my mother for that reason. They were never happy. I shall always remember their bitter quarrels because of the wide gulf between them. I would not have that happen to us.'

'But your mother was an indentured servant!' Roxanna felt that there was a world of difference between that and her own case.

'And your forebears were highly respected merchants,' Dirk repeated calmly and deliberately. 'I know. We have been through all this before. They are of fine stock, I doubt not, but the fact remains that the sons of noble houses do not marry the daughters of traders, no matter how wealthy. It would not work, Roxanna, and we should end by hating one another. I hope to return to England some

306

day and, if I have enough money, redeem my property and title. Then I shall make a suitable marriage.'

Roxanna's face crumpled. 'Don't you love me?' she asked, shaking her head in denial at the same time.

'Sweetheart, do you take me for an utter knave?' His eyes were soft, his smile sad, almost pleading. 'Yes, I do love you, in my own fashion. Do not fret, I shall look after you and the lad.' More than that he would not promise her.

When they dropped anchor in Cayona harbour, Roxanna was in a ferment of impatience. She had nothing to wear, and could not go ashore until either Lucy came with clothes or Dirk went to fetch them. Wafer was alarmed at her sudden fits of temper, gloomily predicting loss of milk and a fever. She was extremely irritable, tears flowing at the slightest reprimand or cross glance from Dirk. Hardly had they been in port an hour, when Lucy came pelting excitedly into the cabin, and both women began to cry as they embraced joyfully.

'Oh, Ma'am, I never thought to see you alive again!' Lucy's round, freckled face glowed with happiness. 'When the news came from Nigger Bay that you had disappeared, I gave you up as lost!'

Roxanna smiled broadly. Lucy was still the same, a deal plumper perhaps, but brimming over with humour, devotion and practical common-sense. 'You surely realized that I would never let Dirk escape me so easily?'

'Lud!' Lucy flung up her hands in mock astonishment. 'Are you still besotted with that wretch?'

Roxanna's grin deepened as she beckoned Lucy to where the improvised crib stood. Amazement registered on her former maid's face. Roxanna stood back, watching her with amusement. Lucy threw her a quick, congratulatory glance. Her voice sank to a delighted whisper.

'Oh, the dear little lamb! Is it a boy?' At the affirmative nod she added: 'And 'tis the very spitting image of the father too!'

She stared, eyes growing round, as Roxanna swiftly told her about the birth less than a week before, and was at once all solicitious concern, taking charge of the situation. They discussed what she should fetch for both Roxanna and the baby to wear.

'And you, Lucy?' Roxanna at last paused long enough to ask. 'How fare you with Dan? Is he kind?'

Lucy's eyes misted. 'Oh, Ma'am, he is a good man and we are very content. The inn flourishes. I keep a full pantry and we are renowned for our food. We, too, have a son! He was born just ten months after we were wed, so we wasted little time.'

Lucy looked prosperous enough in a gown of blue cotton, simple but well cut. She was so immaculate that Roxanna wondered how she managed keeping a tavern in dissolute, roistering Cayona.

'D'you rent rooms to whores?' she inquired, while Lucy was preparing to return ashore.

She shook her brown curls vigorously. 'Nay, that I do not! I leave such like traffic to that slut, Sarah Frisky. If a gentleman wishes to have supper with a lady in a private room, well, that is no concern of mine, but ours is a respectable house and all know it!'

Lucy departed, ticking off the items on her fingers, and before very long Roxanna was standing in a clean shift, with the well remembered crispness of starched petticoats about her legs. Lucy dropped the rustling taffeta underskirt over her head and eased it into place, then the gown followed. Roxanna pushed her arms into the huge, puffed sleeves and squirmed to settle the bodice about her waist. Lucy strained on the busk-laces.

'Oh, Lucy...lace me tighter! You've got to get the waist to meet!' Roxanna's voice was shrill with disappointment. The struggle to close the gap told her plainly that her measurements had increased. The breath left her with a rush as Lucy heaved once again, her knee braced against the small of Roxanna's back.

The gown was a deep turquoise brocade with silver lace frilled in the low bodice and edging the sleeves. Tiny black bows trimmed the front and the wide skirt was caught up at the back to display a black satin lining and lemon underskirt. She painted her face and wetted a black paper rose patch, sticking it at the corner of her mouth. Then, for the first time in over a year, Lucy worked on her hair; again brushed the coppery locks lovingly into a high scroll on the crown, rolling the sides into heavy ringlets. Roxanna hung her latest gift from Dirk in her lobes; a pair of huge opal and diamond ear-drops.

' 'Uds Lud"' she exclaimed in delighted satisfaction. 'I had quite forgot what I really looked like!' Impulsively she leaned forward to plant a kiss on Lucy's cheek. 'Dear friend, thank you for caring for my effects all these months. There is much I must beg you to help me with now. Firstly, the christening which must be done at once!'

Lucy gave a nod. Both women knew that an unbaptized infant might be looked on by a witch and changed into a Gabble Hound to hunt forever the devil whose fault it was that he had not been christened! Roxanna did not for a moment doubt that witches abounded in the Indies as much as in England. She had already taken the precaution of hanging a silver chain with an amber pendant about his neck to prevent the fairies from stealing him. She informed Lucy that Dirk was going to buy a plantation and that she would live with him. Her eyes hardened, deeply unhappy, when she added that he had no intention of marrying her.

At length, she was ready to show herself on deck. Lucy followed behind, carrying the baby as proudly as if he were her own, his long gown hanging nearly to the floor, every tiny stitch and embroidered embellishment worked lovingly by Nan Dob's skilful fingers.

Henri Dubois, who had come aboard to bid them welcome, made Roxanna a deep bow, his eyes frankly admiring. He clucked over the baby, and pressed a silver piece into the small hand. She was delighted, fully expecting everyone to agree with her that this was the most wonderful child ever born. He placed his comfortable establishment at their disposal for as long as they wished and by nightfall they were installed at Lime Close.

The next day Roxanna sought out a carpenter and ordered a cradle to be made. She spent a good hour with him discussing the carving which was to decorate it, wanting the date of his birth and letter C to ornament the hooded head. The initial stood for Charles which was what she had decided to call him, and also for Courtney which she still fervently hoped that he would one day bear.

The church in which Lucy and Dan had been married was chosen for the christening and they drove there in the Dubois coach, ornate with blue and red enamel. Lucy, who had offered to stand as godmother, carried the infant on a lace-edged satin cushion, giving a piece of bread and cheese to a very filthy beggar who squatted on his heels at the porch; this gift was sure to bring the baby good fortune. Roxanna could not prevent the hot blush from staining her cheeks when the parson asked her what the child was to be named. She was determined that he should not carry the hated name of Raynal, and so put on a brazen face and curtly informed him that he was to be named Charles John. The first was for the King, the second for Johnny Comry.

The christening party, a large one, was held at Lucy's tavern. Dubois and Lucy invited friends, some of the officers of the *Hopewell* attended, including Jeremy and Lionel Wafer, who had acted as godfather. Presents were many and costly, and included the traditional apostle spoons, silver mugs, bowls and porringers. Roxanna, conscious that this was an important occasion in her life, wore her finest gown. Her beauty at once singled her out for attention both from old acquaintances and the men who were meeting her for the first time.

She was well aware that this was causing

a spiteful flutter among the women; they retaliated by little scornful smiles which indicated that they were well informed as to her position as Dirk's mistress and that her child, for all his fine christening, was illegitimate.

When Charles was a fortnight old, Dirk and Roxanna resumed their passionate relationship. More enamoured of him than ever, her love was accentuated by his gentleness to her during the birth and his interest in the baby, when she had half expected him to be an indifferent father. It was thrilling to be slender again and she had never felt more buoyant and confident. Dirk had no difficulty in selling his ship, her reputation as a fast and lucky frigate sent him many eager buyers. After this, he spent every available minute in hunting for a suitable plantation. Roxanna passed a good deal of time in Lucy's homely kitchen. She told her all about her travels, and Lucy would pause in astonishment in the middle of some task, the expressions chasing over her honest, flexible face, as she registered horror, alarm and amazement.

Lucy was constantly urging Roxanna to find a wet-nurse for the baby, warning her that she would spoil her figure and that in any case no lady of quality gave suck to her own child. Roxanna flatly refused. Charles was hers and she would have no other woman's milk nourish him, her deepest instincts satisfied to hold him close while his tiny, hungry mouth groped for her breast. She was as jealously possessive of him as she was of Dirk; they both meant more to her than anything on earth.

She had a native girl to help look after the baby but she missed Lucy sorely, and was glad when she recommended another English girl to act as her personal maid and really take charge of the nursery management.

Polly Monk was a fat, motherly, hard-working woman and Roxanna at once took to her merry blue eyes, fair hair and the London twang in her voice which brought home so poignantly near.

One evening Dirk returned to Lime Close, jubilant at having completed the negotiations for a house and land. Roxanna listened to him talking with Dubois far into the night, while the fireflies swarmed in the darkness beyond the veranda and the hot, tropical stars twinkled and flashed.

She had never seen him so moved and excited and felt a prick of jealousy against this land which he already seemed to love more than her. But she scolded herself for being petty and early next morning, when she had fed the baby, she went out with him to view their new home.

She put on her dark green velvet riding-habit, the coat dashingly cut just like a man's. Leather boots encased her feet and she wore a wide-brimmed hat with a great bunch of emerald feathers, an almost exact replica of Dirk's. An ebony, widely-smiling negro was holding two great bay horses for them as they came down the white stone steps into the fresh dawn air.

Dirk helped her to mount and swung up onto the stallion. The beast was high-spirited and the spurs caused him to rear and plunge, lashing out with vicious hoofs so that the groom dodged out of the way. Dirk's voice soon quietened him. He sat this mount with all the graceful ease inherited from generations of horsemen and a father who had ridden in Prince Rupert's cavalry during the Civil War.

The mounts cantered along a rough,

rutted track, through fields of sugar-cane and mango plantations where slaves were already at work, a monotonous droning song rising as they swung their tools in rhythmic beat. As the sun climbed higher the steam spiralled from the dewy grass and dripping branches, while on either side innumerable bird-life rustled the branches of the sapodilla trees.

Dirk drew reign at a pair of wide gates, much in need of a coat of paint and creaking on their hinges. The drive was flanked by trees and blossoms spread in unchecked abundance, the garden weedy and overgrown. The house was big, rambling and neglected.

The workmen, engaged to put it in good repair, had not yet arrived and Roxanna followed Dirk through the echoing, dusty rooms.

'Why, darling...' her eyes were shining excitedly, and her voice rang through the empty hall-way, ' 'tis a fine house!'

She rushed from one room to another, chattering, questioning, and then immediately talking on without waiting for an answer. Dirk watched her and listened, with a slow, quiet smile.

At the back was a large kitchen with a

317

dairy, outbuildings and a kitchen garden. Beyond this, and some distance from the house, lay a walled enclosure to which he took her, lifting the solid iron bar which closed the high, spike-topped gate, holding it open for her to pass inside. Something in his eyes chilled her, although the day was growing increasingly hot. She found herself in a stockade with squalid hutments built against the stone wall. The place was desolate, as if the misery suffered there still clung to the stones. Looking up to make some remark to Dirk, she was shocked into silence by his expression as he stared at the stout whipping-post set in the sun-baked earth.

' 'Tis the first time in years I have entered a barracoon.' His voice was low and harsh, she had never seen his face so bleak.

It was only too easy to picture Dirk lashed by his wrists to the crossbar, his back raw from shoulders to waist, while searing anger and bitterness ate into his soul. He turned on his heel and walked off, back to the house. Roxanna followed him slowly, appreciating his desire for solitude.

CHAPTER 18

In a month they moved into the house at Kingsland plantation. For Roxanna the weeks had been intensely busy and satisfying. With the wise aid of Lucy, she consulted merchants, proving unnervingly canny as she haggled with them for carpets, curtains and furniture. These crafty gentlemen began to watch out for her little retinue. She would step from her coach with a hefty bodyguard, the herculean Jude who had elected to remain with Dirk until some more profitable venture presented itself. The sight of the massive buccaneer striding along at her side, his great broadsword, so heavy that a normal man could hardly lift it, swinging at his side, his formidable whiskers braided with scarlet ribbon, was enough to insure that the vendors reserved their sharp practices for some other customer.

They discovered that, although so dainty and always dressed in an extravagant height of fashion, she was hard and inflexible and could drive a very shrewd bargain indeed. But they liked her, and any particularly fine piece was now always put aside for the inspection of Dirk Courtney's wench. In the purchase of slaves she proved to possess an unerring knack for picking out the weaklings, doctored up by the wily traders. She prodded the black muscles, examined their teeth, eyes and hair and soon Dirk had as healthy a bunch of brawny negroes as any in Cayona. But, though she was spoken of with respect in the taverns and slave-mart, she found herself ostracized by the élite. None of the planter's wives, French or English, came to call on her, particularly when the news leaked out that she had been delivered of her baby by Doctor Wafer and not by a midwife. This tasty scrap of gossip was mouthed behind many a fluttering fan, with a rolling heavenwards of scandalized eyes and brows.

Roxanna shrugged her shapely shoulders, pretending not to care, but inside she was deeply hurt. Dirk's confidence in her abilities, however, compensated her for her neighbours' lack of charity. She was deeply gratified when they stood in their home on the first evening and she saw the growing pleasure on his face.

The furniture was a mixture of delicate French design and the heavier more ornate, Spanish. Roxanna was especially satisfied with their bedroom. Remembering Lucy's boudoir, she had copied the silk ˙ wall-hangings and gilt mirrors, while the bed predominated. It was very wide and extra long to accommodate Dirk's height, and the head and posts were heavily decorated with gold leaf and cupids carved in sandalwood. Roxanna had chosen green brocade for the curtains and canopy, held back by silver swags with massive tassels. As a coverlet she used the jaguar rug from the *Hopewell,* over a bedspread of amber-coloured satin, knowing well that these shades set off her warm colouring and bronze-red hair.

Her days were happy and fully occupied. Although she was not Dirk's wife, she performed the duties of one and the responsibility of maintaining the household rested upon her. With Lucy's help and the advice of Polly, she soon managed with an ever-growing confidence. She set up a still-room which, as the days lengthened into weeks, gradually became lined with jars of preserves, pickles and a good supply of medicines and ointments. She wanted to send home for herbs, but was ashamed that they should know how she lived.

Having received no answering letter from her family, she assumed that Captain Brownrigg had returned to England and told them of her liaison with Dirk. There had been a communication from Lydia awaiting her at Lucy's tavern. She wrote that she had given birth to a daughter and was living in a fine house in the village of Chelsea, just outside London.

Contentment wrapped Roxanna in a dreamy cloud. Dirk worked hard on his land, together with the dozen white slaves transported from France and twice as many blacks. He promised them just treatment and had made their quarters as comfortable as possible in so short a time.

In the evenings, Roxanna made sure that the atmosphere was relaxed and Dirk lounged indolently in a hammock on the veranda, a glass in his hand, watching her as she played the spinet. Sometimes they invited their old friends in for cards and a meal. Lionel Wafer was a frequent caller, as much to see his godson as to talk to the parents. Roxanna's nineteenth birthday passed during October and she began to make plans for Christmas.

Late one afternoon she was in the nursery playing with Charles. He was just beginning to crawl and she pretended to chase him so that he went off at speed on chubby hands and dimpled knees, chuckling with delight. She sat on the floor in a flurry of stiff silk skirts, and snatched the fat brown infant into her arms, where he instantly grabbed at her pearls. Roxanna kissed the back of his neck. His little body carried the smell of warmth and milk and she adored him. He had grown into a very pretty child, almost unbelievably like Dirk, with large grey eyes and a thick mop of black curls. He was like him in temperament too, strong and demanding, with a will and temper. They all spoiled him outrageously and Polly was his devoted doormat.

Roxanna recalled a score of rhymes and songs from nursery days at home, and loved singing them to him.

When he heard her at these games, Dirk remarked that she enjoyed them as much as the baby. Every afternoon she romped with him until it was time for his last feed, and it was the hour to which she looked forward most of all.

She kissed each tiny finger and gently bit off the nails which were growing too long. During the first year of his life, scissors were never allowed near them, otherwise he would grow up light-fingered.

Dirk came in quietly and stood watching them from the doorway, his eyes morose and pensive.

She looked up over the little downy head and saw him. Her face broke into a broad smile of welcome, 'Hello, darling! Marry! How handsome you are looking!'

He was wearing a new coat of claret velvet, with silver buttons all down the front and at the hip-high side vents. It was open, showing the embroidered yellow silk waistcoat beneath and the full breeches gartered at the knee. The coat reached halfway down his thigh and fitted his body and waist closely, the pockets set low and garnished with more sparkling buttons. Polly had made a good job of his white cambric shirt and the lace-edged steenkirk at his throat. He had on red silk stockings and black shoes with silver buckles. Roxanna was glad that he had never adopted the current fashion for wearing a huge periwig, when his own locks would have been cropped.

One of her keenest pleasures was to run her hands through his long black hair.

He came over to kiss her, dropping on his heels and holding out a finger for the baby to grip. 'And how is my young man today?'

'He can stand!' Roxanna declared, proudly. She set Charles on his feet, placing the small hands on a low stool. He lurched for an uncertain moment, jigging a little, his diaper slipping down, then his legs buckled suddenly under his weight and he collapsed. Dirk and Roxanna laughed and he clapped plump hands and gave them a toothless beam. She picked him up and pulled open the front of her bodice; he began to suckle noisily, his tiny, purposeful fingers clutching at the lace on her dress. Dirk sat on the floor beside her to watch him. He loved the child so much that Roxanna rejoiced, never guessing that he could be so tender.

At last, the baby fell asleep, the nipple slipping from his pink, wet mouth, his lashes in dark crescents on his flushed cheeks. Roxanna laid him in the cradle, pulling the net across to keep off the flies and they went softly from the nursery.

In the hall she anxiously enquired the

325

time. Dirk pulled out his jewelled pocket-watch and consulted its enamelled face. She puffed out her cheeks in alarm, 'Hell and Furies! I must hurry!'

They were invited to a gathering at Henri Dubois' that evening and Roxanna was more than a little nervous, this being the first occasion on which she had been called upon to meet the social set of Cayona. Determined either to make them like her or at least to give them something to gossip about, she had spent hours closeted with her French tailor and between them they concocted a gown. It was a bomb-shell of a dress, calculated to make the men stare and the women hate her. Dirk had not yet seen it and she wondered if he would approve.

He followed her into the bedroom. She noticed that certain darkening of his eyes which she had learned to recognize. She went across to the dressing-room, her toes curling luxuriantly in the thick, white fur rug and she left the door open so that she might chat to him while she bathed. But though she kept up a light banter, a tremor was beginning to run through her body, for when he desired her his passion was swift and urgent, accepting no refusal or delay.

Roxanna had learned many tricks with which to excite him, shamelessly pandering to the strong sensuality of his nature.

Now she walked slowly towards him, her négligé clinging damply to her lithe, slender limbs and the high, coraline-tipped breasts. He rose and took her into his arms. A cold thrill stiffened her spine, she caught her breath in almost painful delight, eyes half-closed and langourous.

'Dirk,' she whispered. 'Darling, I love you so much that it hurts!'

He bent to kiss her and for a long moment they stood, bodies locked close together, then he took his mouth from hers and swung her up with an arm under her knees.

'We shall be late for the party!' she reminded, in half-hearted protest.

'Damn the party!' he said.

Roxanna's gown caused every bit of the sensation she had hoped. It was of black velvet with a full skirt and sweeping train over a silver-lustre petticoat, liberally spangled with sequins. The bodice had been cunningly boned so that it appeared to remain in place without any visible means of support, the sleeves being a mere froth of tiffany. Her black gloves fitted like a second skin to well above the elbow and she sweated profusely under them. Both Polly and Hannah, a newly-engaged maid, had fussed over her hair and it glittered like copper, in complete contrast to the sombre gown.

She was nervous as she entered on Dirk's arm. It was useless to chide herself and remember that she had faced Spanish musketeers in battle; she was terrified of the starchy, sour-faced dames and their sedate daughters who sat primly on the edge of Dubois' walnut chairs and looked her over critically. Overwhelmed with panic, she was hardly aware that she was walking forward and being introduced. Then, she caught Lionel Wafer's eye and her chin lifted defiantly, while he gave her an approving nod

After that she felt better and even began to enjoy the stir which she knew her appearance was causing. Wafer came to bow over her hand.

'Madam, you look ravishing!' he murmured, and his dark eyes went down over her gown. 'But confound it, how the devil does it stay up?'

She coloured and then burst in to such

a hearty peal of laughter that even more eyes became focussed on her. He held out his arm and she rested her fingers on it. She spoke to him from the corner of her mouth as they passed a particularly dowdy and disapproving group of ladies.

' 'Tis so long since a man made one of 'em an improper suggestion they've quite forgot what it is like!'

The supper, as usual, was superlative and Roxanna wished that she could engage the services of Dubois' cook. It was a very different gathering from the one when she had first sat there. She knew that Dubois still entertained the buccaneers and almost wished she was in their company instead of this hypocritical, mealy-mouthed assembly.

'My dear,' her host murmured behind his hand, 'talk to the lad on your right. He is newly come from England, visiting his uncle, and he has been pestering me to introduce you!'

She had hardly registered the existence of the person he indicated, having dismissed him as no one of importance and certainly not handsome. Now she turned and her eyes met large hazel ones in a smooth boyish face which was full of frank admiration. Unable to resist such an obvious conquest, she arched her brows and leaned a little closer so that a warm wave of perfume floated up to him. As they conversed, and he lost some of his shyness, she discovered that she liked him. He told her his name was James Cowper and that he was the son of a wealthy squire from Sussex. He had a pleasant voice with a slight, not unattractive, impediment. She could not stop herself from teasing him a little, tapping him flirtatiously on the arm with her closed fan to stress a point. Then she noticed that Dirk was in deep conversation with a young daughter of the one of his planter cronies.

The girl was looking up at him with round eyes, very impressed, and Roxanna could feel her jealous temper rising. She wanted to drive her dinner knife into her. 'Surely,' she thought agitatedly, 'he can have no interest in that insipid-looking ninny!' But she was worried, as she always was when he was with other women. It was not entirely coincidental that all of her maidservants were homely. She was leaving nothing to chance.

Later, they adjourned to the drawing-room where the men played cards, smiling with smug tolerance as the ladies knotted into little groups discussing pregnancies, miscarriages, births and other women with that avidity of females the world over. None of them spoke to Roxanna. She was relieved when, with a bow, Dirk excused himself from the entranced damsel and went off into a corner with Dubois to talk business. Roxanna treated her rival to a raging glare which should have blasted her where she stood and was enormously pleased to see her go red and drop her eyes.

She sulked all the way home in the neat little coach that Dirk had bought. When they reached the house she flounced into the bedroom, furiously slamming the door. Dirk came in slowly.

'Why are you in such an almighty sweat?' he asked at last, sitting on the bed to kick off his shoes and peel down his hose. 'I take you out for the evening and you behave like a petulant brat!'

'There is nothing wrong with me at all!' she shouted, angrily feeling the pull of his strong charm, almost wishing that he were ugly so that no other woman would want him. She slid an opal bracelet from her slender wrist and began to work off her gloves, pouting slightly.

'Come now, sweetheart...' He ran his lips across the nape of her neck and her scalp prickled, every sense in her body responding. But she jerked pettishly away.

He shrugged and continued to undress. Roxanna swung round on the stool, tugging at the pins holding up her hair.

'I saw you tonight, playing the gallant to that simpering little milksop!' she accused, her anger mounting as she tore at the gown which she had worn with such eager anticipation. 'I wanted to strangle her, the mincing bitch!'

'Darling, what a God-damned bother about nothing!' he remonstrated, already lying in bed, beginning to search for the marker in the book he had been reading. 'I have no mind to seduce her.'

'Well, I have a fancy she damned well wants you to!' She twisted the rings on her slim fingers, pulling them off and slamming them down on the dressing-table. Hannah must have gone to bed long before; she backed towards Dirk so that he could unfasten her busk-laces.

'I do business with her father,' he replied casually. 'Barbara was but being civil. She wants me to go and play cards at their house!'

'Cards!' she mouthed jeeringly, tossing off the remainder of her garments and throwing her rose nightgown over her head so that she was briefly enveloped in the scented, flimsy folds, before she wriggled it into place. 'There'd be another game she would want to play, I'll warrant!'

Sometimes Dirk rode out in the evenings giving her no explanation. She had been afraid to question him. Now her anger made her incautious.

'Is that where you go, sometimes, to visit her?' she asked in a brittle voice.

He looked up sharply. 'No, it is not! Where I go, and what I do, is none of your concern!' At her stifled sob he suddenly threw away his book and stretched out an arm to her across the quilt. 'Come here to me, sweeting! Do not let us quarrel tonight!'

Roxanna's resentment melted. She never remained sulky for long. A word or a touch from him could turn her from a flaming termagant into all melting, sighing womanhood. His moods were much more difficult to gauge. On occasions, his temper blazed and crackled, burning out swiftly,

333

while at other times he withdrew into himself, taciturn and cross-grained for days.

They celebrated Christmas in traditional style, although the weather was thunderously humid, preceding the January rains. Roxanna did her utmost to make it a real festival, such as she had always known, and worked with Lucy and Polly for weeks beforehand in preparation.

She sweated in the kitchen, unwilling to trust the preparation of the food to the vagrancies of their genial, but lackadaisical, cook. At the dinner, to which all their friends were invited, she served plum porridge, a kind of soup made of beef-stock, raisins and currants, spices, sugar, a quart of sack and another of claret. The table groaned under a turkey-pie, an elaborately garnished boar's head, oysters, crab and the vegetables fried in butter. Liberal quantities of rum-punch, madeira and highly intoxicating home-brewed brandies soon had the guests, mostly buccaneer captains, traders and their doxies, stamping and roaring choruses, drinking toasts to their hostess.

For three days the house was in an uproar, as the riotous guests stayed on. Music was provided by a fiddler and a piper, and they danced, played cards, made love and drank continually. More than once Roxanna's now famous temper flashed, particularly when a pair of corsairs started to fight with knives all over her best carpet, not only slashing themselves severely, but smashing furniture and spattering her costly curtains with their blood.

Roxanna stood over them, skirts furiously swinging, brandishing Dirk's pistol and threatening to shoot them if they did not pay in full measure for the damage they had done to her property! But even this episode ended in a gale of hilarity and, when the last of them departed, swearing eternal loyalty, she was worn out but very happy. She knew that Dirk, who had never known any celebrating during his bleak childhood days had been well pleased.

CHAPTER 19

In January Roxanna sailed for Jamaica. For months, loath to leave Dirk, she had put off the journey which she knew she must make. She had corresponded frequently with Pieter Van Houel. His letters were reassuring and she felt that she could trust him and leave the management of her affairs in his hands. She was prompted to go by the need for money: Dirk wanted to expand his property to grow sugar, and for the initial outlay, they needed more capital. Roxanna's motives were certainly not philanthropic, she had a sneaking hope that he would marry her out of gratitude.

Accompanied by Polly, Hannah, the baby and a gaggle of nurses and servants, Roxanna boarded a vessel which was going to Port Royal. She would have liked to have taken Jude as a bodyguard, but had to be contented with Will Mitchell, a muscular young house-servant. Dirk arranged for Jim Rackham to cruise in the vessel's vicinity during the passage, the guns of his frigate primed to defend them against any likely attack.

Port Royal was the most important harbour in the British zone of the West Indies. Captured from the Spanish in the early 1650s, it was wicked, shabby and opulent; corrupt throughout, from the governing bodies to the thieves and pimps who thronged the busy wharves. At one time the refuge of buccaneers, it was now taboo owing to change of policy on the part of the English heads of state, who were striving for a peaceful settlement with Spain. Denied the exchange of stolen goods, once brought in by the Brethren, it now depended more and more on the wealth of the planters.

It had a bustling and very thriving market, where a continual stream of slaves passed under the hammer, brought in almost weekly from the Gold Coast of Africa. This was one of the most lucrative businesses in the whole of Jamaica; this trade in human beings, which were in ever increasing demands as the plantations spread.

As the merchantman entered the narrow strait, which was the only entrance to the long harbour, Rackham's gunners gave them a farewell salute and veered off. The Raynal estate, known as Dean Hill, was situated some distance beyond the port. Van Houel expected Roxanna and there was a coach waiting for them on the quay. Quickly, the grizzling baby, the chattering, complaining maidservants and numerous pieces of baggage were packed into the iron-wheeled carriage and they jolted off along the rutted road. Roxanna craned eagerly from the leather-curtained windows, wondering if they were crossing her land. At last they turned into a drive, flanked by the shady palms. Pieter Van Houel came from his office on the ground floor of the imposing white house to greet her.

She at once took a liking to this sturdy, sensible Dutchman. He was around thirty, a widower of some five years, with a square reddish face, shrewd, very pale hazel eyes, and straight brown hair. His pleasure at seeing her seemed perfectly genuine, and he had her conducted to the apartment which had been made ready, so that she might rest and wash away the dust of the journey. There was no reminder of Raynal in these cool, well-furnished rooms and Roxanna found it impossible to believe that he had ever dwelt there. She saw that the fretful Charles was installed in his crib and then bathed and changed into a green foulard gown, very simple and trimmed with white; she was in a mood to get down to business and no nonsense.

That evening, over supper, Van Houel told her how her affairs stood. He had been a faithful partner; the plantation had continued to prosper after Raynal's death and her share had mounted. After they had eaten, he took her to his office and there held up the branched candlesticks, so that she might look through the methodically neat ledgers.

'What then am I worth, in hard cash?' she asked bluntly, unable to make sense of the rows of figures. Van Houel smiled. His new partner had been something of a shock; he had not expected this beautiful young woman. Her face was bent over the pages, absorbed and intent; already he had been surprised by her astute questions, gathering that she was not a pretty, empty-headed creature, but someone who possessed a shrewd wit.

'You are a very wealthy woman,' he said. 'I could sell your share easily for twelve thousand pounds.'

Roxanna flung him a sharp look and delighted amazement broke over her face. Van Houel ran a broad forefinger along the inked numbers.

'See here, Ma'am. The plantation comprises five hundred acres and the mansion is a fine one, well-equipped, covering a goodly area. We have a boiling-house, still-house and a curing house as well as stables, a smith's forge and barns in which to lay provisions of corn and bonavist.'

Roxanna's respect for his planning and foresight deepened with every passing second.

'There are hutments for the negroes and Indian slaves,' he went on. 'And we have ninety-six blacks and their children, besides twenty-eight whites, forty-five grazing cattle, eight milking cows, a dozen horses and as many mares!'

Quickly Roxanna swallowed her astonishment and plunged into an animated discussion with him on the finer points of running an estate of this size. The night grew late and neither of them were aware of it, as, by the light of the spluttering candles, they pored over the accounts and figures and a large map of their land. Van Houel was pleased that she should show such acumen, as he had rather feared that she would be a liability. He promised to take her down to the sugar-mill and refinery first thing in the morning.

When at last she did seek her bed, she could not sleep. The thought of her wealth was like a heady wine. She was sure that Dirk would marry her now, if only to fulfil his own ambitions. The pride of ownership was strong in her. This was her land, her house, even the bullfrogs, making the night hideous with their continual croaking were there in her piece of marsh. Dirk had never lived there, for he had escaped during the upheaval when Raynal transferred his household to this more promising island. It would hold no unpleasant memories for him.

Suddenly she sat bolt upright, remembering that Dirk was branded as a buccaneer and the authorities would be on the lookout to catch him. She determined to take up the point with Van Houel in the morning, already placing a great deal of reliability on this plain-spoken, very systematic Hollander.

Roxanna discussed her problem with him over breakfast. 'I expect you have guessed that I am not alone in Cayona,' she began, finding herself unwilling to let him know that she was Dirk's mistress. Then her words came out in a rush: 'I am the leman of one of the buccaneers who interrupted my journey here. He killed Raynal!'

Van Houel said nothing for a moment, his expression thoughtful. In his eyes there was friendship, not the frank desire which

341

she was accustomed to see in almost every man. It gave her the same feeling that she had with Lionel Wafer, a warm, companiable sensation, which was very pleasant. He raised his coffee cup to his lips and took a sip of the hot, sweet liquid.

'I must admit I already know something of this. Captain Brownrigg informed me when he delivered your first letter.'

Roxanna relaxed as she told him how much she wanted to come back here to settle, and of the fears she had for Dirk's safety.

'Go and see Sir Harry Morgan,' was Van Houel's instant advice. 'If you are prepared to pay a high price, you might be able to buy a pardon for your lover. It may be a little difficult just now, because of that attack of Captain Sawkins' on Santa Maria. Unfortunately, it occurred during negotiations between England and Spain for the Treaty of Windsor. Now, every West Indian governor is alert to punish anyone connected with it, and an act has been passed by the Jamaican Assembly making it a felony for any British subject to serve under a foreign commission.'

Roxanna felt a cold sweat of dread

breaking out all over her. Even she could be apprehended and a noose fastened round her neck. She got to her feet and began to wander up and down, very worried, trailing the skirt of her green gown.

Van Houel also rose, picking up his light straw hat, twirling it easily. 'At the moment Sir Henry is executing any that he can lay hands on. Only two days ago Johnny Comry was hanged!'

At her completely stricken look he ran to take her arm, his eyes alarmed.

'Madam, you are unwell? Let me fetch you a drink!'

'Did you say Johnny Comry?' She was so shocked that she could only whisper the question.

He nodded. 'He was captured in Port Royal last week and tried at once.'

With sick horror Roxanna remembered the gallows near where they had docked. She had turned away in disgust when she'd seen the carrion-eaters resting on the crossarm, from which had swung several bodies in various stages of decomposition. One of them had been Johnny. Agony shot through her as she prayed that Johnny had died swiftly. Van Houel's voice seemed indistinct, and then her attention suddenly sharpened as he said:

'There was a woman apprehended with him, but she pleaded her belly.'

Roxanna came to life. She spun round on her high heels. 'Where will she be lodged?'

He lifted his shoulders in a shrug. 'I assume she will be in the prison. They will not hang her until she is delivered.'

Already half-way to the door, she shouted: 'I must go to her! Will you have me driven there?'

Horrified, he took a step towards her. 'But, my dear lady, you cannot possibly go! The jail is a most appalling place...'

She cut him short. 'I have been in many dreadful places Mr Van Houel. That girl is in dire need! Will you help me, or do I have to go alone?'

Below the Blue Mountains, Port Royal sprawled and sweltered in the morning sun. Van Houel's coach clattered through the market. The prison was beside the fort, both buildings relics of the Spanish conquest. Young Will Mitchell approached the guard at the heavily-studded outer door, exchanged a few words with him, and a purse which clinked invitingly, then went back to the coach to fetch Roxanna.

She wore a cloak over her dress, with the hood up so that she was muffled to the nose. The soldier was curious, but made no comment as he led her across a courtyard and into a dark office. The individual who rose from behind a trestle and came towards her was so villainous that her heart sank within her. From his belt jangled a great bunch of keys, while he swung a heavy bludgeon in his right hand.

He stared owlishly at her, and then flared off into little wheezing chuckles, 'Well, Ma'am, and what do you here? 'Tis no place for the gentry, by troth, unless you be in debt!'

Roxanna felt an almost uncontrollable contempt freezing her face. 'You have a prisoner here!' she rapped out. 'Kate Johnson by name. I want to see her. Are you the chief warder?'

'That's me, Ma'am. Tom Kneebone, at your service,' he grinned. 'So you want to see the pirate wench, eh? I doubt I can allow that.'

Roxanna gritted her teeth. 'I have garnish enough!'

His eyes shot open with surprise that

she knew the term. With a face alive with rapacity, he scooped up the gold coins she slapped down on the table.

Roxanna hurried after the turnkey detailed to escort her, following the torch that blazed in the gloomy passages, glad to have the strong muscles of Will close by her. As they penetrated deeper into the maw of the prison, a choking stench made her clap her handkerchief to her nostrils. It became more than just a stagnant smell; a tangible part of the darkness, foul and polluting. From all sides came noises, cries, shouts, shrill screams of laughter.

The warder stopped abruptly, jamming his flambeau into a sconce by an open door. For an instant as they stepped into the cell Roxanna could see nothing. Then her eyes grew accustomed to the gloom, only a tiny strip of daylight came in from the window set high up in the wall. The room, little more than a damp-swilled cellar, was packed with women.

Like a surge of muddy water, they crept about her, animosity in their sunken, hopeless eyes. With revulsion and growing pity Roxanna looked at them; young and old, white or coloured, she had never seen such despair on human faces. They stared, hostile, envious, hating her because she was beautiful and free. When she moved, her skirt stirred the mouldy rushes on the floor, where mice and rats, completely tame, nosed in the filth for scraps. The walls were green with slime and there was the continual drip of water, as a good deal of the jail was below sea-level. Rising above the coarse voices of the women came the fitful wailing of babies born, and often doomed to die, in this place.

As Roxanna slid the hood down about her shoulders, one of the white women detached herself from the rest and came up close, bringing with her a stench which turned Roxanna sick. She could not have been much over twenty, but looked years older. Her face and neck were covered with open running sores and her hair hung in oily snarls about a face which wore a weary, cynical expression. The bodice of her spotted, sweat-stained dress refused to meet across a stomach swollen with pregnancy and the shift, showing a neck and elbow, was grey with dirt. She paused in front of Roxanna, her mouth twisted into a wry, insulting smile, hands on her hips, and ran a scornful eye down over her fine clothes.

'What have we here?' Her accent was English. 'Some planter's whore!'

Roxanna felt Will's swift, threatening movement, but she put out a hand to restrain him. Her voice was unusually gentle as she asked; 'Please, can you lead me to Kate Johnson?'

The dull eyes brightened, the fetters on her wrists clinking as she held out a dirty hand. Roxanna placed a gold piece in it.

'She's over yonder,' the woman gave a laconic jerk of her head. 'You'll find she is in a sorry state.'

Roxanna started across the cell and the prisoner walked at her side, biting down on the coin to see if it were false before tucking it into her bodice.

'And who are you...?' she began, before being seized with a violent paroxysm of coughing, so distressing that Roxanna stopped short helplessly. The woman, purple in the face, thumped herself on the chest. She hawked out a gob of bloody phlegm on to the floor.

'My God!' Roxanna burst out indignantly. 'You are sick! You should never be in this damp hole!'

The wench gave a strangled laugh. 'I've

no money for garnish. If I had I could get better quarters.'

Impulsively, Roxanna turned to Will, pressing money into his hands, quickly telling him to take her to the taproom and buy her a drink, assuring him that she would be quite safe.

The prisoners of both sexes had freedom to roam within the confines of the prison. If they had the money they could drink themselves insensible. The women were usually able to earn enough for bribes, to obtain the necessities of life, by the simple expedient of prostitution. Roxanna was not afraid. She passed unmolested to the dark corner where she could distinguish a huddled form lying on a heap of straw. Beside Kate crouched what, at first glance, looked like a bundle of old rags, then a gnarled, grotesque face stared up at her, with eyes that glittered at the sight of her jewels.

A wheeze reached her ears. 'Mrs Trapes, the midwife, Ma'am.'

Roxanna's nostrils dilated at the rank breath blown into her face. She gave her a narrowed, warning stare and leaned over Kate.

It was so dark that she spun round in

exasperation to thunder at the midwife. 'Bring a glim, you useless old windbelly!'

Grumbling and complaining, Mrs Trapes shuffled off, returning to hold the rush-light high. Kate was almost unrecognizable. Roxanna drew in a deep breath, and then hissed it out through her teeth. 'Satan spare us! Is she dead?'

'Like to die. She's been in labour for two days, ever since they cast her man, not full term either, so I doubt she'll live, or the babe for that matter, if it's born at all!'

'What mean you, you filthy old bawd?' Roxanna rounded on her.

The midwife shrank back and her voice rose to a whine. 'Now, Ma'am, 'tisn't my fault! I've done all a body can! But the child is coming out arse first, and 'tis stuck fast and I can't move it. Look for yourself!'

She reached out a hand, the nails long and curving like claws, and twitched up Kate's ragged skirt. Roxanna stared down in growing dismay, and a sense of helplessness which released itself in a scathing outburst.

'Where's that damned quod cull?' She stormed to the door and shouted till the warder appeared, then rapped out smart orders, supplementing her demands with money while the other women gaped at her. Within a short while, Kate had been transferred to a small, private cell and Roxanna had paid for a pallet, sheets, candles, water and linen rags. The iron manacles were knocked from Kate's wrists and ankles. As the jailor left, she began to remove her cloak. She saw that the nurse had crept in.

'Get out!' she spat, busy making Kate as comfortable as possible. Mrs Trapes began to cringe and fawn.

'Madam, you'll have need of me. I'm the midwife. Let me stay, I need the money sorely.'

'You'd get a fee?' Roxanna was not really interested, and had little hope that this repugnant creature would be of much help to her, but she was suddenly too disgusted to argue. 'Oh, very well. But do as I tell you and no peery tricks!'

By the stronger light Roxanna studied Kate. She looked very ill indeed, her face had an alarming hue. Lying on her side she had not moved since the warders put her there, but sometimes a long moan escaped from her pale lips.

'Kate! 'Tis I! Roxanna! Wake up!' She

could not prevent the urgent, frightened note from entering her voice.

Unwilling to return from the dreamy realms of delirium to a world which held nothing but physical torment and mental pain, Kate shuddered and attempted to shrug off her hand. But at last her lids quivered, then rolled open. Her almost lifeless eyes looked up into Roxanna's face, which swam mistily above her. For an instant there was no flicker of recognition, then the shadow of a smile fluttered over her mouth.

'Well, if it isn't Mrs High and Mighty,' she whispered. 'What are you doing in the quod ken? Have they snabbled you too?'

Roxanna shook her head. 'Nay, I'm no new prisoner. I've come to help you, Kate.'

A great sob tore through the exhausted girl. 'No one can help me!' Her voice gathered strength and the tears slid across her dirt-streaked temples, falling onto the sheet beneath her head. 'They've nubbed Johnny!'

'I know.' Roxanna bent to wipe the sweat which stood out in great drops on Kate's forehead. 'But I can get you out of here. You've got to give this child birth, Kate.'

'I don't want to live any more.' There was the finality of utter despair in Kate's voice and she turned away. 'Let me sleep. I'm so very tired.'

Never had Roxanna felt so inadequate and ill-fitted to deal with a situation.

Desperately, she sought for words which would jerk her into action. 'Johnny would be ashamed to hear you say that!' she suddenly blazed, tart and scornful. 'He never believed you a coward!'

As she had hoped, a fire smouldered in the eyes dark with pain and misery. A sudden spasm of labour made her writhe, her voice rose to a protesting scream which sent Roxanna cold. She gave a frantic nod to the midwife, but after a sharp, panting effort Kate collapsed. The baby had not moved. Mrs Trapes' hands, hovering about Kate, were so nauseous in their dirt that Roxanna frigidly ordered her to stand back. Then she herself worked in an attempt to get hold of the child.

After what seemed an interminable struggle, Roxanna was able to grasp the infant and within seconds it was born. It lay, pale and flaccid, completely still.

Several weeks premature, it was the smallest baby she had ever seen. With a hand on the minute back, and another at the little chest, she tried to make it breathe by gently squeezing, terribly aware that with each passing moment the chances of its surviving were dwindling. As hysteria began to swell in her throat, she tried hard to remember what Nan Dobs might do in such a crisis.

Seizing the pale heels between her fingers she dangled the child upside down and slapped it, hard. It gave a convulsive jerk, the ribs rose and fell, and a weak, strangled cry escaped from it for an instant.

The midwife had been occupied in kneading Kate's abdomen and, terrified, Roxanna stared at the blood which would not stop flowing. She hastily wrapped the child in one of the dubious rags and held it up so that Kate could see it.

'Look, Kate! You have a daughter!'

Reluctantly, almost grudgingly, Kate looked at her child. Her mauve lips moved, and Roxanna had to bend close to catch the words. 'Poor little jilt, it will be as well if she dies.'

'She's not going to die!' Roxanna insisted. It was of absolute importance to her that this little scrap survived. 'And neither are you!'

The shadow of her old, scoffing smile played about Kate's mouth. 'I feel so very comfortable...' she murmured. ' 'Tis like lying in a warm bath. But tell that old sot to stop prodding me!'

Offended, Mrs Trapes sat back on her haunches and began to pick at her teeth with her fingernails. Kate's fingers were plucking fitfully at a fold in her sodden skirt. Her head rolled to look at Roxanna again. 'And you...you did this for me and didn't ask for garnish.'

'Of course not!' Roxanna spoke sharply, although the tears were burning in her eyes. She held the quiet baby hard against her. Kate lifted her head and fumbled at her bodice, drawing out a small leather bag.

'Here...' she offered it to Roxanna. 'Here is your chummage. 'Twill be of little use to me where I am going.'

Roxanna opened the draw-string and tipped the contents into her palm; her emerald ear-rings flashed in the sullen candlelight. She heard Mrs Trapes, greedy exclamation from behind her.

Nonplussed, she stared at Kate. 'But you could have bought easement with this.'

The dark head moved. 'Nay, I liked

them too well. But you have them back now.'

A tear splashed down onto the gems and Roxanna wiped her cheeks with the back of her hand, trying to be practical. 'The babe must be baptized at once. What would you like her to be named, Kate?'

Kate seemed to be summoning up enough strength to speak and then Roxanna caught the words: 'I've always thought Louise a mighty pretty name.' She turned away, towards the wall, with a deep, sleepy sigh.

Roxanna, her slanting eyes wide and frightened, clutched at Mrs Trapes' arm. 'What can we do for her?'

The midwife shrugged. 'Nothing, Ma'am, she's dying.'

Roxanna opened her mouth to give her a slating when she was arrested by a curious, uncanny sound; a bubbling rattle as Kate drew in her last breath. Roxanna stood perfectly still for a moment. Then, gritting her teeth, she went across and rolled Kate on to her back. In death she looked quite different, her thin body empty and deserted.

Numbed, too tired to think or feel, Roxanna began to tidy up, pulling on her cloak and picking up the silent infant, unsure whether it still lived. Mrs Trapes put out her hand and clutched at her skirt as she went by to go to the door. Roxanna whirled round and the old woman jumped back, cringing and grinning.

'Ma'am, please, do I get my fee?'

'Fee!' Roxanna glared at her with hatred and disgust. 'And what did you do, pray? You let her die, damn you!'

Mrs Trapes protested indignantly. 'Indeed, I did not, Ma'am!' Then her voice became ingratiating. 'I need that cole. A poor old lady like me can't pay garnish for the few small comforts she needs. A beaker of brandy, that's all I want to keep the ague out of my bones!'

Her eyes filled with crawling entreaty. Roxanna stared at her without pity, then abruptly tossed over a coin.

'Now mark you, Mrs Trapes, I want that girl laid out properly. You will see to it.'

The midwife snatched up the gold piece. 'I'll see to it, madam, and God bless you! Never fret, leave it to old Trapes!'

Master Kneebone proved unhelpful when she demanded that he give Kate burial in consecrated ground. But when she rattled the money in her purse he became more amenable.

'If you carry out my instructions you shall have this now, and another later if you see that the pirate Johnny Comry's body is interred near her.'

Kneebone shook his head. 'That I dare not do, Ma'am. He's to remain there, hanging in chains until he rots, as a warning to other malefactors. That is part of the sentence.'

Roxanna gave a snort of exasperation. 'Come now, Master Kneebone, d'you mean to tell me that the law cannot be wheedled around? I'll make it worth your trouble. Substitute another body.'

She raised her price till eventually the head-warder consented to do what she asked. As she departed, Roxanna flung him a warning. 'Mind that you do not cheat me, sirrah! I am not without influence in Jamaica and if I find that you have not carried out your part of the bargain, I'll see that *you* swing for it!'

The alarm and respect in Kneebone's watery eyes assured her that she had managed to lie convincingly. She did not mention the baby which was concealed beneath her wrap, and he did not ask, presuming that it was dead.

Roxanna stepped from the purple shadow of the great gate into the unslacking sunlight of noon. The town was very still, wallowing in the drugged sleep of siesta. The blinding glare scorched her eyeballs after the dimness within, and Will guided her to the waiting coach. The interior was stifling and Roxanna lay back against the scalding leather, exhausted, as the driver flicked his whip and the coach lurched along the road to Dean Hill.

CHAPTER 20

Pieter Van Houel tirelessly gave all of his time during the following day in teaching Roxanna everything she could wish to know about her plantation. She was eager to be occupied so that she might forget the scenes in the jail and Johnny's death. They rode for miles, starting early before it became too hot. Gradually, the reality that these acres of rich pasture land and thick woods were really hers, began to permeate her mind. He took her to the sugar works where, in spring, the crude wet Muscavadoes was boiled and refined till it resembled the white sugar demanded by the merchants. He told her the important points to remember in producing a successful crop; the manner of planting, the time of gathering and the right placing of the coppers in the furnaces so as to conserve the fuel and prevent the flames reaching and setting fire to the boiling syrup.

Over two hundred acres were devoted to sugar-cane, eighty acres for pasture, one hundred and twenty for forest, twenty for tobacco growing and five for ginger. The plantation was practically self-supporting. They cultivated corn, potatoes, plantains, pineapples and many other fruits.

From the first moment when Roxanna had staggered into the nursery, clutching the baby, Polly had taken the waif to her warm motherly heart. Roxanna stripped off her garments, to which the prison stench clung persistently, giving orders that every garment had to be burned. It took her hours to get rid of the lice which teemed on her body and in her hair. With every minute that passed the baby's hold on life grew stronger. Roxanna's requirements for a wet-nurse were exacting; the woman must be clean and healthy, two qualifications difficult to come by. But at last they found that one of Van Houel's white slaves had lately been delivered of a child. Roxanna saw her and pronounced her satisfactory. She gave the girl new clothes and many instructions, and left her to feed Louise under the strict supervision of Polly.

A parson had been sent for to baptize the infant as soon as Roxanna brought her home; they hung a necklace of anodyne around her neck and settled her in a crib made of ash and sprinkled with salt. Roxanna took the added precaution of tucking an iron nail into the pocket of her robe; everything had been done to aid her survival and insure her preservation from bad luck. Roxanna had an interview with Henry Morgan, going to see him on a particularly humid morning. She found him a rather pitiful hulk of a man; all trace of the brilliance and resourcefulness which had enabled him to crush the tremendous power of Spain in the Indies, had vanished in his dropsical middle-age. He lived surrounded by doctors, peevishly disregarding their advice and drinking himself to death. Roxanna thought it best to lay all her cards on the table and she told him, as accurately as she was able the details of the Sawkins' trip, although she knew that by so doing she incriminated herself. Dirk's pardon cost her two thousand pounds and Sir Henry let her know, with a leer and a spark of the gallantry for which he had once been famous, that, had it not been for the gout which was crippling him, she would have been asked to pay for her lover's freedom in a very different coinage.

Dirk seemed very pleased to see her when at last she was in his arms again on the wharf at Cayona. She began to cry with happiness at seeing him and the release of emotional tension under which she had been living since the deaths of Kate and Johnny. She did not know how to begin to break the news to him and was very worried. 'Lord!' she thought, 'if I tell him before, he won't want me because he will be so upset and if I wait until afterwards he'll grumble because he wasn't told straight away!'

There was a smile in his eyes when he saw the small baby carried by her nurse to the coach. 'Roxanna! Were you brought to bed again in Jamaica?' he teased, his arm pressing her waist briefly as he helped her in. 'Or maybe 'tis yours, Polly?'

As he settled in, close beside Roxanna, she gave him a glance from the corner of her eye. 'I'll tell you all about it when we reach home,' she said.

He took his son on his knee, where he wriggled and bounced energetically. He was so very strong and healthy that Roxanna found him wearing to hold and was looking forward to the time when he could walk. She chattered about Jamaica while they jolted along, but even while she talked his dazzling good-looks enraptured her. He handed the child back to Polly and his arm went round Roxanna, under her cloak. She clung to his hand, her cheeks flushing as she met his eyes. She stopped short in the middle of a sentence, wanting nothing so much as to be alone with him, filled with the same intense irrational excitement that she had known on the very first time they had met.

Polly took the children off to the nursery when they reached Kingsland; Hannah supervized the unpacking and Roxanna and Dirk went straight to their bedroom. As the door shut behind them, his arms went about her, the fingers of one hand thrusting through the glossy mass of her hair, his mouth coming down hard on hers.

'Darling, I've missed you so,' he murmured against her lips, and her heart gave a great joyful bound. They stood together for a long time, bodies straining, thighs pressed close. She ached with desire for him, yet she knew that she could not fully enjoy union until she had broken the sad tidings and released herself from his demanding arms. He cocked a questioning eyebrow at her; it was unlike her to be reluctant. Slowly she paced to the bed, flinging aside her cloak and kicking off her shoes. She sat down, tucking her feet up under her and Dirk came swiftly across, shrugging off his coat and jerking at his cravat, fully expecting to make love to her without preamble. But she put up her fingers and laid them gently across his lips, a pleasurable thrill creeping down her spine as he seized her hand and began to kiss her wrist and arm.

With all the tact and tenderness she could command, she told him about Johnny. He grew very quiet, and when she had finished he still made no comment, staring blankly at the floor. Dirk got up suddenly and she put out her hand in a little, helpless gesture.

'Darling, I did all that was in my power.' She wanted to draw his head down and kiss away the strained look from his shadowed, grey eyes. Still with his back to her, his shoulders sagged, he spoke:

'I am sure that you did, and thank you, my dear. We will bring up their child as our own.'

With hurried strides he was gone and Roxanna made no attempt to stop him. She knew that he would make straight for his study where he could remain for hours, quite alone except for a rum bottle. When he came out there was no knowing what his mood would be. She heaved a sigh and went into the nursery. Little Charles, over-excited, would not settle to sleep and insisted on pulling himself up in his cradle, rocking it violently. Roxanna felt like spanking him. Louise, too, was wide awake and Roxanna picked her up carefully; she was so fragile that she was always afraid of hurting her. Her blue eyes were very pale, her face was like a tiny pink flower, while her head was covered with fluff, so fair that it was hardly noticeable.

The wet-nurse hastened to assure Roxanna that the babe was sucking strongly and sleeping well. Roxanna gave a satisfied nod and went off to inspect the rest of the household.

Next morning she was awakened by the sound of Dirk talking outside to one of the servants. His voice always thrilled her and she turned over and lay on her back listening, eyes half-closed, in delicious strained expectancy, like a cat having its fur stroked. He entered the room and appeared from the other side of the bed, smiling down on her, one hand pulling back the curtain. It was the first time that she had seen him since telling him of Johnny's death. She smiled widely and held out her arms to him. He sat down and she ran her fingers over his freshly-shaved cheeks and down his wide muscular shoulders and chest.

'My love, 'tis so wonderful to be back with you again,' she whispered with a catch in her voice. His expression was filled with sadness, but her arms were about him, demanding and passionate, and their mouths came together in a sudden violence which stamped out every thought but satisfying the urgency of their desire. Some while later, he lay quietly beside her, while she soothingly fondled his hair, breathing in the scented, personal fragrance of it. When at last he sat up, she opened her eyes and gave him a lazy smile.

'You don't have to hurry away, do you? There is so much I want to tell you.'

He was putting on his shirt, tucking the tails into his breeches, fastening the lace-trimmed cuffs. He gave her a sudden, searching glance. 'I, too, have a matter which I would discuss with you.'

Still smiling, idly wondering what it was, she caught hold of his hand in an indolent, intimate grasp. 'What is it?'

He moved away, watching her while he slid his shoulders into his waistcoat, eyes narrowed slightly. 'I want to bring my son to live here.'

Roxanna looked across at him with stunned incomprehension. 'Your son?' She had not taken in the full import of his words; her brain refused to believe them.

Dirk fastened the buttons and sat down to put on his hose. 'Yes, he is fourteen and it is time I had him with me.'

'Fourteen!' Her lips were stiff. Then, suddenly, everything seemed to collapse, all the hopes and dreams she had been building of a new life for them in Jamaica crumbling away. He had a son of fourteen, just five years younger than herself. 'Oh, my God!' she whispered.

He turned to face her, unwillingly, as if he knew that what he had to say was going to hurt. 'Do not be so upset, my sweet. He was born when I was little over seventeen. There is no reason why it should distress you so much.'

'No reason!' Her voice rose to a shrill wail. 'Are you mad?' Her eyes were suddenly hard and malicious. 'Were you married to his mother?'

'Good Lord, no!' She saw the look on his face change to one of warning and withdrawal. He stood up and thrust his arms into his coat-sleeves. 'I lived with her when I first escaped to Cayona. For years now I have visited her only to see the boy, and I have provided her with money for him. Her present keeper has offered her marriage. He wants to take her back to France, but the child will be an added complication.'

Roxanna had begun to pride herself that she knew him very well, but now she realized that he was as secretive and independent as when she had first seen him and he needed her no more than then. She had counted heavily on his love for Charles eventually persuading him to wed her, now all her hopes were shattered.

'You will make him your heir?' her voice was bitter.

He turned to the mirror and began to comb his hair into place, so calm that she wanted to kill him. 'Yes,' his voice was steady. 'He is my elder child.'

Roxanna flounced off the bed. 'Damn you, Dirk!' she exploded savagely. 'How many other bastards have you that you may suddenly spring on me?'

'None that I know of.' His grey eyes did not flinch and he spoke with gentle irony. 'Please, my dearest, do not feel so hurt. It does not affect how I feel for you. I just want to have the boy here, now that we have a real home. Our baby will be treated in the same way as usual.'

Roxanna pulled up short, her mouth twisted in a sneer. 'Oh, will he! Small thanks for that! Listen to me, Dirk Courtney, if you insist on bringing another woman's brat here I shall go! I am not dependent on you for money. I shall take Charles and Louise away!'

Dirk did not answer at once, he buckled on his sword and picked up his hat, the jewelled clasp flashing in the bright sunlight which was beginning to stream in between the slats of the shutters. He slowly walked across the room, moving with that easy, fluid stride which stabbed at her heart, reminding her of how much she loved him.

'Do as you think best, my dear,' he said. 'But remember that he is my child as well as yours.'

Roxanna's face was ugly with hatred and wounded pride, 'Your child? Once you doubted it! Well, maybe you were right!'

Dirk ignored this insinuation, 'I shall be bringing Paul here within the week.'

There was no change in his tone as he paused, his hand on the brass door-handle, but there was a dangerous spark in his eyes which she knew only too well.

When he had gone Roxanna stood for a moment, eyes brilliant with furious tears, then she fell on her knees beside the bed, sobbing wildly. The knowledge that another woman had enjoyed his great powerful body and borne him a child was more than she could stomach. She had been miserable and despairing often enough before, but never like this. If that child's mother had been unable to marry Dirk, after all these years, how could she hope to succeed? If did not occur to her that perhaps the woman did not wish to become his wife.

Anger and indignation began to storm through her. She sat up and blew her nose hard. Damn him! she thought, I'll show him! She scrambled to her feet, shouting for Hannah and rushing through to the nursery in search of Polly. Dirk would be busy all morning and when he returned she was determined that he should find her and the babies gone. Fortunately a great many of her belongings had not yet been unpacked from the Jamaican trip; the cradles and luggage were hastily piled onto the coach and, without giving herself time to relent, Roxanna climbed in. It was only when they came in sight of Dubois' white house that her fury abated and she began to have doubts; but it was too late to turn back.

The planter asked no awkward questions at her abrupt arrival, putting his house, his servants and himself at her command for as long as she wanted. She could easily have gone to stay with Lucy, but she hoped that Dirk would get to hear that she was living with Dubois and be hurt by it. But she had no intention of becoming the mistress of that over-amiable Frenchman. For five weeks she was courted and petted by both Dubois and James Cowper, who called to see her at the slightest pretext; but every moment of the time she never stopped longing for Dirk, sick at heart and miserable enough to die.

Daily, she looked for a message from him, but no word came and she realized, with dull, leadened pain, that with his stubborn pride he would make no move towards a reconciliation and that if she returned to him it would be on his terms. Her depression was deepened by the growing conviction that she was pregnant again. She had several disquieting symptoms and, within the past few days, Charles had begun to scream with displeasure at her milk, turning his face away. Polly said this was a sure sign. This complicated matters; returning to England with one illegitimate child was bad enough. It was unthinkable that she should go to Jamaica, it being far too tormentingly close to Dirk. Whatever she did she was in a fix and spent long hours lying on her bed, brooding despondently.

Dubois and James did their utmost to coax Roxanna out of her gloom. They took her driving, bought her presents, arranged parties for her, and she went everywhere that they suggested on the hope that she might hear news of Dirk or catch a glimpse of him. And, when James received an unexpected summons back to England, he asked Roxanna to marry him and go with him. This was, of course, a perfect answer to her dilemma. He was a loving gullible fool, no match for her wiles, and she knew that if she yielded to him at once, she could easily convince him that the coming baby was his. Yet, somehow, she could not bring herself to do it. She was revolted by the thought of lying in any other man's arms.

It was only a visit from Lionel Wafer which brought her to her senses. She had called him up to look at Charles who seemed feverish and unwell, and he took the opportunity of giving her a straight lecture on the foolishness of her behaviour. He told her to pocket her pride, since Dirk would not do it, and go back to him. Gladly she took this advice.

When, later that evening, she arrived at Kingsland, Dirk was not there. She left Polly to settle the children and hurried off to find some of the servants. She reached their quarters out of breath, a stitch clawing at her side. Several of them were lounging in the doorway and she picked out Jude, his pipe glowing against the darkness.

He told her that Dirk had gone down to the harbour and she was at once off, back to the Dubois coach, determined to find him now that she had made up her mind. Jude heaved his hulking shoulders from the porch and followed her. Their first stop was Lucy's hostelry and she came running out.

'Nay, he is not here. Is aught amiss, Ma'am?'

But Roxanna was already out of the coach and giving the driver sharp instructions to wait there for her. She set off in the direction of Sarah Frisky's house, walking as swiftly as her heels would allow, Jude loping easily at her side. The narrow alleys were sharp with the contrast of mauve shadows and the flares in brackets out side of the taverns and brothels. The smoke wavered in every movement of the

374

hot air and the tumult of the quarrelling, laughing, fornicating crowd was like the surge of an angry sea. Roxanna regretted leaving the carriage; in her haste she had forgotten how brutal the port was at night.

She swallowed hard to keep back the frustrated tears, angry with the mob who jostled her, unreasonably furious with Dirk for not being at the plantation. Jude had to use his great fists to clear a path for them through a crowd who blocked the way. They were watching two men who rolled in the dust, knives flashing in the smoky glare. Roxanna felt faint, the smell from the open sewer running down the street rising in a hot nauseating wave.

Jude took her arm and guided her across the roadway and she recognized the sign outside Sarah's house. As she entered the men turned to stare and the tousled doxies eyed her, making slighting remarks, summing her up as a more fortunate whore who had strayed on to their preserves. Quickly she scanned the faces, but Dirk's was not among them. It was only then that she fully appreciated the protection which Jude offered. Had he not been with her she knew that the chance of escaping molestation by the drunken rabble of buccaneers, log-cutters and hunters would have been slight.

She made her way between trestles and benches, dexterously weaving past two sailors who were dancing a jig with drunken solemnity, and stopped near a gaming table. She looked over the cards spread out, the pile of coins, the familiar faces of corsairs whom she knew, and straight into Dirk's eyes. For an instant the room swam and she rested her hands flat on the table, weak in the knees. When her head cleared, leaving her cold and trembling with excitement, she saw that he was absorbed in the game, just as if he had not seen her.

This roused her anger and she deliberately flashed a bright smile at his companions, glad to see that Lionel Wafer was there. He obligingly stood up so that she could slip along the bench and sit beside Dirk. Roxanna arranged her skirts, let her cloak slide down and fluttered her fan. Dirk ignored her, but she saw that his fingers were unsteady as he dealt.

For what seemed an eternity, she watched the money mount in front of him, tribute to his skill, his hands

376

flashing over the cards. Her pulse raced, turbulently affected by his nearness. With growing longing she knew that she would commit any mortal sin if they could be reunited. He appeared to be dead sober in spite of the brandy in his glass. She feasted her eyes on the profile turned stubbornly away from her. She gloated on every familiar, attractive feature; the straight nose, sardonic brows, sensitive, tormented, strong-willed mouth. His hair had grown longer, well below his shoulders, curling over at the ends into great rings, and he was wearing a leather doublet, with the neck of his shirt open, well-cut breeches and black riding boots.

The intensity of her desire for him alarmed her, it rendered her completely vulnerable, unable to break free of him. She knew that if she were to rise and walk out of the tavern he would make no move to stop her, whereas, whatever happened, she could not live without him, no matter the cost to her pride and self-respect.

The strong fumes of wine were driving away the remnants of her control, his body acted like a magnet, she could not refrain from touching him. With all the force of her being she willed him to look at her,

her hand pressing against the long sweep of his thigh, feeling the coarse texture of the cloth, the supple softness of leather and the tough strength of the muscles beneath. Slowly he turned his head and they exchanged a glance. His eyes were dark and unfathomable, but his words were like a slap across the face.

'And how do you like being Dubois' whore?'

Her eyes snapped open in surprise.

'I am not!' She shook her head. 'Oh, Dirk, you must believe me!' He shrugged, his mouth twisted into a cynical smile, and she added, urgent and pleading: 'Can't we go somewhere...? I must talk to you!'

Sarah grinned knowingly when he paid for a private room. As Roxanna followed him up the staircase she felt a surge of primitive pride, seeing how the women looked him over, the interest of the prostitutes not only professional. In the dingy bedroom he lit the candle, and they stared at each other. Then suddenly all Roxanna's resolve broke. She reached out her hands to him.

'Oh, Dirk, I've been so miserable.'

He moved and she threw her arms about him, dragging his mouth down to hers. She clung to his kiss, feeling him tremble as he held her and she began to cry, hammering on his chest with her fists, hardly knowing what she was doing in her desperate need for him.

'Can I come back with you?' she asked a little later, as she lay curled in his arms on the bed. Her tone indicated quite clearly that she did not expect a refusal. 'You will send the boy away, won't you? For you must see, Dirk, that I cannot look after him. It would be too distressing.'

There was the starting of a frown in the eyes that had been watching her indulgently. The chill finger of doubt touched her. Just now his need for her had seemed as great as, if not more than, hers and she had been confident that this time she would make him yield in his purpose.

'I cannot do that, Roxanna,' he began finally. 'The boy needs me. He misses his mother and it would be cruelty to deprive him again.'

She was quiet for a moment, then: 'Are you still going to make him your heir?' she demanded, crossly and unwisely.

He stood up, eyeing her shrewdly, wishing to avoid a scene. 'Yes,' he answered with that quiet determination which she knew was immovable. He looked down at her and there was compassionate tenderness in his eyes. 'I think, my dear, as I have said before, you should plan your life without me. We shall never be happy for long together.' As she started to speak he shook his head. 'I shall never spoil, adore and cherish you, which is what you need. Marry this James Cowper and go home to England.'

'I can't...' The fact that he was completely serious and meant every word that he said, tore at her heart. 'I love you!' He picked up his sword and baldrick. 'You will forget me. You are a very lovely and desirable woman, and there are no heights which you cannot reach. Get that young ass to wed you, and your way will be open to court. You could be the King's mistress yet!'

'But you know that I want to marry you,' she whispered.

A shutter seemed to drop over his eyes. One hand started to move in an involuntary gesture. He was about to speak when there came hurried footfalls in the passage outside and a furious knocking at the door.

It was Jude. He came in, his battered face concerned. 'Madam, 'tis the baby. A messenger 'as come down from Polly! It seems that 'is fever 'as worsened.'

Her heart turned over in fright and she was already gathering up her things. 'You did not tell me Charles was ailing!' There was anxiety and anger in Dirk's voice. 'And you left him with a servant!'

Guilt jarred through her as she started to explain. 'I thought 'twas nothing, a mere teething trouble...'

But he had swung round abruptly and was already half-way along the corridor. She fled after him to the stables. He leaned down to heave her up onto his horse and she was aware that Wafer was leaping into the saddle on another. In a kind of nightmare frenzy they galloped along the moonlit road. Roxanna huddled against Dirk, her mind empty of everything but conscience-stricken panic and a dreadful anxiety.

In the nursery Polly was watching out for them, her plain features very worried. Wafer began to question the maid-servant, quietly and efficiently, and Roxanna went to the cradle. Dirk was close behind her and she shot him a glance; there

381

was something almost frightening in the way that tenderness could soften this domineering, ruthless man. Charles gave a little whimper, his cheeks were flushed and there was moisture on his forehead. His breathing was hurried and irregular. He looked very sick.

'Have you moved Louise away?' Roxanna asked sharply. If it was an infection she could not risk that very delicate infant catching it. Polly nodded and there were tears on her face. The baby woke and began to cry. Roxanna lifted him to change his diaper. She found that his stools were unformed, offensive and streaked with blood. As he lay across her lap, he suddenly vomited. Roxanna was thoroughly frightened now.

Wafer prescribed another mixture. Roxanna handed the child to Polly and rushed off to the kitchen to brew up one of Nan Dob's concoctions. When she returned. Dirk was gone and the baby lay in his crib again, moaning as he breathed. In anguish Roxanna hung over him, wondering if the fact that she had been trying to wean him was the cause of this. Polly had been giving him goat's milk and paps, possibly one of these had disagreed with him. She knew only too well how vulnerable infants were, the shadow of the coffin haunted every cradle and many a baby died in its early months. She tried to push this dread away from her, afraid that even to think of it might bring it about.

She crept away to her own room and took off her elaborate gown, slipping her dressing-gown over her shift and petticoats, then sent Polly to rest and kept watch herself, changing the bedding frequently as he was sick.

At about three in the morning Dirk came in. He did not speak for a long time, staring down at the sick infant. Roxanna felt desperately sorry for him, and yet she could not understand why this pity flooded her.

'Poor little lad,' he murmured, reaching out a gentle finger and briefly touching the sweat-beaded brow. 'My God, but I feel most horribly to blame for this. Lionel says that we must be prepared to lose him.'

Charles stirred feebly and Roxanna picked him up, soothing him against her shoulder. 'Hush, sweeting...' she whispered against the small, damp head. She was scarcely aware of Dirk any more, all of her energies concentrated on the baby.

383

She thought about her life, which now seemed sickeningly hollow, worthless and selfish, and her petty refusal to accept Dirk's child shamed her beyond belief. It became very silent just before dawn. Dirk had restlessly wandered out. Roxanna started, goose-flesh rising on her skin, aware of a change, almost as if there was an unseen presence in the room. She forced herself to hold high the guttering candle to examine Charles. A sobbing prayer escaped her.

He was sleeping peacefully, the hectic flush replaced by a pallor and his forehead felt cool and dry. Although minutes before she had been so tired that every nerve seemed to hurt, now she ran to rouse Polly, telling her to watch while she sped down the still-darkened passage to find Dirk.

He was slumped in his large leather armchair, a nearly empty decanter on the table at his elbow, the candles almost burnt out. He looked up dully as she came in, then he half-rose. 'Roxanna! The child is dead?'

'No!' She was on her knees beside him, her face haggard with strain and weariness but glowing with joy. 'No! He will live, darling.'

His hands, lean and hard, gripped hers. She lay her head down against him and he reached over to stroke her hair. Relief and gratitude had drained all other emotion from them and it was some time before Roxanna could stand and walk to the window.

It was very cool, the garden dripping with dew and turning very faint blue. Away in the east the sun was beginning to rise, melting the frail whisps of cloud, blinding the pale sickle moon in a glory of vivid greens and purples, through the haze of gold and dissolving greys. In the top of an oleander tree a bird began to carol.

Roxanna leaned against the window-frame, feeling the cool pane against her forehead. 'Dirk,' she said slowly. 'There is much I must say to you, things which I intended to tell you on that morning when I left here. Firstly, you are a pardoned man. I bought your reprieve from Harry Morgan.'

He gave a startled exclamation and she heard his step behind her. Then his arm came across her shoulders, turning her to face him.

'My dear, I know not how to thank

you.' He seemed confused, as if unable to believe her.

'You are now free to settle anywhere in the Indies.' All pretence, scheming and spite had dropped away from her. She gave a shrug and a little grin. 'I must admit that there have been times a plenty during the past weeks when I all but tore it to shreds.'

'But you did not?' There was a most curious expression in his eyes as he stood and watched her and waited.

She shook her rumpled curls, 'No, 'tis safe. Dirk, I am a rich woman and the plantation in Jamaica is very fine. Can't we give up this one? In any case, if we want to cultivate sugar, there is not enough room here. Come with me to Jamaica and let us settle. Wed me, Dirk. There is no end to what we can achieve together.'

Her tiredness was forgotten in her passionate enthusiasm as she talked on, telling him everything about Dean Hill and her hands went up to bite into his arms, her voice urgent and pleading. 'My father will help us to market our goods in England, and later we can send the boys to be educated in London. My money and property will become yours if we wed, and

386

perhaps we may yet be able to buy back your father's estates in Cornwall.'

When she paused for breath he asked slowly. 'And what of Paul?'

Roxanna spoke humbly and sincerely. 'I will do everything in my power to make him happy.'

He was looking at her with anxiety, and a kind of pity. He gently smoothed her fingers with his. 'You must want this most deuced badly, darling.'

He was strained and in need of a shave and his eyes were reddened with lack of sleep and too much rum. It was impossible to tell what he was thinking and hopeless frustration worked over her. She made one last desperate try.

'Dirk, we could be so happy and think what a home we can make for these children and Johnny's little one.'

He gave her an odd, doubtful smile, his face sceptical, as it always was when she made extravagant entreaties, promises or threats. He stretched, throwing wide his arms and yawning. 'God damn it, but I'm tired. I will go and waken Paul, then you can meet him. As for these other matters, we'll go into them more fully later. And with regard to our marriage, you must give me time to think on't.' Roxanna's heart gave a great leap of happiness. In a blinding flash of clarity she was certain that she would get her way. In this issue her will was stronger than his. She felt it, she knew it! For the first time ever he had not flatly refused her. She reached up on tip-toe and he bent his head and kissed her softly, briefly, before he went out of the room.

Roxanna almost floated on air back to the nursery. For two and a half years she had been struggling to accomplish this end. Now it seemed nearly too good to be true. Her head buzzed with eager plans although her back ached, her eyeballs felt prickly and raw as if there was dirt under the lids and she longed to sleep more than anything on earth. There was so much work ahead to move the entire household to Jamaica, that her mind balked at considering it. And, most difficult task of all, she would have to conquer her jealousy and get to know Paul, who might well be a surly, resentful lad.

She hoped that they might be able to reach Dean Hill during 'crop', that important period in the spring when the cane was cut and milled and the sugar made. Van Houel had told her that it was a happy, intensely busy time. She felt sure that it would be good for Dirk to arrive in the midst of this activity, when there was cane to chew, rum allowed or stolen, excitement and bustle and usually at the end—some sort of feast. Dirk would see the plantation at its happiest and best, when every available hand was needed.

Regretfully, she knew that friends would have to be left behind in Cayona, including Lucy, Lionel Wafer, Jude and Jeremy; this was going to be a wrench. But she had already decided to write to Lydia suggesting that she join them at Dean Hill. On these islands a marriageable female was a rarity and Van Houel would make a good husband. Roxanna was already busy matchmaking.

In the nursery, Polly was rocking the cradle with her foot. A peep at Charles assured Roxanna that he was well on the way to recovery. Wafer's angular form was stretched out on the truckle-bed. He sat up, digging his knuckles into his eyes, as she came over to stand in front of him. She told him excitedly that she was going to marry Dirk.

His comment surprised her. 'Darling, are you sure that is a wise course to take?'

Her tilting eyes widened incredulously. 'But naturally! It is what I have set my heart on! And, anyway, 'twas you who suggested that I came back to him!' He got to his feet, buttoning his shirtsleeves and reaching for his coat. 'Ah, yes, but I did not tell you to wed him. There is a vast difference, my sweet, between passion which you feel and a sound basis for a successful partnership. Love has very little to do with marriage, and life has a nasty trick of giving us what we think we most desire, but not in the way we want it!'

Roxanna pulled a scornful, disbelieving face. 'Pah! That I will not grant you!' She would not admit for a moment that being Dirk's wife could give her anything but blissful, unbounded happiness. It was the summit of all her ambitions.

As he collected up his case, hat and cane, she asked him to stay and breakfast with them. He shook his head, saying that he must go back to his lodgings before calling on other patients. She strolled along with him. Outdoors, it was almost light and she could hear the servants talking and moving about, clattering pans in the kitchen, beginning the daily chores. The slaves would already be on their way to the fields. In the next room Louise set up a shrill hungry squalling, heartening to hear.

Roxanna stopped in the hall-way, reaching up to tweak Wafer's cravat straight; it was nearly always awry. Then she gave him a gay wave as he went out through the open front door, before turning towards the study to join Dirk and his son.

The publishers hope that this book has given you enjoyable reading. Large Print Books are especially designed to be as easy to see and hold as possible. If you wish a complete list of our books, please ask at your local library or write direct to: Dales Print Books, Long Preston, North Yorkshire, BD23 4ND, England.

Other DALES Romance Titles In Large Print

Other DALES Romance Titles In Large Print

JENNIFER HYDE
Arabesque Of Daisies

STELLA ROSS
Fly Home With The Swallows

FLORENCE STUART
The Right Kind Of Man

PEGGY GADDIS
Nurse In Flight

FRANCES McHUGH
Vow Of Love

JEAN DAVIDSON
Spring Fever

GIULIA GRAY
Lure For A Falcon